THE ~~...~~ **RIGHT FOR HER**

Men had never been a problem for Saskia. She had successfully evaded their entreaties for all of her young womanhood. But now she had reached the ripe old age of twenty-one, and they were closing in around her.

There was Mr. Kneighley, the loquacious curate who uttered words of adoration in a torrent that Saskia couldn't turn off.

There was Captain Durrant, the gallant seaman who set full sail after her with all charm blazing to make her his prize.

And then, of course, there was Derek Rowbridge, who clearly wouldn't even dream of desiring her, just as she couldn't conceive of considering him . . .

. . . until the unthinkable happened, and two hearts ruled by cool heads went out of control. . . .

The
Unlikely Rivals

More Regency Romances from SIGNET

The Unlikely Rivals

by
Megan Daniel

A SIGNET BOOK
NEW AMERICAN LIBRARY
TIMES MIRROR

Publisher's Note

This novel is a work of fiction. Names, characters, places, and incidents are either the product of the author's imagination or are used fictitiously, and any resemblance to actual persons, living or dead, events, or locales is entirely coincidental.

NAL BOOKS ARE AVAILABLE AT QUANTITY DISCOUNTS WHEN USED TO PROMOTE PRODUCTS OR SERVICES. FOR INFORMATION PLEASE WRITE TO PREMIUM MARKETING DIVISION, THE NEW AMERICAN LIBRARY, INC., 1633 BROADWAY, NEW YORK, NEW YORK 10019.

SIGNET TRADEMARK REG. U.S. PAT. OFF. AND FOREIGN COUNTRIES
REGISTERED TRADEMARK—MARCA REGISTRADA
HECHO EN CHICAGO, U.S.A.

SIGNET, SIGNET CLASSICS, MENTOR, PLUME, MERIDIAN AND NAL BOOKS are published by The New American Library, Inc., 1633 Broadway, New York, New York 10019

First Printing, November, 1981

1 2 3 4 5 6 7 8 9

PRINTED IN THE UNITED STATES OF AMERICA

For Marilyn—sister, comrade,
and best of friends.

Chapter One

Magdalena's hands were raw and bleeding as they clung to their tenuous hold on the rock. Her foot groped gingerly for a firmer foothold on the crumbling, narrow ledge. If only she could stop trembling so!

She froze in terror as the pounding hooves approached. Had he followed her so easily then? She mustn't even breathe lest she declare her presence to the mustachioed ogre. She heard him dismount, the jingling of his heavy spurs like thunder over her head. The blackness of the night was like a cloak, hiding her from his probing eyes, but still she tried to flatten herself further against the sheer, unyielding cliff face. A picture flashed through her agonized mind, her battered body crashing onto the ugly rock so far below. Even that was preferable to what surely awaited her if Count Almendoro discovered her.

"Achoo! Drat this pen," muttered Cornelia Crawley, scratching her tickled nose. She reset the spectacles that had been knocked askew by the sneeze, tucked an errant silver-blond curl under her cap, and resolutely dipped her quill in the standish again and applied herself to her work.

> Suddenly her foothold was gone. The ledge had crumbled below her, sending a shower of rock crashing into the gorge. The footsteps above her stopped dead at the sound, and Magdalena, now clinging desperately, sent up a silent prayer.
> A scream came. Magdalena realized it was herself. A hand like steel closed round her wrist. The Count's voice, like oiled ice, spoke.
> "Such a pity, my dear Magdalena, if such perfect beauty were wasted on the rocks. I've a much better fate in mind for it."

"Achoo!" It was no good. The spell was broken. How pleasant it would be, thought Cornelia Crawley, if someday she could afford a good right-wing quill. These left-wings she used were undoubtedly far cheaper, but they did tickle her poor nose unmercifully, and she feared she was growing just the tiniest bit cross-eyed from having to peer around the end of the feather as it curled up into her face.

She stared vacantly at the fading green damask draperies at her elbow, trying to recapture the creative impulse, but it had apparently flown out the window, traversed the gay little garden, and quite disappeared. She chewed the end of her already mangled left-wing quill.

It was with something very like relief that she heard a gentle tapping at the door. "Come in, come in," she cried, dropping the long, curved plume onto the Queen Anne desk and spraying her work with inky freckles.

The door creaked open a bit, and a golden mop of curls peeked around it. Below the curls was a pair of large, limpid eyes of a quite startling blue, twinkling over a perfect upturned bow of a mouth.

"Mama?" came the musical voice. "You're not too terribly busy, are you?" The girl tripped lightly into the room and gave her mother a happy hug, sending the lady's spectacles quite charmingly askew once again. "Saskia has the *most* interesting news to tell you. May we come in?"

Before any answer could be vouchsafed to this question—which was, in any case, rather a rhetorical one as the asker was already *in* the room—a second young lady entered in the wake of the first.

"Trix! You know you mustn't disturb Mama when she's working. Come away, do."

"But, Saskia, it's such very exciting news! I'm sure Mama will want to hear it at once. You do want to hear it don't you, dearest Mama?" she pleaded prettily.

With a little mental shake, Cornelia Crawley, Authoress, pushed away her manuscript, rubbed her ink-stained fingers on her already sad-looking smock, set her spectacles aright, and became Mrs. Cornelia van Houten, mother, all eagerness to hear her daughter's news.

Her interest was not in the least feigned. There were two things in the world that had the power to capture her attention. One was her work. Indeed, when fully immersed in the tribulations of one of her romantic heroines, the ceiling might fall in on her without her knowledge.

The other consuming passion of this well-known Authoress of Gothick Tales was her children. She knew very well that they were all five quite superior specimens of the species, and though she might not have a perfectly clear understanding of the everyday necessities involved in running a household and raising a lively family, particularly on the meager funds provided by her novels, which were the family's sole source of income, she was entirely convinced of the felicity that such children provided to their parent.

"Well, my dears, and what is this extraordinary news?" she inquired.

"I am sorry, Mama, for allowing Trix to disturb you when you're working. It can easily wait for another time," said Saskia van Houten in her clear, well-modulated voice, and she began to usher her younger sister from the cheerful, if somewhat shabby, room.

"Nonsense, my darlings. I hope I am never too busy for my own children."

Saskia, who knew quite well that her mother was often very much too busy, or at least too lost in her work, to even be aware of another presence in the room, be it daughter, son, or gardener, gave her a shrewd look from the fine pansy-brown eyes that were the best feature in a long, rather angular face. Heroine Magdalena must be misbehaving today, she thought.

"It's a letter, Mama," chirped Beatrix happily. "Quite the most extraordinary letter, from my Aunt Eccles. Only wait till you hear."

"Eccles? Eccles? *Do* you have an Aunt Eccles? Have I met her? Eccles . . . Hmmm." She laid a finger alongside her nose in thought, leaving a rather pronounced ink spot where it touched.

"She is your Aunt Eccles, too, Mama," explained Saskia patiently. "You remember now, I'm sure. Lady Hester Eccles. She is your papa's sister, and you have never met her because she has been traveling for years and years. You told us all about her."

Mrs. van Houten sat dumbly a moment, eyes focused on a point some four inches before her nose, and Saskia knew that she was thinking. "Ah, yes," she exclaimed finally, and with a suddenness that made her bounce. "Lady Eccles, to be sure. My Aunt Eccles. Yes, yes, and how is she, dear? I hope she is well. A letter you say? How odd."

"Decidedly odd, I should think," said Saskia matter-of-factly, "since she has never written to you in all your life, so far as I can tell. And why she should do so now . . ."

"Yes, yes, I remember perfectly now," continued her mother. "She lives in Arabia somewhere and consorts with sheiks and such."

"She lives in Bath," corrected her eldest daughter

gently. "And quite alone, as far as I can tell. But I do believe she is only recently returned to England."

"Well, well, in Bath you say? Extraordinary, quite extraordinary. I made quite sure she lived in Arabia. My Aunt Eccles in Bath. Hmmmm. Are you sure she didn't mean Baghdad?"

"Oh, Mama," bubbled Beatrix. "Of course she is sure. And you will never guess why she has written. Saskia is invited to come and see her!"

"Rather say commanded," replied her sister dryly. "It is a most odd letter, to be sure. She seems a somewhat eccentric woman. Why on earth she should wish me to visit her I cannot imagine."

"Eccentric?" said Mrs. van Houten. "Oh yes, I should think she is certainly eccentric," she pronounced with the air of paying a high compliment. "I believe there is rather a strong strain of it in the family," she added proudly. "And so you are going to Bath, dear. You must have a new gown, of course. That one is sadly dowdy. I can't imagine why you are still wearing it."

Saskia allowed her eyes to wander for only the smallest instant to the plain steel-blue calico dress she wore, no longer in its first, or even its second, season. But she shook off her frown of distaste at once. "You know, Mama, that we cannot afford any new gowns just now, and this one suits me well enough. And in any case, I'm not at all certain that I shall go to Bath. But here. Let me read you the letter. *I* hardly know what to make of it."

> "17 Royal Crescent
> Bath

"My dear Miss van Houten

"Having recently returned to the shores of Merrie Ould England, after some forty-odd years abroad, here to sink into my dotage and fade gently away, I am desirous of acquainting myself with the younger generation of our esteemed (or should I say notorious?) family. Despite your sadly heathen name, I believe you to be a bona-fide member of said family.

"Though we have not met, I shall assume that my name is not unknown to you. You have most likely heard a great deal of nonsense about my exploits of past years, but you really must not believe all you hear. The truth is generally *so* much more amusing. I do hope you are not the sort of milk-and-water miss to be shocked by such things, for I adore to recount my adventures.

"For the purpose of determining your personality and acquainting you with a service you may render me, the quite private particulars of which must wait until we meet face to face, you may call upon me at Bath. And, as a sop to my advanced age and peculiarity, at my convenience rather than your own. I shall expect you on the 17th, after two in the afternoon. A chaise will be sent for you on the previous day.

"At the age of seventy-four it seems a bit presumptuous to sign myself as humble servant to what I can only assume to be a mere slip of a girl and probably silly into the bargain. I am, therefore,

> "Your aged and notorious aunt,
> Hester, Lady Eccles"

"What do you make of it, Mama? I am sure it is quite the oddest letter I have ever received."

Cornelia van Houten did not reply but stared cross-eyed into space again. "Hmmm," she muttered in her vague, murmuring way. "Arabia. I wonder if she has ever lived in a harem. I should quite like to know what life is like inside a harem. I must remember to ask her." She reached for her pen, dipped it with a splash, scribbled a quick note to herself muttering, "Arabia, harem," sneezed, then turned to her daughters once more.

"Well, and so you are going to Bath," she repeated. "And in a private chaise, too. Quite proper."

A tiny furrow creased Saskia's brow. "I don't like to

leave you, Mama. Jannie is sure to try and slip you some of that mugwort she sets such store by but which always gives you the headache. And who will look after the twins?"

"I will," piped up Beatrix. "Of course, they don't mind me as well as they do you, just because I'm only seventeen, but I *will* deal with them. And you can wear the cashmere shawl Tante Luce sent me last Christmas, and my new chip straw bonnet."

Saskia, fully appreciative of the enormity of these sacrifices on the part of her sister, smiled her thanks, but she was still uneasy at the thought of leaving, even for only a few days, a household that seemed to fall apart if she so much as spent the day in bed with a cold. The van Houten family, for all its good qualities, was not particularly noteworthy for its practicality and manageability. The source of Saskia's hardheaded realism and common sense was a mystery to them all, but if they ever bothered to consider the matter they would have been thankful that at least one of them possessed sufficient stores of these qualities to keep them all from sinking.

"It will be the very thing for you, of course," her mother went on.

"What do you mean, Mama?"

"Your Aunt Eccles is disgustingly wealthy, I understand. One might even say she was rolling in sauce if one were inclined to be vulgar, which with all my failings I hope I have never been called. The Rowbridge family may have come under a bit of a cloud in its time, but at least we have never been *that*. Oh yes, she is most decidedly rolling in sauce." She gave a great sigh, only very slightly tinged with the tiniest note of regret. "I fancy it comes from outliving three husbands."

"Obviously outliving only one does not suffice," said Saskia dryly, but not without very real sadness behind her fine brown eyes.

Beatrix looked at her sister. "I do wish you wouldn't speak so—so coldly of poor Papa."

"You know very well, Trix, that I adored Papa, as much as any of us. Maybe more. But you must own that he was like a child when it came to money matters, and he did not serve us very well by dying just when things were at their worst and leaving us with nothing at all to manage on." It was that death that had caused the van Houtens to flee Amsterdam, leaving behind them a large pile of bills and a raging war, to live in this little corner of England.

"Poor Papa," sighed Beatrix.

"Such a very handsome man he was," sighed her mama.

All three of them sank into a reverie, seeming to dwell on the myriad fine points of the late Pieter Maurits van Houten, financial speculator, sometime merchant and shipbuilder, beloved husband and father, with his round Dutch cheeks, his ever-present clay pipe, and his laughing blue eyes.

But Saskia was not thinking of the beloved papa who had been dead for nearly three years. Her mind was more attuned to the worries of the present and the hopes for the future. "She's very wealthy, you say?" she said at last. "Whatever do you suppose she wants of me? What service can I render her?"

"It would seem quite obvious to me, my love," said her mama with her usual blind optimism. "She wishes to make you her heiress, of course. You must know that my aunt has no children of her own, so what could be more natural? It does seem about time something good came of my having been born a Rowbridge."

Beatrix clapped her hands in delight and gave a squeal that set her lovely golden curls to dancing. "Oh, Saskia! Would it not be wonderful? Do you suppose it can be true?"

"I can think of no reason at all why it should be," she said calmly. She turned a gentle smile on her mother. "I'm afraid, Mama, that I am not one of your heroines for whom things always so conveniently turn right in the end." She regarded her sister with an affectionate smile.

"Now if it had been Trix, I just might have believed it. If anyone was cut out for a heroine, it's she. With those eyes! But whoever heard of a too tall, rather angular heroine, with hair of mousy brown and an overdeveloped streak of common sense?"

"Nonsense," exclaimed her mama. "*All* my children are particularly handsome. I quite pride myself on the fact. And besides, dearest," she added with an unwonted twinkle, "heiresses are always beautiful. Didn't you know?"

Saskia regarded her mother with respect for the rare flash of insight from one who generally suffered an almost impenetrable vagueness about the realities of life.

"An heiress," sighed Beatrix, drinking in the dream of grandeur that the word implied.

"Well, *I* am certainly no heiress," said the practical Saskia. "Nor am I at all likely to become one. And at my age it no longer matters much whether I am a beauty or not."

"Pooh!" said Beatrix. "To hear you talk one would think you a positive ape-leader."

"Well perhaps not yet," laughed Saskia. "But at one-and-twenty I am scarcely in the first bloom of youth."

"Pooh!" repeated Beatrix and gave her sister a teasing grin. "Mr. Kneighley doesn't seem to mind it a bit that you are practically in your dotage. And I daresay he has scarce noticed that you are a positive antidote."

A ripple of mirth she could not suppress escaped Saskia. "Mr. Kneighley is by far too wrapped up in admiring his own oratory to notice even the color of my hair. I daresay whatever admiration he feels for me has more to do with the flattering degree of attention with which I seem to be listening to him on Sunday mornings. I must *look* like I am listening when I am concentrating so *very* hard on staying awake. Poor Mr. Kneighley is a very good sort of man, I'm sure, but he is such a hopelessly prosy bore."

"Well, he shan't have you, in any case," said Beatrix with unusual emphasis. "You are far too good for him.

And you *shall* go to Bath. Our aunt is sure to adore you. Don't you agree, Mama?"

The two girls looked expectantly toward their mother. But Cornelia van Houten was no longer with them. That particular look of concentration, a tiny frown appearing over the vaguely crossed eyes that focused on some inner muse, proclaimed quite clearly that Cornelia Crawley, Authoress, had returned in her stead.

"Come, Trix," whispered Saskia. "We shall leave Mama to her work. You can help me decide what to pack."

As the two girls walked softly from the room, the older woman reached for her pen and her notes and began to scribble: "Harem, eunuchs, camel's milk . . ."

Chapter Two

The next few days saw Saskia van Houten in a mighty struggle with her conscience. She did not feel she ought to go jauntering off to Bath, leaving her family to shift for themselves. But her more selfish side longed to grasp at the chance of a few days free from the constant demands of running such a clamorous household. Her baser self finally won the battle, goaded on by the prospect that perhaps her wealthy Aunt Eccles might, after all, be induced, or cajoled, or at least goaded, into doing something handsome for the van Houtens. So she packed her few simple gowns into the least battered valise that could be found in the attic, held a long colloquy with Mrs. Jansen, the round Dutch housekeeper, left pages of instructions with Beatrix and lists of admonitions with the twins, and prepared for her holiday.

The whole family was in front of the snug (a euphemism for *far too small*, Saskia thought wryly) cottage in Eynshant, the Oxfordshire village which the van Houten family called home, to see her into the elegant chaise-and-four which her great-aunt had sent for her. Even Mama had been pried away from the exciting trials and tribulations of her poor Magdalena to wave a handkerchief in farewell.

Rembrandt, the family dog, made it as far as the porch where he settled into a half-snooze, opening one eye every now and then to see if anything of interest was going forward, then closing it again when he discovered that it was not. To be sure, the unusual arrival of a coach-and-four had warranted an investigation, a few snuffles, and a loud bark or two for the horses' benefit. But even such a magnificent equipage could not hope to compete with his very own well-chewed pillow pulled into a bright patch of sunshine on a warm spring morning.

Mrs. Jansen, who was much more a member of the family than a mere housekeeper, bustled about the carriage like a hen. She must make certain there were enough rugs to ward off any chance draft and place a hot brick for Saskia's feet. She loaded the overflowing hamper which she had filled with enough bread and cheese, oranges and sour pickles, hard-cooked eggs, macaroons, and cream buns to feed six hungry men, then she engulfed Saskia in an enveloping hug.

"*Pas op, lieveling,*" she warned in Dutch.

"Of course I will be careful, Jannie," replied Saskia. "What can happen to me, after all?"

The twelve-year-old twins frisked about the luxurious coach, Willem admiring the beautiful team of bays and sneaking them lumps of sugar from the kitchen, Mina oohing and aahing over the postboys, in their silver and grey livery, who were scarce older than she. Give that one a few more years and the gentlemen would be pounding down the door. Despite a still-strong hoydenish streak, she was already bidding fair to outdo Beatrix in beauty.

Cornelius, the oldest boy in the family at eighteen (going on eighty, Saskia sometimes thought) had strolled out of the library and stood in his usual stance, a book under one arm, a finger tucked securely between the pages to mark his spot. Neil was the scholar of the family and it was obvious he was eager to get back to his book. It was probably some terribly exciting tome on the romance of higher mathematics.

"Say, Sask," he said with sudden interest. "Do you think you might look out a copy of Carey's *Basics of Aerodynamics* for me while you're there? Couldn't find it last time I was in Oxford, and I really must have it, you know. It's got all his theories and his diagrams of bird flight. Give a look, will you?"

"Carey, *Basics of Aerodynamics*," Saskia muttered, mentally adding it to an already absurdly long list of trifles she'd been asked to "look out." "And yes, Trix," she cut off her sister before she could speak. "I have your blue muslin for matching. I promise not to return without your ribbons. And Mina's sugarplums. And Willem's new crop. Some camphorated spirits for Jannie and Miss Austen's latest novel for Mama. Now, have I forgotten anything?"

"Of course you have, silly," cried Beatrix. "You are to bring us back Aunt Eccles's fortune, of course." The smile that brought the pert dimples to Beatrix's face erased any taint of selfishness her words might imply.

"And shall I look out for a rich husband while I'm about it? Why stop at only one fortune, after all?" she teased.

"That would be very nice, darling," said her optimistic mama, who saw no reason at all why the feat should not be easily accomplished. "I'm sure you would like it very well."

"In any case," Beatrix went on, "you are to buy yourself a new spring bonnet, an extravagantly fetching one."

"Oh, but there is no need to now, when yours becomes me so mightily," teased Saskia, adjusting the ribbons on the pretty confection of yellow chip straw that was perched at a jaunty angle over her brown waves. The bonnet went some little way toward dressing up the plain brown merino pelisse, beginning to fray at the cuffs and hem, which covered an equally plain orchre muslin round dress of several summers' wear. While she looked neat as a pin and entirely proper, Miss van

Houten was scarce a threat to the fashion queens of the day.

With a final round of embraces she stepped up into the chaise and rolled away at last, waving out the window until she rounded a bend and could no longer see the little family group dispersing into the house.

The first primroses were already peeking out of the hedges, and the rolling hills glowed with the rich new green of spring as Saskia began her adventure. She leaned back against the luxuriously upholstered squabs and wallowed in the freedom of this unexpected holiday. She began to hum a little tune, some vague accompaniment to the birdsong that followed her.

This mellow mood lasted nearly half an hour and carried her the half dozen or so miles that separated Eynshant from Oxford. But even before the towers of the university town were clearly in view, she had reverted to her usual mental stance of worrying what was to become of her family.

As the oldest and most sensible offspring of two very merry and impractical parents, it had long since fallen to Saskia to run the household. They all acknowledged her as its actual, if not titular, head. To be fair, it was the exertions of Mama, toiling over her annoying left-wing quill, which put bread on the table, and Saskia was at great pains to create an atmosphere to encourage her prolific output.

But the London publishers of this, the enlightened nineteenth century, were still medievally clutch-fisted when it came to paying their authors enough to live on, especially when they were women. More than once, Saskia had been forced to make the incredibly dreary trip to London on the Common Stage to tussle with a particularly recalcitrant publisher over the question of monies due.

One could not exactly call the van Houtens poor. Their cottage, though more than a little cramped with five children and a dog, was cozy and comfortable. The neat little kitchen garden that was Beatrix's special domain provided fresh vegetables and berries and other good things, and Mrs. Jansen, who had adamantly refused to allow them to leave Amsterdam without her, always contrived to fill the larder and the table with the most delicious of treats and to keep the boys in hand-knitted socks.

True, the draperies were definitely threadbare, and they had recently taken to using smelly oil lamps in a few of the rooms. It was shocking how high the price of wax candles had climbed. But they managed to go on quite cozily for all that. The present was not the problem. It was the future that caused Saskia endless anxiety.

What seemed to be her most pressing worry just now was brought to mind by the august towers of the colleges of Oxford rolling into view. Neil, her oldest and most brilliant brother, would soon be ready for university and how on earth it was to be paid for was a mystery. But he absolutely *must* go; his brilliance must not be wasted. He had long since outstripped Mr. Kneighley's efforts to teach him. The pompous young rector struggled to believe himself on top of the situation, but it was abundantly clear that Neil had learned everything the man had to teach. Why, he could already talk three strong men to distraction in any discussion of aerodynamics, and once give him a sticky problem in mathematics and his deep blue eyes glowed with the pure joy of searching out the answer.

And though Neil's education might be the most pressing of her worries, it was by no means the only one. The twins were both in need of stronger guidance than she could provide. Willem would never be a scholar like his brother, but a stint in a good school might go a long way toward curbing the wild streak that had grown so markedly the last two years.

Saskia knew well that she should have disciplined the boy with a sterner hand. But it had seemed impossible somehow. When Papa had died, mischievous little Willem, the quintessential Dutch boy and so much his father's son, had been knocked totally off-balance. He had climbed into a shell thick as a tortoise's, where even his twin sister, so much a part of him, could not reach. And when, after nearly a year, he had finally begun to emerge and show signs of his former liveliness, Saskia hadn't the heart to put the least curb on him.

Unfortunately, Mina (Wilhelmina when she was naughty—which was lamentably frequent—because she disliked the name heartily) idolized her twin brother and followed him into every sort of scrape and start. The girl had turned into a regular hoyden. It was high time she had a governess who could instill in her the proper sort of behavior that her sister seemed unable to do.

And then there was Beatrix. Saskia could never help smiling when the image of her sister crossed her mind's eye. Who could contemplate such perfect beauty, such a lively spirit, and such a completely amiable nature with anything but joy? Trix was like the colorful wildflowers lining the road Saskia was traveling, seeming to laugh brightly as they bobbed their heads to the breeze.

But Saskia's smile quickly soured and the tiny frown lines appeared on her smooth, wide brow. What was to become of Trix? Such beauty should—indeed *must!*—be allowed to shine. The girl should, by all rights, make a brilliant match if only one absolutely necessary attribute were not totally lacking. There would be no fortune, no dowry at all, to go with the soft hand and sparkling eye of Beatrix van Houten. In her more optimistic moments, Saskia believed that such a handicap could be overcome if only Trix could be *seen* by the right sort of gentleman. Surely a man of birth and fortune who truly loved her wouldn't let her lack of dowry stand in the way of marrying such a treasure. And her birth was certainly good enough to marry into the highest of families. Her mama had been a Rowbridge, after all.

But what chance was there for Trix, to even *meet* such a gentleman, stuck away as she was in Eynshant, totally *wasted* in the little country hamlet? Mr. Kneighley seemed blind to her charms—indeed Saskia sometimes suspected him of being more than a bit short-sighted, for he did have a terrible squint, though he was far too vain to be seen in spectacles—and there were few other single gentlemen in the neighborhood.

Of course there was Freddie Winslow, the Squire's son. He was as smitten with Trix as it is possible for a young man of nineteen to be, which is to say considerably. But he was a desperately silly, frippery sort of fellow much given to such fancies as Cossack trousers of a vitriolic yellow, cut so full he looked like he was swimming whenever he strolled down the village High Street, and cravats grown higher and stiffer and more intricate daily till they threatened his sight if he turned his head too quickly. In short, he was an impertinent young coxcomb, and Saskia couldn't bear the thought of her beloved young sister sinking to *that*. The young man was currently up at Oxford, but their close proximity to the university town made it simple for him to toddle home whenever he liked. And he liked far too often for Saskia's peace of mind.

Even Mama needed looking after, for when in the throes and tales, she was prone to forget that night follows day and that one must eat and sleep if one is to work effectively.

Whichever way Saskia twisted her mind in thought, bending it to the task of finding the perfect answer to all her worries for the future, it inevitably led her back to the only real solution that seemed viable. She must marry. The thought gave her no joy. Not that she didn't believe in the efficacy of marriage. Her own parents had been perfectly suited and deliriously happy together. Perhaps it was that which caused a frown to shade her face now. She had had a wonderful example of what marriage *could* be, and she had no desire to settle for less.

It might seem odd to the casual observer that Saskia van Houten had been allowed to reach the ripe old age of one-and-twenty still single. She had certainly not lived a life entirely devoid of suitors. In fact, Papa had used to tease her unmercifully about what he called the flocks of unfledged young 'uns, or their Dutch equivalent, fluttering around the door. She had turned down several very advantageous offers for a quite simple, straightforward reason. She had never yet been in love.

She had actually tried very hard to fall in love once with a certain French cavalry officer stationed in Amsterdam, and she came fairly close to succeeding. Papa, thoroughly anti-French, had been set against the young man, which of course made falling in love with him that much simpler and more attractive. But when it became evident that the fortune he expected to go with her hand would not materialize, and it was borne in on the young man that a half-English wife would do his military career no good, Saskia's charms seemed to hold less appeal than before. He quickly forsook them for those of a well-dowered, well-connected Dutch lady and began his rapid rise in the ranks.

Saskia, try though she might to mourn his loss, couldn't seem to force herself to grieve more than a week. She lost not a single ounce over the affair, and cried considerably less than a whole bucket of tears over his defection. She thus easily recognized that she had not really been in love at all.

Now, at what she considered her advanced age, she truly thought herself beyond romance. Any marriage she might contract now would be one of convenience only, entered into with a steady hand and an eye toward bettering the future of the family that depended on her, and with no frippery considerations such as love allowed to color her decision. She knew she was being very common-sensical to consider it in this light. She couldn't think why the notion should make her feel so horribly low.

She gazed out of the carriage onto the bursting green countryside in an attempt to give her thoughts a brighter direction. This was supposed to be a holiday, after all, and she *would not* spend her entire time in these constant worries. She tried to fix her attention on the passing beauty, and even succeeded in noting that the English countryside, which she had never tired of, was at its very best in April.

A quick movement caught her eye. She turned her head just in time to catch a glimpse of a weasel darting across the road and disappearing under a hedge. As the carriage rolled past the spot, the pointy little face of the creature bobbed up to peer at her, looking for all the world like Mr. Kneighley peering over the top of his pulpit of a Sunday morning, and she was plunged right back into her unproductive train of thought on the question of marriage.

For Mr. Kneighley seemed to be the only current candidate for the post of husband to Saskia and savior and protector of her family. Though only a country rector, his post was a well-remunerated one, and he also had an independent income from his family. And though Beatrix insisted that the squinty-faced little rector was not nearly good enough for Saskia, he *had* offered and must in all conscience be considered.

There were certainly inducements to accepting him. He had often hinted that he would have no objection to sending a brilliant brother-in-law to Magdalen College, his own *alma mater,* and he *might* be able to exert some steadying influence over Willem—even though the boy loathed him. And then, the rectory was but a five-minute walk from the van Houten cottage, and Saskia would be able to run the household almost as effectively as she did now.

But, oh dear, he was as dull as ditch water and so unbearably pompous and prosy that Saskia often wanted to scream with vexation. What a dreadfully *boring* life such a marriage would be. She wasn't at all sure she could bear it.

She gave an involuntary grimace as the scene of the evening before sprang to mind, for it was then that Mr. Kneighley had chosen to make his declaration in form. Saskia had, with some trepidation, seen it coming for months and had been at great pains to keep him from

coming to the point. The Lord knew why he had chosen
to speak at last unless, Saskia thought with a wry smile,
he felt somehow threatened by this holiday of hers in
Bath. Indeed, one never knew what mischief such as she
might get up to in such a gay place. She might take it
into her head to elope with a gouty grandfather—provided he could be urged away from the curative Bath
waters long enough for the ceremony to be performed—
or waltz the night away with an aged baronet, romanti-
cally discussing the various manifestations of chronic
indigestion.

In an effort to be fair to Mr. Kneighley, she admitted
the improbability of his harboring any jealous fears
about her trip. He was far too filled with self-impor-
tance and had far too high an opinion of his own worth
to entertain the vaguest notion that Miss van Houten
could find anyone she might prefer to himself. He had
paid her the supreme compliment of asking her for her
hand in marriage, and what more could a young woman
in her position desire?

It had been the sheerest mischance that Mr. Kneighley, walking up through the garden from the Rectory,
had come upon Saskia quite alone in the morning room,
penning a letter with becoming concentration. The os-
tensible reason for his visit was to bid her a final adieu
and to bring her a copy of *Fordyce's Sermons* to beguile
her weary hours in the carriage, which book she had
unaccountably left behind.

But the rector had never been a man slow to recognize opportunity when it faced him head on, and finding
Saskia alone, he put on his homily-speaking voice and
plunged into his long-prepared sermon on the felicity of
marriage and his admiration of her person. Saskia, momentarily struck quite speechless by his eloquence—or
was it his absurdity?—could make not the slightest move
to staunch the flow and the rector, before he was many
minutes into his monologue, was so encouraged as to
somewhat gingerly lower his unromantically scrawny
person to its knees. His mama had informed him that

ladies appreciated—nay required—such courtly touches
to their wooing, and he wished not to be found backward in any little gesture which might please and convince his chosen bride. His words, though fluidly,
rollingly spoken, were somewhat less romantic than his
stance.

"I consider it as incumbent on myself to set the proper
example of felicitous matrimony for my flock, who
naturally look to me for guidance in such matters. I
deem it the first responsibility of a clergyman to show,
through his own actions, the benefits to be gained by the
wise choice of one's life's mate, and the good manage-
ment of his household such a mate can provide."

At this point Saskia did finally make an attempt to
speak, if for no better reason than to get the poor man
up from his extremely unbecoming posture. "Dear sir, I
beg you . . . ," she began, but her effort was doomed.
The rector's fatuous smile broadened and he held up a
hand.

"Ah, no, no, you must not thank me yet, Miss van
Houten, as I flatter myself you are about to do. Hear me
out, first, I pray you. I would have you know the bad as
well as the good, so as to make your decision an informed one."

Saskia was effectively silenced by this. She could not
imagine Mr. Kneighley owning up to a fault, and was
bursting to know which one he would choose to acknowledge.

"I fear I may be just a bit too fond of gaiety for a man
in my position, as my sainted mama has, on occasion,
hinted to me. For you must know that I dearly love to
spend an evening at whist with companionable friends
and have been known to lose as much as six shillings of
an evening. In my own defense, I must plead the loneliness of the single life"—which single life Saskia knew
very well included an overbearing mother and a stiffly
pious spinster sister residing at the Rectory—"and give
my solemn pledge to set aside such frivolities, except in
those cases where to refuse to join a card table would be

considered a social solecism, when I have the more appealing alternative of my own wife beside my own fire."

"Oh, get up, do, Mr. Kneighley," Saskia burst out before he could go on. "I am convinced you cannot be comfortable in that absurd position." She was longing to put a period to his rhetoric, though she was not at all certain what she would say when she did. But she could not bear him longer on his knees.

He rose painfully and gratefully. "Ah, you are a sensible woman, Miss van Houten. A man in my position stands greatly in need of a sensible wife. I am sure it will flatter your good sense to hear that it is my chief reason for choosing to honor you in this manner. And of course, you always make a very creditable appearance. I hope you know that I am not a worldly man, but in my position it is of the first importance that my wife should be able to mix well at every level of society. I should not like it bruited about, mind, but . . ."

It was evident from his expanding smile, his thin blue lips stretched almost to the breaking point over his mouthful of teeth, that Mr. Kneighley was about to play his trump card. ". . . I have no compunction in telling *you*, my dear Miss van Houten, that I harbor rather high and, I may humbly say, not unfounded hopes that I shall not long remain a rector in a small country parish. What would you say to the idea of moving to, say, Oxford, as wife of the chaplain?"

He puffed up his tiny chest till he looked very like a turkey-cock. Saskia half expected him to gobble.

"The position," he went on, "as I am sure you are aware, stands in direct line to a bishopric. So you can see the importance of my having a wife of whom I need never feel the least shame. I am entirely confident that, married to such as you, and once you have a bit of experience behind you, I need never blush for the behavior of the lady I have honored with the title of wife."

Saskia might well have been insulted had she not been so amused at Mr. Kneighley's absurd posturings. In her attempts to hide her smiles, she could not be offended at the back-handed compliment.

"And so it remains," he said, finally winding to a conclusion, "for me to assure you of the violence of my affection and admiration for your own esteemed person"—anything less violent than the regard thus exhibited would be hard to imagine, she thought—"and to ask you to name the date on which I may expect to be made the happiest of men." And myself the most depressed of females, continued her unruly mind.

The possibility of a refusal of his flattering offer was obviously the furthest thing from Mr. Kneighley's narrow mind. But in defiance of the several stern talkings-to she had given herself, Saskia was unable to give him the acceptance he so patently expected. Every finer feeling revolted at such an action.

But she had been equally unable to refuse him outright. With a large and needy family depending on her, she didn't feel she had the right to do so. How could she sacrifice Neil and Trix, the twins and even Mama, to her own selfish dreams?

And so she had prevaricated. To gain time for ordering her thoughts, or for accustoming herself to her bleak future, she had mouthed all the expected inanities about being truly sensible of the honor done her, et cetera, but her final answer had been that she would consider his proposal during her short stay in Bath and give him her answer on her return.

Mr. Kneighley was obviously more than a bit surprised that there should be the slightest question in her mind, but he agreed to the short put-off with alacrity. He complimented her on her good sense in wishing to fully consider such a profound step as marriage and was totally confident of her final acquiescence on her return from her holiday.

Finally he went away, leaving behind him far more food for thought than was contained within the covers of Mr. Fordyce's *Sermons*.

Now riding along in the carriage, it didn't seem to

Saskia that she should even be pondering the question of such a marriage amid the bursting fullness of an English spring, all new and bright and full of promise. Surely a marriage to such as Mr. Kneighley should only be considered in late autumn, among the dead and dying leaves, when everything was turning grey and all living things were steeling themselves for the ordeal of the harsh season ahead.

Now she thought of it, Mr. Kneighley bore an uncanny resemblance to a scrawny tree, stark and forlorn, shorn of its summer's growth. And his mama was very like the hawk that was drifting slowly over her head, riding the currents and looking out for a nice soft victim for its razor-sharp talons.

An involuntary shudder escaped her and she pulled one of the soft carriage rugs more firmly about her. With strong resolution, she pushed the image of the rector away and picked up the copy of *Pride and Prejudice*, which she had brought along, *quite* by mistake, instead of the *Sermons*. She snuggled down to beguile the remaining hours, blithely unaware that she was hurrying—albeit at a sedate and proper pace—toward her fate.

Chapter Three

Saskia van Houten's comfortable chaise-and-four was not the only equipage of interest moving steadily toward Bath on that lovely spring day. In another quite similar carriage an auburn-haired, serious-looking young gentleman who might have been called handsome with more than a grain of truth, particularly when he smiled which was unfortunately rare, was bowling along the Bath Road at a fair clip. He had left his London lodgings that morning still in some confusion about the purpose of this rather tedious trip. Now, with the same primroses and robins passing unheeded outside his window as greeted Miss van Houten, he pulled out the very odd letter from this totally unexpected great-aunt of his and read it through yet again.

Until three days ago Derek Rowbridge didn't even know he *had* a great-aunt by the name of Eccles, and he had at first been much inclined to suspect that the eccentric letter had been directed to him by mistake or as some sort of prank. But a close check of *Debrett's Peerage*, 1815 edition, convinced him that Hester, Lady Eccles, *née* Rowbridge, was indeed his very own relation. Further inquiries had elicited the information that not only was she a Rowbridge born, sister of his scandalous grandfather and even more eccentric than he was reputed to have been, she was also enormously wealthy.

He learned that she had left England more than forty years before and had spent the ensuing period jauntering about the deserts of the Holy Land, the jungles of Africa, the sandy hills of India, and assorted other heathen and uncharted wildernesses. She'd gone through three husbands, each wealthier than his predecessor, and cut a swath through the sheikdoms, sultanates, and pashalics of the Exotic East that would not soon be forgot by those lucky enough to have encountered "the Divine Hester."

Now she had returned to England disgustingly rich, and, what Mr. Rowbridge considered very much more to the point, without any living relations other than himself, at least so far as he could determine.

In fact, before the arrival of her letter, Derek had believed himself to be totally without relations in the world, if one discounted, as he continually tried to do, some quite distant and thoroughly obnoxious cousins on his mother's side.

There had been days, of course, when he had thought longingly of how useful it could be to have an aged and wealthy godfather. But it had always been an idle daydream, certainly not one he expected to assume any aspect of reality. Now, he thought happily and with his rare and truly enchanting smile fleeting across his well-defined mouth and brightening his hazel eyes, a wealthy aunt might do just as well.

It must be said in Mr. Rowbridge's defense that he was *not* a money-grubbing sort of gentleman. His greatest pleasures were quite simple ones, really. He enjoyed good food and good company, liked to look at a pretty girl now and then, and could be quite as happy on a fine horse amid a beautiful countryside as he had been on the deck of a fine ship amid the waves over which his nation ruled.

Unlike many young men of his birth, he had never tried to divorce himself from the idea of hard work. He had been a reliable and occasionally innovative young officer in His Britannic Majesty's Royal Navy for several years, helping to bottle up the French in their attempts to take over the seas, and rising rapidly from midshipman to the rank of first lieutenant. He would have made a conscientious landlord of the estate on which he had been raised had he been given the chance.

He had never felt the need to cut a dash, nor to be a Corinthian, and certainly not a Tulip, a race of gentlemen he held in contempt. He did occasionally and wistfully wish that he could replace his coats more often, keep a carriage of his own, and generally live the sort of existence he had been born to and would have enjoyed had things turned out differently.

But as it was, Derek Rowbridge was what might euphemistically be called purse-pinched and could more realistically be called poor. Despite this sad state, it was not greed or an extravagant nature that made a little beam of hope glow in his eyes at thought of the wealth of this unexpected aunt. The deprivations he had suffered in the last year were, to his mind, minor ones. He hadn't learned to like them, but he had discovered how to live with them, allowing them to dampen his good humor only a little now and then.

He did, however, have one character trait which was very strong and, through no fault of his own, very expensive. He was an honorable man.

Now honor, under normal circumstances, needn't cost all that much. But in Derek's case there was an extenuating circumstance. His father, like his grandfather, had been an inveterate gamester. A popular man with a ready wit and a bright laugh, he had been heard to chuckle merrily as he won and lost fortunes at the tables. Unhappily, he lost one or two more of them than he won, and at his death, just over a year ago, he had been deeply in debt.

Derek, during his Navy years, had been so seldom at home that he was not fully aware of the extent of his father's losses. But when Napoleon had finally been de-

feated once and for all and sent off to St. Helena, and
Lieutenant Rowbridge had come home, a half-pay officer, to deal with the estate of his recently deceased father, he had been appalled to learn the true state of
things. The old man had been badly under the hatches.
Instead of inheriting the snug estate that should have
been his, Derek was left with nothing but gaming debts
mounting into the thousands of pounds. The young officer, full of ideas and prize money, was quickly reduced
to a near-pauper status.

Derek Rowbridge, an honorable man, and proud of
the ancient though slightly tarnished name he bore, had
unhesitatingly refused all offers from his father's credi-
tors to forgive the outstanding debts. He was determined to pay back every penny.

How this was to be accomplished on the six shillings a
day allotted to a naval lieutenant on half pay did
present something of a problem.

He was not afraid of work, and in a port as busy as
London there was always work in plenty for a strong
and willing pair of hands. He had occasionally, when
things were really desperate, turned his hand to loading
cargo, hauling canvas, and transporting warehouse stores
on the London docks, his powerful frame stripped to the
waist and trickles of perspiration glistening on his
bronzed chest. But the miserably few pennies these ac-
tivities returned went no distance at all toward reaching
his goal.

He'd then considered the idea of marrying an heiress,
and had even gone so far as to appear at a few *ton* parties with that object in mind. But though he liked to
dance with a pretty girl as much as any ripe young
gentleman did, he had never been much in the petticoat
line. His years at sea had given him little experience in
the art of dalliance and his lack of sisters had left him
with a paucity of understanding of the feminine character. He'd encountered several girls who fit what he supposed to be the ideal of womanhood: all softness and
smiles and clinging helplessness. But fifteen minutes in

their company soon sent him running. The inanity of their conversation bored him; their missish simperings drove him to distraction; and he soon found himself running for the safety of his male cronies.

Perhaps he might have steeled himself to the idea of a life spent with such a creature, for many of his friends had just such marriages. Livelier female company could always be found outside one's home, after all. But his lack of fortune meant that the only likely candidates for the position of Mrs. Derek Rowbridge were the daughters of wealthy Cits and merchants desirous of marrying into an old and noble family. Since nothing like love had touched his heart with any of the hopeful young ladies, it was a simple matter to decide he could not marry so far beneath himself. He was, after all, a Rowbridge and very, nay insufferably, proud of it.

And so he had lighted on the only reasonable alternative left him. Gaming, though it bored him unutterably, was, after all, in the blood. Why should he not use it to his advantage? So he settled into a tedious routine. Each month, on drawing his half pay, he would count out the miserably few shillings he allowed himself for his own needs. With the rest he would stroll off toward one of his clubs, generally Arthur's or the Naval (White's and Boodle's, while certainly not above his touch socially, were well above his pocket), and seek out a "friendly" game of piquet with one of his willing and well-heeled superior officers. The pleasure he might have felt in participating in a game he knew himself to play remarkably well was offset by the determination, the absolute necessity, of winning.

And win he did, with just enough exceptions to keep from scaring off his partners. And nearly every penny of those winnings was immediately funneled into paying off his father's debts. He was making progress. It might be as little as thirty years till he was free and clear and able to get on with his own life. He would only be, let's see, fifty-six, he thought wryly.

He pushed the utterly depressing thought firmly from

his mind. Here he was riding along in a well-sprung chaise-and-four, leaning back on the most luxurious of velvet squabs, and looking out on a countryside bursting with the optimism that only comes at the end of a long hard winter. Surely he could allow himself some small share of that optimism.

The carriage rolled through Savernake Forest, cool and dark, then began the long climb up Forest Hill. The mesmeric bobbing of the postillions' capped heads as they gently nudged their steeds up the steep grade sent Derek to dreaming of a rosier future for himself than the one he now imagined was his almost certain due. In this mellow mood he closed his eyes and soon drifted off.

Chapter Four

It was nearing dusk when Derek Rowbridge's carriage reached Marlborough. Although he had told the postillions he would put up there for the night, he was taken by surprise when he found himself being swept around the circular drive before the elegantly porticoed grey brick facade of the famous Castle Inn, renowned as one of the finest hostelries on the Bath Road. Here was none of the bustle and clamor found at a more plebeian stopping place. No ostlers shouted profanities to each other; no squawking chickens pecked about the yard; no disreputable piles of luggage awaited the carrier's cart. At the Castle Inn all was dignified stateliness, understated elegance, and seemly behavior.

Such opulence of accommodation was far beyond Mr. Rowbridge's pocket, and he reluctantly leaned forward to motion the postillions to drive on to some humbler and cheaper hostelry. But before he could do so, he found the door of his chaise eased gently open by a very superior footman who proceeded to let the steps silently down, then favored the passenger with a grave bow.

"Mr. Rowbridge, is it not?" he said, to that gentleman's great surprise. "Your rooms are ready, sir. This

you please. The boy will attend to your bags."
Mr. wbridge, speechless, could only follow.

In moments he was in the graceful entrance hall and
the landlord himself was bowing a welcome. "Ah, Mr.
Rowbridge. I do hope you will be comfortable with us.
The rooms bespoke by Her Ladyship for you are quite
ready."

Mr. Rowbridge, taking in the opulence that had at
various times housed the likes of Lord Byron and the
great Beau Brummell himself, fervently hoped that in
this case "bespoke" also meant "paid for" and considered
the pitifully few shillings in his purse. A few hopefully
subtle questions and some definitely discreet answers
reassured him, and he relaxed and allowed himself to
enjoy the experience. He followed yet another footman
to his rooms to prepare for what he was certain would
be an excellent dinner. He would follow it with a glass
of port and a cigar, and sleep the sleep of the just on the
finest of linen bedsheets.

Apparently Her Ladyship had been quite busy "be-
speaking" rooms at the Castle Inn. It was while Derek
was beginning on that very fine dinner, enjoying the
genteel bustle of the public dining room, that Saskia van
Houten descended the grand staircase of the inn. Her
slippers stepped noiselessly on the thick crimson carpet;
her gloved hand slid easily over the polished mahogany
banister. Oh, she would have such wonders to relate to
Mama, and Trix, and all of them. Cornelius *might* even
be impressed by the fact that his sister had slept in the
very room that had housed the great Walpole so many
years before. How very kind it had been of her great-
aunt to engage such superior accommodations for her.
She was determined to enjoy every moment of such unexpected luxury.

She stepped to the door of the large gilt-chandeliered
dining room and paused, unsure, on the threshold. She
knew that, even in this enlightened era, it was more
than a bit unusual to see a totally unaccompanied young
woman in a public inn. How she wished she had Trix

with her—though then the gentlemen would be certain to stare!—or Mama, or at the very least an abigail.

But surely here, Saskia told herself, in such a very genteel and respectable inn, she might eat her dinner in public without undue embarrassment. Valiantly as she had tried, she found she couldn't bear to sit in solitary splendor in the private parlor her aunt had so thoughtfully engaged for her. It was a lovely room, all pastel stripes and white wainscoting, but its loneliness soon led to the following rather one-sided conversation.

"Hello, wall," said Saskia cheerfully. The wall did not deign to answer. "My, what a very handsome wall you are. I do think green and yellow suit you especially well." Silence. "Tell me, wall. Do you not think yellow will give way to pink this season?" The wall didn't seem to have an opinion on this important point of fashion. "Oh well. I suppose I shall have to wait and see, though I fancy you should prefer the yellow."

This conversation didn't seem to be leading in any very promising direction, and Saskia's unruly mind soon reverted to the unfruitful thoughts that had plagued it for most of the day.

"No!" she exclaimed, either to the wall, to the air, or to herself. "I will *not* sit here fretting away the evening in this ridiculous fashion."

And so she donned her plainest evening dress—even the gayest was pretty plain, she admitted ruefully—swallowed hard, and descended to dinner.

"Miss van Houten," exclaimed the landlord as she paused on the threshold of the dining room. "How may I serve you? Some problem with your private parlor, perhaps?"

"Oh, no, sir. None at all, I assure you. It is wonderfully comfortable. It is only that, after so many hours in a carriage with nothing but my own thoughts to occupy me, I find I cannot bear another moment of my own company. And it occurred to me how much I should prefer to eat my dinner down here, surrounded by other wandering souls."

If the landlord was displeased at the notion of an unescorted lady in his dignified dining room, it showed by not so much as a flicker of an eyelash. Any connection of Lady Hester Eccles must be assumed to be slightly eccentric, and the landlord had no wish to offend Her Ladyship in any way. In any case, the young lady *looked* quite modest and respectable with her hair wrapped in neat braids around her head and a small cameo on a velvet ribbon about her fine long neck. And times were changing—he allowed himself a little inward sigh of resignation at what the modern world was coming to—and he supposed he must change with them.

"Of course, miss," he said with a bow. "There is a quiet table near the fire which may suit."

Another superior servant appeared at her elbow as if by magic to show her to her table. She followed in his wake, feeling like a freak in a sideshow and trying to look as inconspicuous as possible.

If she roused much curiosity in the other guests, they were too well-bred to show it, and she soon began to relax and look about her. There was much to see. The room itself was lovely, beautifully proportioned and elegantly appointed. But it was the people who caught and held her attention.

Saskia never tired of observing her fellow creatures in all their wondrous variety. She had long ago developed the game, or quirk, of assigning appropriate names to those she observed. She indulged in it now with abandon.

The lady just rising from a table she christened Mrs. Zebra. In a vain attempt to minimize her bulk and maximize her not very considerable height, she had dressed herself all in stripes: claret on a chartreuse-striped petticoat under a cherry-on-white-striped overskirt, topped by an evening spencer of an unfortunate shade of pink on buttercup yellow. The poor thing looked like a padded maypole, forlornly waiting for some frolickers to come pick up its ribbons.

Spooning up white soup across the room was Sir Cipher, a thin man so pale of face and hair that he almost wasn't there. And beyond him, making a somewhat heartier meal, was a jolly-looking fellow she immediately named Mr. Burgher because of his good Dutch burgher face. He was round-cheeked and ruddy with a smile straight out of a Frans Hals portrait, an altogether open, honest face, but also one not likely to miss anything of importance in the world and certainly not one to be imposed upon. Yes, she thought, very Dutch.

The waiter brought her a tureen of heavenly scented soup, and she turned her attention to her dinner. Usually a light eater, tonight she feasted on *semelles* of veal in piquant sauce and roasted guinea fowl. There was a deliciously tart red jelly which she learned from the waiter was made from an American fruit called the cranberry. There were broiled mushrooms and roasted new potatoes, and the whole was crowned with a ribbon blancmange and coffee cream in a chocolate cup. Saskia really fancied she could learn to enjoy the kind of wealth that allowed one to eat such a meal whenever one chose.

The dinner, in all its splendor, had deserved her full attention. But now, as she spooned up the last of the blancmange, she let her eyes wander again. This time they lighted on a gentleman near the door, a young gentleman with auburn hair.

The young man held her attention because there was something vaguely familiar about him. Nothing pronounced certainly, nor even very definite. She was quite certain she had never seen him before. But there was an expression about the eyes, a tilt to the jaw that she thought ought to remind her of someone she knew well. She couldn't for the life of her think who.

The waiter was just removing the remains of a roast leveret and a dish of artichoke bottoms from the gentleman's table and offering a delicate orange soufflé and a plate of Chantilly baskets. The young man waved away the sweets and motioned the waiter to pour him another glass of wine.

A ripple of annoyance went through Saskia. The fellow probably ate like this every night of the week, she thought. No wonder he could wave away such a treat with barely a glance. There would always be another tomorrow, should he want one, and another after that.

There was an air of assurance, of arrogance even, she thought, in the way he lifted his glass to the light to examine its rich ruby color. He was probably wondering if just such a claret-colored coat would suit him, she mused. At the moment, he was wearing hunter green, which did in fact suit him very well. From this distance she could see only that it seemed to be well cut and that his cravat was a snowy white.

A fashionable fribble, she decided. She would call him Lord Fribble.

Just as a smile tilted up her mouth at the thought, the auburn-haired gentleman looked up and surprised her gaze. With a little blush, she looked quickly down and began studiously worrying her blancmange.

She didn't look up again, but she could see from the corner of her eye that he was still looking at her, staring in fact, quite impertinently. So he was ill-mannered as well as vain. He became Lord Rudesby Fribble.

Derek Rowbridge was thoroughly enjoying his dinner. How many times had he dined on biscuit, salt beef, and brackish water in his years aboard His Majesty's ships? The Castle Inn was certainly a come-up. It had been many a long month since he'd had such an excellent wine, and the food had been so delicious that he'd had to decline that tempting orange soufflé. He simply could not eat another bite.

He felt eyes upon him and looked up to see a young woman across the room staring at him. He quickly planted his feet, which he had allowed to sprawl slightly, firmly on the floor. She must have noticed the incipient holes in the soles of his Hessians. He also lowered his hands to his lap, hoping to hide the cuffs of his coat. More than once lately he'd had to take a pair of scissors to their fraying edges. No wonder she stared!

One did not expect to see shabbiness in the exclusive confines of the Castle Inn.

He sat looking at her for some minutes before he realized she looked almost as out of place as he did. Not that there was anything *wrong* with her appearance, exactly, but she didn't look at all wealthy. Most of the Castle's patrons were very wealthy indeed, or very powerful, which comes to the same thing.

He knew as little of female fashion as he did of female character. But he could clearly see that the young lady's gown of rust-colored crape, though tasteful and with an able air of propriety about it, was far from new and had obviously never graced the parlors of the *ton*. It was severely cut, long sleeves demurely buttoned to the wrist, and its neckline was modestly filled in with a gauze scarf. She was neat as wax and looked like a governess or a paid lady's companion, neither of which could hope to afford so much as a breakfast at the Castle Inn.

What was still more unusual, she seemed to be quite alone. Perhaps she was one of those disagreeably independent, *modern* young women he'd heard about. Maybe even a bluestocking! He decided not to approve of her.

He watched her rise from her table—she *did* move gracefully, he noted—and leave the room. She favored him with not so much as a glance as she brushed past his table. Yes, definitely governessy. That was precisely the word for her, he decided.

He laid down his fine linen napkin and took himself off to the smoking lounge. He would have his brandy and his cigar and then off to bed.

Both of Lady Eccles's young guests decided on an early start the following morning. Saskia, having condescended to eat her breakfast upstairs in her rooms, was just stepping off the grand stairway and into the entrance hall when Derek emerged from the public breakfast room, having sufficiently broken his fast with lavish helpings of kippers and eggs, grilled ham, cold sirloin, muffins, and plenty of strong, hot coffee.

At sight of her he inclined his head ever so slightly in greeting, to which she responded with the smallest of coldly civil nods. They turned apart simultaneously, Derek to allow a servant to assist him into his greatcoat, Saskia to pull on her brown kid gloves and tender her thanks to the landlord for his kind attentions.

But the landlord didn't seem to be at liberty to attend to her just then. He was in conversation with a garishly dressed young man whom Saskia had noticed the previous evening in the dining room. She had labeled him Mr. Tulip.

His dark hair was curled, pomaded, and brushed into the fashionable Brutus. His greatcoat sported the requisite sixteen shoulder capes and large buttonhole, in which Saskia could name honeysuckle, cowslips, geraniums, myrtle, and a daffodil. His curly beaver possessed a crown of staggering height, and his double-tasseled Hessians gleamed smartly.

The gentleman was not smiling. The landlord had just handed him his not inconsiderable bill, which he had immediately handed back again with cold arrogance.

"You may send the bill on to me at Bath. Here is my card. I'll have my man deal with it." He tossed an engraved *carte-de-visite* in the landlord's direction, who allowed it to flutter to the floor unheeded.

"I would much prefer, Mr. Tolliver, if you would be so kind as to settle with me now," he said with an extreme civility. It seemed that Mr. Tolliver's reputation had preceded him to the Castle Inn.

"My good man, don't be absurd! I dislike carrying money excessively. But you may be very sure of your payment within a day or two. A week at most. Send the bill on." He began drawing on his smooth yellow gloves preparatory to striding from the room.

"It quite grieves me to cause you the least inconvenience, but I'm afraid I must insist on settlement of the account now." The landlord gave a slightly discernible lift of the eyebrow in the direction of an attendant waiting at the door, who proceded to slide silently from the room. Not many more minutes of argument had passed, Mr. Tolliver growing more loudly adamant, when he noticed that the horses had been unhitched from his phaeton, waiting before the door, and were being led quietly back to their stable.

"What the deuce! Here! Where are you taking those horses?" he called loudly out the window. "Hitch them up again at once!"

"With infinite pleasure," said the landlord with a smile, "the very moment the bill in question has been settled, sir."

Several more splutterings from the dandy, and a profoundly smiling silence on the part of the landlord, led at last to the gentleman reluctantly pulling out his purse. "Mind you, I've no intention of paying so much as a ha'penny for that abominable bowl of slops you called a ragout. Nothing but salt and grease, 'pon my word, and stone cold into the bargain."

"As you wish, sir. Of course, sir." The benevolent landlord smiled; his charges were, in any case, quite high enough to cover the small loss of the price of the stew.

Mr. Tolliver, having grudgingly and incompletely paid his shot, turned a dazzling smile on Saskia, a smile of comradeship, a smile that clearly said, "What *is* the world coming to when a gentleman is not to be trusted for a paltry innkeeper's bill?" The smile faded dramatically as he turned back to the landlord and flipped him a coin.

"Here's for your trouble, my man," he sneered, and having favored the company with a well-studied bow he strode from the inn.

The landlord, examining the single farthing in his hand, grinned in the direction of the other two people in the hall.

Mr. Rowbridge, who had watched this little scene with growing contempt for a fellow who would try to shab off a landlord in such a scaly manner, could not keep an exclamation from his lips. "Well, if that don't beat the Dutch!" he cried, turning an expectant face toward Saskia for confirmation of his opinion.

Instead of the answering smile and agreement he expected, however, he discovered that the young lady across the room had stiffened visibly, martial lights shooting from her remarkably fine brown eyes.

"As it happens, sir, that *I* am half Dutch I cannot agree to the validity of such a statement. I have never found the Dutch to be half so boorish and silly as many Englishmen I meet!"

Really, she thought as she turned away in disgust, this young man was beyond impertinence! Lord Rudesby indeed! She had named him well. She thanked the landlord prettily for his care of her, favored the young man with a final lifted eyebrow, and stepped out to her waiting chaise.

For his part, Mr. Rowbridge just offered up a shrug which clearly implied his opinion of uppish females, and, waiting only long enough for the young lady in question to disappear up the road, followed her from the inn.

Chapter Five

Saskia's first view of Bath was one of pure delight. Every care, every worry, vanished in the beauty of the city, glowing there in the sunlight as her chaise crested a hill and Bath stretched out before her. Saskia loved Holland, the land of her birth. But a life spent in the never undulating remorseless flatness of the windswept polderlands had given her an insatiable taste for hills, mountains, valleys, dales, vistas, inclines, and glens. Bath might have been designed with Saskia van Houten in mind. Its steeply climbing narrow streets—which were the bane of many a coachman and insured the survival of the old-fashioned sedan chair—suited her temperament exactly. The pinky-yellow Bath stone, of which nearly every building was constructed, glowed invitingly in the bright sunshine of an afternoon in early spring. The sparkle of the River Avon provided the perfect harmonic accompaniment.

The vista slid from view as the chaise rolled down into the valley and was soon replaced by the reality of a bustling spa town. The carriage bumped along the cobbled streets, rolling past elegant shops, grand public buildings, beautiful people, invalids in Bath chairs, and dogs on the sniff. Almost before she could take in their magnificence, the expensive shops were left behind and the chaise was climbing the hill into the most elegant of the elegant residential streets. She swept around the graceful curve of the Circus, rode down Brock Street, and finally emerged into the Royal Crescent.

Now Saskia really did catch her breath, for never had she seen so elegant, so beautiful a terrace of private houses. It swooped gently round in a vast, graceful arc. What seemed like hundreds of glistening windows looked out with a serene sense of their own superiority onto a field full of placidly grazing cows and across to the Lower Town over which it so obviously reigned as the Queen of Streets.

The chaise drew to a halt before number seventeen; the steps were let down; and Saskia, pulling herself from her wonderful musings, set foot in Bath.

She wasn't certain from her great-aunt's very odd letter what to expect. She was reassured by the elegance of the house itself and the obvious superiority of its situation, as well as by the absolute Englishness of the heavy lion's head knocker on the door.

Before the sound of that knocker had echoed through the house, the door slid open to reveal an awesome figure at least six feet in height, with dark polished skin and ebony hair and a very large ruby glittering in the center of his forehead. He was very properly, though seemingly a bit uncomfortably, garbed in basic butler's black. At mention of her name, white teeth flashed briefly in his chocolate face, and he gave her a bow that might have done credit to a courtier of Old Queen Bess. She stepped into the hall.

This room was decorated in a style that could only be called eclectic, even to Saskia's untutored eye. An inlaid Adam table, an Aubusson carpet, and a pair of satin striped Hepplewhite chairs would have been at home in the most modern and elegant house in Bath. This could not be said, however, for the dominant feature of the room. It was a huge bronze statue of a skimpily clad dancer, one foot uplifted in an acrobatic posture, who seemed to enjoy the advantage of eight arms, a circumstance Saskia had frequently thought would be a real benefit. Bubbling just below his sandaled feet was a small, blue-tiled fountain. Flower petals floated about on its surface, and small jets of water created delightful water music. The fountain was flanked by a pair of ferocious-looking and very large Oriental jade dogs. The total effect was dramatic to say the least, but surprisingly effective and dignified for all that.

The voice of the butler intruded on Saskia's enjoyment of the setting, calling her to attention in deep, clipped, and heavily accented tones.

"Of Eccles House we bid you most welcome, miss. My Ladyship, she is at three o'clock awaiting you in the Divan. First you go now with Mrs. Beach to be comfortable." He bowed again, his right palm to his forehead, and gave her over to a rather more ordinary and altogether more comfortable woman in black bombazine and a white bun. After a thoroughly English curtsey, Mrs. Beach bustled up the stairs with Saskia in tow, bestowing kindly and vastly reassuring smiles all along the way.

Saskia's bemused thoughts must have been mirrored in her face, for the housekeeper turned to her with a twinkle in her eyes.

"You needn't be alarmed by Rahjim, miss," she said with just a hint of a conspiratorial whisper. "He's really a good sort of chap for all he's a heathen. Only takes a bit of getting used to, is all. It's a mite easier now he's given over wearing that white robe of his—kaftan *he* called it—and the turban or whatever it was on his head. We'll turn him into a proper Englishman before long, we will." She became suddenly conscious that she was chattering rather too much for the dignity of her station and closed her lips with resolution, but her eyes still twinkled. Saskia liked her immensely.

The corridor through which they passed bore mute witness to its mistress's travels in the form of luxuriant Persian carpets, intricate ivory carvings on sandalwood pedestals, and porcelain bowls filled with exotic, sweet-scented flowers. From the wall at the end of the hall, the head of a large and proudly antlered gazelle watched their progress.

The room into which Saskia was finally ushered encouraged her to think the best of her eccentric aunt. It was thoroughly modern, elegant, and comfortable. The only touches of the East which had been allowed to intrude were thoughtful improvements: a lovely red silk canopy prettily draped over the bed like a tent, some dozen of embroidered cushions and pillows in jewel tones piled on the windowseat, and a set of combs in mother-of-pearl set out for her use. And, most thoughtful of all, large bowls of tulips were dotted about the room. How could a Dutch girl resist such an attempt to make her feel at home?

She turned her most gracious smile to the housekeeper. "Thank you, Mrs. Beach. I'll come below to join my aunt at three, then. In the . . . the Divan, did he say?"

"That's what he *said*, miss. Don't see why he can't just call it the drawing room, for that's what it is and always will be. Or the Crimson Saloon, as Lady Hartingdale used to call it. Still and all, it don't rightly *look* like any drawing room I've ever seen, as you'll discover for yourself, I fancy."

"My aunt. Is she a trifle . . . well, eccentric, would you say?"

"Oh, Lord yes, miss! Balmy as a meatball, that one!" The complacent smile on the housekeeper's face said clearly that this was a quality to be cherished. "Why, she's the loveliest mistress I've ever served, miss, and I've served a good few in my time."

"You don't mind the . . . the oddity?"

"Oh, not at all, miss. That's just what I like best about Her Ladyship. Unexpected, she is. Why a body never knows what to look for next. And the *stories* she can tell! Well, you'll see soon enough, miss."

"Yes. I imagine she must have many interesting tales of faraway places."

"Oh, miss," sighed Mrs. Beach, enraptured at the idea of the life her mistress had led. "I always wanted to travel myself, you know. Had the wanderlust on me ever since I was a girl. My brother too. Of course, boys are always luckier that way. Joined the army, he did, and went jauntering off to Spain and Belgium and I don't know where else besides. But my skirts kept me close to home. Never been much of anywhere. But living in a house with Her Ladyship, it's, well, it's real *adventurous*, if you know what I mean, miss."

Saskia stifled her amusement sufficiently to show it only in a benign smile. "Yes, I fancy I do."

"Well, and just listen to me prattle on! I swear I never opened my mouth to a guest when I served old Lady Hartingdale. A regular Tartar *she* was. The house is ever so much more *comfortable* now, if you know what I mean. But I'll leave you to rest from your journey now. Rina'll be up directly with some nice hot water for your bath. She's a heathen too, of course, but a good girl all the same, and learning fast. She'll take fine care of you, miss, never fear."

With that, Mrs. Beach bobbed out the door. Clearly Lady Eccles's eccentricity was catching.

What followed her introduction to the Eccles's household was two delicious hours of unaccustomed luxury. Mrs. Beach hadn't been five minutes from the room when a soft scratching at the door heralded the entrance of a dark-haired young serving girl whose face seemed all huge black eyes and shy smile. With a sort of dipping bob that might have been a curtsey, she glided into the room with an economy of movement and innate grace, moving silently about as though she had rollers for feet.

She set out steaming water scented with orange blossoms for Saskia's bath, unpacked her valise with a degree of care that Saskia unhappily knew the simple gowns and muslin underthings did not warrant, and gently scrubbed her back as she soaked in the soapy water. Then she carefully combed out her soft brown hair, pinned it up again with deft fingers, and made Saskia feel very much pampered in general. Saskia loved it.

Her bath finished, the next treat in store for Saskia was a delicious nuncheon, brought to her room on a silver cart, consisting of cold meats, little unleavened breads, exotic fruits, molded rice balls sweetened with honey and nuts, and a heavenly water ice flavored with raspberries. She wondered how she would ever be content with Eynshant and Jannie's Dutch stew again.

She ate the meal at a satinwood table set by the window. As she munched contentedly and gazed down on the sweep of street and the lush field beyond, a chaise drew up below. A gentleman stepped down and entered the house. From her vantage point she could see only the top of his hat and a pair of broad shoulders encased in green wool. She could clearly see, however, that a portmanteau followed him into the house. It would seem that she was not her aunt's only houseguest. Curious, she thought idly.

The little clock on the mantel chimed three just as Saskia began to make her way down the long, curved staircase to meet her aunt in the Divan. She was much refreshed and was looking her best in a simple but neat afternoon dress of ecru muslin.

The majesterial Rahjim appeared as if from nowhere as her foot touched the bottom step. He showed her not into the mysterious Divan but into a smallish anteroom, ornately paneled with lattice screens and filled with ferns and palms. Then with a bow he left her to wonder what was to come next in what was rapidly taking on the appearance of a carefully staged performance.

Her wondering had little time to take her anywhere as she perceived almost at once that she was not alone in the room. Sitting at his ease in a large fan-backed wicker chair was an auburn-haired gentleman with a look of astonishment on his face which nearly equaled Saskia's own.

She recognized at once the fine broad shoulders of the gentleman who had entered the house an hour earlier. But she also recognized the face. It was the rude young man with the odious opinions from the Castle Inn.

He immediately recognized her as the disagreeably independent and snippy young woman who had sneered at his worn boots and made him feel altogether ridiculous that morning.

"Lord Rudesby . . ." she began before her manners could overcome her surprise.

"What the deuce . . . ," Derek spluttered, springing from his seat as though burned.

Saskia was the first to regain her lost composure. Seating herself stiffly in the opposite chair and folding her hands primly in her lap, she cast furiously about in her mind for some explanation of the presence in her aunt's house of this disagreeable fellow.

"I collect you are here to see Lady Eccles, sir?" she finally asked in an effort to cover her confusion.

"I am. Am I to understand that you are here for the same reason, ma'am?" he asked coldly.

"I am." Neither could then think of anything further to say, which was just as well, Saskia considered, as she had no desire to further her very limited experience of him. They sat thus a few moments in a stony silence until Rahjim appeared once more, the ruby in his forehead seeming to glow with malice.

"My Ladyship, she sees you now," he intoned, not making it clear to which of the two he was speaking. He crossed the room to a set of double doors, threw them wide (rather dramatically, thought Saskia) and proclaimed loudly, "Miss van Houten and Mr. Rowbridge, Ladyship."

With so many new sensations and surprises this day, Saskia was still not ready to hear *that* name attached to *this* gentleman. She stopped and stood stock still on the threshold, staring at him. As he was very properly wait-

ing for her to enter before him, their progress was effectively halted.

"Well, don't just stand there with your mouths at
half-cock. Come in. Come in!" came a deep, gravelly,
but strangely musical voice from within. Drawn from
their reverie, the two young people did as they were
told. The double doors closed silently behind them as
they entered the Divan.

Chapter Six

Whatever Saskia had expected, and now she thought about it she wasn't sure what she *had* expected, her fertile imagination could never have outdone the reality that was her great-aunt Hester. A tall, angular, well-bronzed lady, she peered down at them from atop a sort of platform, fully four feet high, ornately carved and decorated, piled high with cushions in rich jewel colors, and canopied in sky-blue silk caught up with silver cords and tassels.

Here Great-aunt Hester perched, very erect, her legs crossed beneath her. Her feet were bare, excepting only some half-dozen rings adorning her toes.

It was rather difficult to determine just what it was she wore, but it quite clearly bore no relation to any feminine garment her young relatives had ever seen before. A sort of tunic, high at the throat, fell in embroidered magnificence nearly to her knees over a pair of crimson silk trousers, very voluminous, caught in and banded at the ankle in gold. A small jeweled dagger glittered on her belt. Her exposed arms displayed a myriad of bangles in silver and gold, ivory and jade; rubies and sapphires glowed on her fingers. The vision was topped with a gossamer veil shot with gold, draped over abundant silver hair.

All in all, she was quite the most magnificent sight Saskia had ever beheld.

She didn't speak for a full minute, but raised a snaky hose to her lips, inhaled deeply, and expelled a series of perfect blue smoke rings to waft toward her guests and mingle with the subtle fragrance of incense that permeated the room.

Finally she laid her pipe reluctantly aside and spoke. "Rather as I expected."

She didn't seem inclined to elaborate on this elliptical remark just at present, and reverted to her scrutiny of them. Saskia, undaunted, stood comfortably at her full, not inconsiderable height, projecting calm self-assurance, tinged with just the right touch of curiosity and obvious admiration. Derek Rowbridge was rather too busy being amused at his aunt's performance to be disconcerted by her odd manners. A hint of a smile touched one corner of his mouth and twinkled in his eyes.

Lady Eccles, apparently satisfied with what she saw, broke into a deep, warm, and endearing laugh.

"Yes, yes, that's all very well, children, and I dare say we shall get on quite well. Sit down, sit down."

The two guests were quite willing, and even anxious, to comply. There seemed, however, to be a marked shortage of chairs in the Divan, the furnishing consisting instead of a pair of large stuffed peacocks in full sail, various pieces of statuary in sandstone, limestone, and uncomfortable-looking poses, and any number of cushions, pillows, and hassocks dotted here and there around low tables.

"Gladly, ma'am," said Mr. Rowbridge, "if I wished to put my neck permanently out of joint by being obliged to gaze up at you from an ignominious position on the floor. As it is, I prefer to stand, thank you."

Lady Eccles allowed an enchanting smile to steal across her fine features. "Well," she said happily, "I am glad to see you're not a simpleton, Rowbridge, nor a man easily cowed. Can't stand that sort of niminy-piminy behavior." She turned to Saskia. "And, based on first impressions, which I long ago learned to trust implicitly, I nourish some hope for you, my girl, though I've yet to hear a word out of you."

"I do beg you will forgive me, ma'am," replied the girl with cool self-assurance and a neat curtsey. "But as we have never met I thought it would be prudent to assure myself as to your identity. You *are* Lady Eccles, I assume?"

Derek was amazed at her audacity, but Saskia's instincts had not led her wrong.

"Hah!" Her aunt laughed delightedly. "Served with my own sauce! I *am* Lady Eccles, my girl."

"Oh. I really thought you might be a genie and was only looking about for your lamp. Are we to be granted any wishes, ma'am?"

"Pert! Well, I'm glad to see you've a clever tongue, but I'll thank you to keep it between your teeth, and you may get a wish after all." To this Saskia gave another curtsey.

Lady Eccles slid to one end of the howdah (for such it was on which she perched) and swung her long legs over the side. Then she picked up a brass hammer that lay next her and struck a resounding blow on a massive gong. The sound filled the room, and almost at once Rahjim appeared. At his gesture, a pair of footmen entered and speedily shuffled the haphazard arrangement of cushions dotting the room into something strongly resembling three chairs. Rahjim himself crossed directly to the howdah, pulled on a silver cord, and Lady Eccles was slowly lowered, as if by magic, until she could stand upright on the floor. She took a silver cane from the butler and motioned him away.

"Give me your hand, Rowbridge," she demanded. "Damned camel broke my leg last year. It has not healed properly. Persian doctors, you know." She walked stiffly but grandly to a chair, and soon they settled, Saskia having to concentrate only a very little on sitting

directly in the center of the pile of cushions so as not to
throw off her balance and send herself toppling.

Lady Eccles gestured to the elaborate tea set which
had just glided in on the strong arm of Rahjim. "You
may pour us some tea, girl, and I suppose I'd best introduce you to each other, though you've the look of folks
who've met and were none too pleased about it."

Saskia poured the smoky amber liquid and refrained
from looking at Derek, turning instead a slightly incred-
ulous smile to her aunt.

"Oh, no, ma'am. We have not met. At least not in a
formal way. Of course, we did just chance to pass each
other at the Castle Inn, as I rather fancy you knew we
would."

"Just so," said Lady Hester, not displeased by the
slight brittle edge in the girl's voice. "In any case," she
went on with a negligent wave, "Miss Saskia van
Houten, meet Mr. Derek Rowbridge . . . your cousin."

"Cousin?" said Saskia faintly.

"Cousin?" said Mr. Rowbridge, somewhat more force-
fully.

"Yes, cousin," said their aunt calmly.

"But I haven't got any cousins!" demanded Mr. Rowbridge. "That is to say, no Rowbridge cousins."

"And who, pray, was your grandfather, young man?"
asked Lady Eccles.

"Your brother, ma'am, Edward Rowbridge, as you
very well know," was his stiff reply.

"Just so. And you, miss?"

"*My* grandfather, ma'am, was Edward Rowbridge.
Your brother."

Derek was on his feet now. "That is impossible! My
father was Edward Rowbridge's only child. My grandmother died when he was born." He turned to his aunt
in some disgust. "I understand he was a frisky old
gentleman, ma'am, which I don't condemn. But if you
are seriously asking me, as head of the family, to acknowledge the offspring of my grandfather's by-blows,
you're fair and far off!"

By now, Lady Hester was the only member of the party seated. Saskia had sprung to her feet in anger. "I suspected this morning, sir, that you were *not* a gentleman! You have now entirely convinced me! I won't pretend not to understand the meaning of your offensive language, and I take leave to tell you, sir, that my mother was born with as much right to call herself a Rowbridge as you. Her mother was my grandfather's *second* wife."

He stared at her a moment, then shook his head with finality. "No, no, impossible! My grandfather died within a year of their marriage, I'm told, and she went away—*childless*—to the Continent and never came back."

"Quite true," said Lady Hester. "Your knowledge of the family history is commendable, Rowbridge, but incomplete, I fear. Within six months of her arrival in Brussels, Susannah Rowbridge was delivered of a daughter, Cornelia who, some twenty years later, married a Dutchman by the name of van Houten. I daresay you can figure out the rest."

"Precisely, ma'am," said Saskia, reseating herself primly, and making a strong, and to all appearances successful, attempt to rein in her temper. "Much as I may loathe the connection, sir, we *do* appear to be cousins. But, *pray*, do not let it disturb you! I have as little wish to recognize the relationship as you."

The young man was silent a moment. His outburst had been understandable. He had been trying so hard to restore the name of Rowbridge to respectability, and he simply could not deal with any of his grandfather's dirty linen. His father had left quite enough of *that*. Relief that the linen was not at all dirty made him no more eager to hang it on his line. As head of the family he had all the responsibility he could handle.

He did realize, however, that he had spoken too hastily of the young lady in question and, even more serious in his mind, he had been guilty of a breach of manners. He offered her a short, stiff bow.

"My apologies. I did not know."

"Well, no," put in Lady Hester. "How could you, indeed? Susannah didn't wish any of her family to know. She'd been treated remarkably shabbily, you know, when she ran off with Edward. Detestable fellow, her father. Rich as Croesus and cut her off without a shilling. And Edward his best friend, too! But there, I'm getting ahead of myself. I fancy you're wondering what you're doing here, in the home of a slightly deranged old lady who never troubled herself about either of you and expected you to return the compliment. And I daresay I may tell you if only you will settle down a bit. My hookah, Rowbridge." Luckily this bewildering demand was accompanied by a gesture toward her two-foot-high standing pipe. It was fetched and lit; the room began filling with curls of smoke; and Lady Eccles began her story.

"I am an old woman. I have lived a splendid life. And now I've taken a fancy to the idea of dying in the home where I was born. I have returned to England to purchase Rowbridge Manor and there to quietly, or at least inevitably, fade from life."

"I trust, Aunt," interjected Derek, "that that will be many years from now."

"Hah! You may not hope it when I tell you why I've brought you here. As even I cannot hope to go on forever, I feel it incumbent upon myself to name an heir. One of you will be it."

The two young people would have been less than human had their eyes not sharpened by one or two degrees.

"Hah! I thought that would make you listen. Quite true. One of you shall be my heir, a privilege, I might add, not to be lightly disdained as I am currently worth something in the neighborhood of a hundred thousand pounds. But you will have to earn it first. And whichever of you earns it will get it."

Both of the cousins were very proud, and their eyes narrowed in suspicion. Saskia spoke first.

"Just what would you have us do, ma'am?"

Her cousin added, "I'll not deny such an event would be most welcome to me, ma'am, but I fear I am no false flatterer."

The old lady laughed, the deep, hearty laugh that might have been thought vulgar in anyone else, but in her was totally charming. It lightened her dark eyes with warmth and animated her face, and it was easy to see how she had managed to capture three peers in succession and leave a trail of broken hearts clear across the Levant.

"Oh, have no fear," she said at last. "I am no Lear, looking to see my young relations toady to me to a disgusting degree. I'm not in my dotage *yet*, and I should dislike excessively being fawned over by some young snip who was waiting for me to die. No, no. I have quite a different sort of requirement in mind, I assure you. And I daresay you may not find it so distasteful, for you seem rather to have taken each other in dislike. That should add some spice to the undertaking. For you see, what I am proposing is in the nature of a contest."

"A contest?"

"Or call it a race, if you like, or a gamble. But only one of you will win, and that one shall be my heir."

Their surprise at this may be imagined. Curiosity was written clearly on their faces; their eyes met for a moment, a moment of study, perhaps, of their would-be opponent. Whatever sort of contest could Lady Eccles have in mind? Derek was confident of his abilities in any sort of card game she might name. Saskia knew herself to be well-read and educated enough to stand up creditably in a test of information.

Added to their speculations were perhaps a few niggling doubts about the propriety of any contest at all, but Lady Eccles *did* have the right to dispose of her own fortune as she saw fit. And if she wished to make game of it, they might well be willing to play. *If* they knew what the game was and if it turned out to be one that did not jar against their consciences, which they fervently hoped would prove to be the case. The questions flitted across their features, and Lady Eccles enjoyed the moment immensely. At last she spoke.

"As I have said, I wish to finish my days in Rowbridge Manor. I wish to buy it. I *intend* to buy it. I am prepared to pay *any* price to obtain it." Her voice had grown determined.

Derek thought he understood. "And is the owner not disposed to sell it to you, ma'am, at any price? Surely you, with your personal qualities, could endeavor to change his mind."

"Humph!" Lady Eccles's frustration was showing. "I daresay I might, for I've managed to talk my way around a good few wiziers, moguls, and caliphs in my day. But my 'personal qualities,' as you call them, are no good whatever to me against a shadow."

"A shadow, ma'am?" Saskia was puzzled.

"Who is the owner, Aunt?" asked Derek.

"A fellow by the name of Banks, I'm told, though I've never laid eyes on him. Nor has anyone else as far as I can tell. He doesn't live in the house. Indeed, no one has lived at Rowbridge Manor since Susannah left it nearly forty-five years ago. It is managed by an agent here in Bath, and there is a pair of caretakers to keep it from going entirely to ruin. But of Mr. Banks not a hair has anyone seen."

"Could you write to him, perhaps, through the agent? Explain why you want the house?" said Saskia.

"I am not a *complete* fool, girl! That has, of course, been tried. The answer is always the same. Rowbridge Manor is not for sale."

"Just how did this Banks fellow come to own it in the first place?" asked Derek.

"Well, I fear my brother was an immoderate gambler. The Rowbridge blood, you know."

"I do know," he replied with a grimace.

"He settled down amazingly when he married Susannah, but by then the damage had been done. He was up to his ears in debt. When he was killed in a freak accident, it was discovered that Banks held all the mortgages on the estate. He'd bought up several of Edward's other debts as well. In any case, everything that was left went to him, and Susannah went off to an aunt in Belgium. I understand Mr. Banks is still alive and still the owner of the Manor. The problem is to locate him and convince him to sell it to me. I have made no headway whatever. Now you will try. One of you will get me that house, by whatever means you must. And that one will have my fortune."

"What leads you to suppose," said Derek, "that we shall succeed? Would it not be more certain to hire an agent of some sort, an investigator with experience in such matters?"

"Well, I had considered it, but I must own to yet another reason for asking two young relatives to take on the task."

"And that is?" asked Saskia.

"I have been in England six months now, and never, *never*, have I been so heartily bored! I promise you I am quite weary of it. I expect to be excessively diverted by this little contest I have concocted. I rather think there will be more than one false step between you. It should be quite a show."

"Perhaps you should employ a troupe of mummers, ma'am," said Derek with an acerbity his aunt chose to ignore.

"Also there is the matter of my fortune. It must go to someone. You represent the two branches of the family, and I fancy I've hit on as good a means as any of determining the worthier of you. I expect it will take a good deal of cunning and more than a little ingenuity for one of you to succeed. They are qualities I admire."

"And supposing neither of us succeeds?" asked the practical Saskia.

"Well then, there are one or two charities in Turkey I fancy could find a use for the money," said Lady Eccles airily. "But I don't expect you to fail, and I shall enjoy watching your efforts. Yes, indeed. I expect the next few months to be very diverting."

"Few months!" gasped Saskia. "But . . ."

Lady Eccles cut her off. "I shall expect regular progress reports, of course, as you get into it, and . . ."

"Excuse me, ma'am," Saskia said firmly, "but you must not go on. I thank you for your kind offer, and do most bitterly regret that I must decline to take part in your scheme."

Derek looked at her in amazement, as did her aunt.

"Nonsense, girl!" she snorted. "Have you taken leave of your senses entirely? You will never be offered such another chance in your life!"

"I realize that, ma'am. Please believe I am most dreadfully sorry. But it is out of the question. My family depends on me rather heavily to manage things at home. To be away from them for so long is beyond considering."

"And what of your mother?" asked Derek. "Is that not her responsibility?"

"Mama has much to occupy her. And she is, well, a bit . . ." She trailed off, unwilling to betray Mama.

"Dotty, is she?" asked Lady Eccles. "Most of the Rowbridges are."

"Certainly not! She has supported us single-handedly since Papa died. She works very hard indeed!" The anger and pride in her dark brown eyes shot out wonderful sparks. "It is just that she, well, she requires a great deal of time and concentration for her work."

"And just what is her 'work'?" asked the old woman.

"Mama writes," Saskia said proudly.

Lady Eccles nodded and muttered, "Dotty. I should have known it. Very well. You shall bring her with you. And there is a sister, is there not?"

"Two sisters, ma'am, and two brothers."

"But, good God! There are *five* of you?"

"Five, ma'am," she answered in her matter-of-fact way. "Managing such a household is a full-time occupation."

"So I should think. Clearly you cannot stay here with me, then. I detest children. You will need a house. I believe there is a habitable one in Laura Place. The Duchess of Rushford has just left it."

"Laura Place? But . . ."

"Now don't go all highty-tighty on me, miss! If Laura Place is good enough for Her Grace of Rushford, what objection, pray, can you have to it?"

"You misunderstand me, ma'am. It is far too fine! Not to wrap it up in plain linen, we cannot afford it. I fear you will have to proclaim Mr. . . . . my *cousin*, winner by default."

But Mr. Rowbridge, being a man of honor, could not allow this. "I beg pardon, Aunt, but I could not accept the prize under such circumstances. If my cousin cannot take part, I, of course, must also refuse. I'm sure you will agree."

"Are you?" said the old woman, a look of unholy amusement in her dark eyes. "But then you do not know me very well, do you? Enough of this! I meant, of course, that I will cover all the expenses involved. It is my contest, after all."

"You are very generous, ma'am, but naturally I could not allow such a thing," said Saskia proudly but stupidly.

"Nor I," added Derek.

Lady Eccles harumphed in exasperation. "The Rowbridge pride! I might have expected such foolishness. Were you both trying to make me think you completely bird-witted, there would be no surer way. If you let pride convince you to turn down this chance, I shall wash my hands of both of you. You may run back to your respective holes with your tails between your legs and forget that your *very* wealthy aunt ever returned to England, as she will most assuredly forget you!"

Derek bristled. Saskia stiffened. Lady Eccles glared at them, daring them to speak. They didn't.

"Good," she continued. "Now these are my instructions." Her voice took on the tone of command that had stood her in good stead throughout a long life filled with would-be tyrants. She had out-tyranted them all.

"You, miss, will send to Eyewash, or wherever, and

summon your too numerous family at once. The house in Laura Place can be made ready in a very few days. You will see to clothing yourself suitably, for I'll not be seen going about Bath with a young lady who looks like a governess. You will find a carriage, hire servants, and so on. I suppose the others will need new wardrobes as well, if that dress is any indication. Very well, see to it."

"As for you Rowbridge, you will get yourself rooms at the York House. You will also get yourself some decent clothes and a valet to care for them. You'll need a carriage, and I expect you'll want a riding horse as well.

"One week from today both of you, settled and looking respectable, will start your search, and the contest will begin. I shall assume responsibility for every reasonable cost, and probably for several unreasonable ones as well, for three months, or until one of you succeeds. The winner will be named my heir and given a healthy allowance until I condescend to die. The other will have had a quite luxurious holiday in Bath at my expense."

She saw that Derek's face had grown steadily darker, for he was unused to being spoken to like an errant schoolboy. "And I'll bear no skimble-skamble stuff about the expense. I am well able to stand the nonsense, I promise you. I want Rowbridge Manor, and you are my best chance of getting it. All I want from you is a simple yes or no."

Derek brought his indignation under control with difficulty, but he was no fool. Here was a chance to turn his life around. "As you wish, ma'am," he said with a stiff bow.

"And you, miss?"

Saskia's mind had been racing. Three months in Bath, in such comfort and luxury! Companions for Mama; a chance to present Beatrix with real elegance; and none of the constant, nagging worries about money. She made a curtsey. "I should be honored, ma'am."

"Humph! I am glad to see that you are not total fools. That is settled then. Now shake hands with each other as opponents are supposed to do before entering the 'fray." The two young people eyed each other warily. Finally Saskia held out a neatly gloved hand. Derek took it, and they gave one short, firm handshake.

"You may go away now," said Lady Eccles. "It is time for my afternoon meditation." Her eyes closed. "I shall see you both at dinner." They were dismissed.

They looked at each other again, dislike and sympathy strangely mixed in their expressions, and walked silently from the room.

Chapter Seven

With their heads in such a whirl, one might expect the cousins to sleep badly that night. But to two such serious individuals, nothing so frivolous as insomnia could be allowed. Derek had spent far too many hundreds of nights slung in a hammock on a crowded deck to have his night's sleep disturbed by anything less than cannon thunder. And Saskia had always been much too busy to waste time or energy tossing and turning in her bed. They both slept like the proverbial rocks.

Exhaustion might offer some explanation for this shocking want of sensibility. They had, after all, made a tedious journey and their first evening in Bath had been eventful.

Based on their experience of the Divan, they had both entered the dining room in some trepidation, fearful of what they might be expected to eat and fervently hopeful that they would not be asked to take their meal reclining on a sofa or to eat with their fingers. With Lady Eccles one ought not to be too sanguine.

They were vastly relieved, therefore, to see a conventional dining table set with a full complement of recognizable china, glass, and cutlery. A reassuring baron of beef and some familiar roasted pigeons helped to set them at ease. Even their aunt's introduction of such un-known delicacies as lentils with hot peppers, red caviar salad, and a layered confection dripping with honey did not materially diminish their enjoyment of the meal. Saskia loved them all. Derek did not try them.

The conversation consisted of a series of pronouncements, recommendations, and verdicts from their aunt—Lady Eccles was a woman of strong opinions—regarding their stay in Bath. Soon their heads were swimming at the luxury, extravagance even, their life would offer, at their aunt's expense, during the next three months.

There were servants to be hired—"Get yourself a good valet, Rowbridge, and a groom. I expect you'll know what you want." There were horses and carriages to plan for—"I've a number of good Arabians in my stable, most likely going to seed. They need exercising. You may do it." Lodgings must be procured. And there was shopping, shopping, and more shopping.

"Whatever you may think about such frippery concerns as fashion and appearance," she said, "I have a reputation to support." She thought a moment, then added, "I don't suppose that's precisely true, is it? If I do have a reputation of sorts, it is as an oddity, in which case whatever strange starts you get up to would be no more than expected. Well, that's neither here nor there. Put it down to a desire not to be surrounded by shabbiness, for I must say, Rowbridge, that coat is sadly shabby."

"I am aware of it, ma'am. Not all of us have been blessed with your good fortune," he replied stiffly.

"Oh, I know. No need to poker up on me. The world is a remarkably unfair place. A pity there is no time for you to go to London. You'll not find Weston's like in Bath. But Ossett, in Union Street, is said to make a tolerable coat." Boots, shirts, hats, gloves, in short everything a gentleman of fashion might require, were well covered in her inventory.

"And you, miss," she went on, turning to her niece. "We must see at once to changing your prim and proper image. Fleurette, in Milsom Street, has reasonably deft fingers and some sense of style. She can manage several dresses on short order. Now for hats . . ."

On and on it went till Saskia considered pleading a headache and retreating to her room. Instead she retreated to a quiet corner of the drawing room to which they repaired after dinner—an *actual* drawing room this time, with chairs and tables and all—and busied herself with the making of numerous lists of details to be seen to in the coming days.

Derek spent the evening allowing Lady Eccles to win a close game of piquet. At least, he *thought* he had allowed her to win. He was admittedly uncertain. She was a devilish sharp player.

And so both young actors in the coming drama were reasonably fresh and ready to begin their adventure when they met over breakfast after a good night's sleep. Saskia was the first to appear. She'd always been the earliest to stir in the van Houten household. She cherished the quiet moments lingering over her morning coffee, accompanied only by a book or her own thoughts. It was the only part of the day that was truly *hers*.

Discounting the presence of a snarling tiger with unpleasantly sharp teeth just over her head, she settled down with her cup and the final volume of *Pride and Prejudice*. She felt sure this was the last such leisurely breakfast she would enjoy for some time to come.

It was with a definite twinge of annoyance that she saw her cousin enter the room soon after she'd settled into her book. Good manners forbade her continuing to read at table in his presence, and the volume was reluctantly laid aside. So much for the precious time to herself!

"Good morning, Miss van Houten," he said gravely, helping himself to the strong, delicious coffee and taking a seat.

"Good morning, Mr. Rowbridge. I trust you slept well?"

"Quite, thank you. And you?"

"Quite, thank you." This channel of conversation didn't seem too promising. Saskia buttered some toast. Derek carved a slice of ham. They ate. They stared at the table. "I trust I do not interrupt your reading?" he said at last.

"It is of no moment. I may finish it another time." Another silence. They sipped their coffee. This time Saskia spoke. "Do try some of this cheese I brought our aunt. It is Dutch, but *quite* innocuous, I promise you." This last statement was unhandsome of her, but she couldn't resist, nor keep the light of challenge from her eyes, even as she smiled.

Derek had no desire to come to points with her so early in the morning, and he refused to rise to her bait. He accepted the wedge of creamy yellow Edamer cheese with a nod of thanks. In hopes of turning the conversation into less dangerous channels, he picked up her discarded book.

"You are a reader, Miss van Houten. Excuse me, but may I call you Cousin? I fear Dutch names are too much of a mouthful for me."

A pause. "As you wish . . . Cousin."

"I see you have been sampling one of Miss Austen's efforts. *Pride and Prejudice* is my favorite of her works. Are you enjoying it?"

Her face lit with genuine and admiring surprise. "Why yes, very much. Have you read it? I thought gentlemen did not enjoy such lighthearted nonsense."

"If it comes to that, I cannot imagine *you*, Cousin, indulging in anything nonsensical. But I cannot agree to your description of Miss Austen's work. They are much too true to life to be called nonsense."

"Oh, yes. To be sure they are. But then I find much of real life nonsensical. My own family certainly is." She began to warm to her topic. "I suppose in many ways we might have been a prototype for the Bennet family in *Pride and Prejudice*. Of course, two of us are boys, and Neil isn't the least bit flighty. But if Mary Bennet—

you know, the plain and terribly serious one—had been a boy, she might well have been my brother Cornelius. And the twins are quite silly enough to serve for the youngest sisters."

He was actually smiling now. "And you?"

"Oh, I am Eliza Bennet, unquestioningly. She is very down-to-earth, you know. And, like her, I enjoy laughing at people's foibles."

"But you are the eldest, are you not? Was it not Jane Bennet who filled that role? I believe I preferred her to all the others."

"Why, how unhandsome of you, when I have just admitted my own likeness to Eliza!"

"But I did not mean . . ." She cut him off with a laugh.

"Oh, I know what you meant, Cousin. You need not apologize. I am sure many gentlemen would prefer a Jane, all compliance and amiability. Never a harsh judgment or acid comment. And pretty into the bargain! For myself, I find such sweetness a bit cloying and such compliance insipid."

"Yes. I do not believe anyone could call *you* compliant."

"Not in the least!" she cheerfully admitted. "I expect it comes from being so long in charge of things. I *do* hope I am not stubborn, when shown to be wrong in my judgments." With a moment to consider she might have blushed, for she knew very well that she *was* occasionally stubborn. "Like Eliza Bennet, I have strong opinions, but I am willing to have my mind changed when the evidence warrants. Were I a man, I should much prefer a woman with opinions to one who simply agreed to my every pronouncement, however inane. What a shocking bore that would be!"

"But then you are *not* a man," he said coolly. "Gentlemen like to have their superior judgment deferred to and to feel that their protection is needed. I have difficulty imagining you standing in need of protection from anything." Except your own rashness, he nearly added, but bit back the words in time.

She gave his words serious consideration. "No, perhaps not protection, for I am usually well able to look after myself. Support, perhaps, would be a better word. Someone to lean on, an ally. And companionship, of course. A friend to trade thoughts with, to bandy opinions about with, even when they are wildly awry." As she spoke, the words struck her with their truthfulness. This was her view of the ideal marriage, even though she had never so expressed it before, even to herself. Could she even imagine such a relationship with Mr. Kneighley? The thought made her giggle, and she choked over her coffee.

As if reading her mind, Derek said, "And was there not a cousin in the story, a preacher? Quite ludicrous as I recall. I hope you do not see me in the role?"

"Oh, no! You would not do at all for Mr. Collins, cousin or no. Besides, we already have one pompous, prosy rector *exactly* like Mr. Collins, and I promise you one is quite enough!" She banished the hapless Mr. Kneighley from her thoughts, and concentrated her attention on her cousin. "I rather think you must be Mr. Darcy. He is very stiff and proud, you know, so I think he'll suit you very well."

"Now who is being unhandsome?"

"Do you not admire Mr. Darcy? I rather thought you might."

"I do, very much, though he is perhaps a trifle toplofty. But I consider him to be a thorough gentleman."

She smiled. "Yes. I imagine you would."

This interesting discussion was interrupted by the entrance of Lady Eccles. Even leaning on her cobraheaded cane, she was a very grand sight in a day-dress of claret-colored *gros de Naples*, a striped shawl of red and gold silk tied around it as a sash, and another, of finest cashmere, wrapped about her head into a large, enchanting turban. Saskia surveyed her impersonally, marveling that anything so flamboyant could be so tasteful and so, well . . . so *right*.

She had breakfasted in her room and was looking quite as fresh and rested as the young people who were less than half her age, and quite as ready as they to face the day and beat back any and all resistance to her wishes, by main force if necessary.

"It's time we were off. Rowbridge, I leave you to your own devices. Just do not, I beg you, come back looking like a fop with your collar up about your ears. You, miss, will come with me. We will begin with Fleurette, then move on to that clever little French milliner. Then up Milsom Street to . . ."

"I beg pardon, aunt," Saskia interrupted, "but I really believe we must begin in Laura Place. It is of the first importance to make arrangements for Mama's reception there. My wardrobe can easily wait."

Fond as she was of shopping, Lady Eccles had to admit to the logic of this. "Very true. I should have considered it myself. Where do you get this common sense of yours, girl? It can't have come from your mother, for never did a Rowbridge have a grain of sense or practicality that I could see. *I* certainly had none, unless you consider the very desirable results of marrying three wealthy gentlemen. But I might just as easily have fallen in love with a string of paupers and *then* where would I be now?"

As she spoke she donned a quite remarkable cloak of silver-grey astrakhan and picked up a huge muff of the same. She was not as yet acclimatized to the horrid English weather. "Are you quite sure you're a Rowbridge, girl?" she asked. "You've the look of one, no denying. All angles and brown eyes. But you're sadly common-sensical, it seems."

Saskia could not forebear smiling as they made their way out to the waiting carriage. "I expect it comes of my being half Dutch, ma'am. Of course Papa hadn't a particle of practicality, nor does Mama. But I do have at least one good burgher uncle and an aunt, Tante Luce, who, though *very* kind, is the absolute soul of boring practicality." She cast her cousin a beatific smile as he made to hand her up into the carriage. It was far more wounding in its assumed innocence than the most blistering scowl. "Surely you know, ma'am, the Dutch reputation for hard-headed business sense. Why, I even believe *some* people think us clutch-fisted in the extreme! Good morning, Cousin Derek."

It was a totally unscrupulous Parthian shot, as she well knew. After all, he had apologized for his *faux pas* in the inn. But she couldn't resist. She was rewarded by a wounded look which smote her conscience the whole of the morning.

Her guilt would have faded rapidly and completely had she been privy to the smile that replaced his look of hurt as the carriage rolled away. Pricked pride slowly gave way to some degree of admiration and a softly muttered *"touché"* as Mr. Rowbridge made his way down the street.

Chapter Eight

That morning began one of the most incredible and frenziedly active weeks of Saskia van Houten's young life. The house at Number Two Laura Place was beautiful, elegant, and entirely overwhelming. It required a small army to run it. She had to see to the hiring of an intimidating butler, two footmen, a housemaid-nanny for the twins, a pair of kitchenmaids for Jannie, plus the abigail that Aunt Hester insisted was *de rigeur*. A comfortable desk must be found for Mama and new hangings ordered for the back sitting room where she would work. One look at the bilious green damask now draping the windows and not a word would she be able to write.

Rooms must be allotted, linens and china checked, pantry staples ordered. Letters must be written to one and all with explanations and instructions. Saskia handled it all with an outward calm that belied her harried spirit.

On top of this, hour on endless hour was spent with milliners, mantua makers, bootmakers, and linen drapers. Saskia was amazed, appalled even, at the number of dresses, gowns, habits, shoes, bonnets, scarves, and reticules her aunt was intent on ordering for her. She demurred at every purchase, asking the price of every bolt of muslin, until she finally put her aunt out of all patience and was roundly admonished to "Stop all this claptrap and put on that dress! I want no more nonsense from you, my girl!"

Two circumstances encouraged her finally to go along with her aunt's high-handed dictums. The first was a promise that an equal number of beautiful and costly gowns would be provided for Beatrix. And second was a realization that Lady Eccles was enjoying herself enormously. Despite her "limited mobility" Saskia was hard put to it to keep up with the woman! It seemed that her leg only bothered her when confronted with anything she wished not to do. Then she became the veriest cripple.

Derek took the week at a more leisurely pace, not having the imminent arrival of a large family to worry about, but he accomplished nearly as much.

With a natural good taste he had never had the money to indulge, he outfitted himself with style and quiet elegance and with none of the exaggerated quirks of fashion that marked the Dandy. The rugged and healthy shipboard life he had lived so long had given a lithe grace to his sturdy form, and the molded coats of Bath superfine, Melton wool, and kerseymere showed off his broad shoulders to advantage and boosted his self-confidence.

An experienced valet was located; a groom was engaged. A gig was procured, but at his aunt's look of disgust was none too reluctantly exchanged for a sporting curricle to be pulled by a pretty pair of match bays from his aunt's stable. There was also a beautiful and spirited roan which had instantly become his own.

The cousins met daily, as they were still sharing their aunt's roof. They generally shared breakfast, chatting about books or music, safe topics not given to controversy, which interested them both. Their animosity was curbed slightly with the familiarity of daily contact. Saskia still thought him odiously proud and stiff; Derek still found her pert and managing. But they had learned to be civil to each other most of the time, snapping at each other no oftener than once or twice a day.

Lady Eccles had seen their first sparks of animosity with gratification. She watched them tread warily around each other with a growing sense of amusement and carefully noted the occasional look of admiration of which they were not themselves even aware. This prank of hers really did look to be even more diverting than she had imagined.

Derek had agreed to choose a horse for Saskia to ride, and this added yet another chore to the harried girl's week. Although she had at one time been a notable horsewoman, she had not ridden in years. Keeping a horse at Eynshant had been far beyond their means. But never, *never*, would she admit to her cousin her fears that she might have lost the ability to sit a horse creditably.

And so every afternoon saw her stealing off for an hour or so to Mr. Ryle's Riding Establishment in Monmouth Street to practice and regain her confidence.

It was a lucky thing she did so, for the horse her cousin chose for her from Lady Eccles's large stable was no placid lady's ride. It was instead the prettiest little golden mare Saskia had ever seen with the spirit of the Arabian deserts where she had been born.

"I thought somehow you'd not be satisfied with a slug," said Derek as Saskia gazed in admiration at the animal. "She's called Sunshine."

Saskia stroked the sleek neck and patted the velvety nose. "*Goede morgen, Zoonschijn*," she greeted it softly. *Goede morgen, nieuwe vriendin.*"

Curious, Derek watched her with the animal and saw how well the horse responded. "What are you saying to her?"

"Just good morning, and telling her what good friends we are going to be. She is beautiful, Cousin. Thank you for bringing her."

"She's a high-spirited animal. Do you think you can handle her?" he asked with a lamentable want of tact.

Saskia answered in a voice tinged with sarcasm. "I shall do my poor best, Cousin."

Trying to make a recover he asked brightly, "Well, would you like to try her now?"

"Oh, yes!" she said with enthusiasm. "Only . . ." She suddenly recalled the sad state of her wardrobe. None of her new habits had arrived, and she had nothing decent to wear. For her riding lessons she had worn an old black habit which Mrs. Beach had managed to borrow from a friend, a governess to a family farther along the Crescent. It was devastatingly ugly and made her look thirty at the least.

But she did so want to get on that horse. And why should she give a fig for what Derek Rowbridge thought of her appearance? He could scarce think worse of her than he already did. And besides, she had no reason to care if he did. His opinion was of absolutely no consequence to her.

"Yes, of course. I will ride her now," she said snappishly. Derek wondered what he had said to get her hackles up. With such a waspish female it didn't take much. "If you will give me ten minutes to change," she continued, "I will be with you directly."

He should have known that when she said ten minutes she meant ten minutes, but he was nevertheless surprised to have her reappear so quickly. He was not in the least surprised by her appearance, however. That severe black habit was just the sort of thing he would expect her to own, all prim and serviceable and unlikely to show soil. Its bone buttons marched in regimental order straight up the center of her jacket; the high neck and long cuffs of the skirt showed nary a touch of softening lace. She looked dowdy and mannish and exactly as he had imagined she would look.

"Shall we go?" Sternly as she had told herself she cared nothing for his opinion, she could not keep her voice from sounding stiff with her self-consciousness.

"Certainly," he replied with an equal lack of warmth. He tossed her up into the saddle, surprised at how light she was, and adjusted the length of her stirrup leather. Then he swung himself up onto Pasha, his marvelous roan, and they headed up the hill to the open fields.

Derek quickly saw that he had chosen the right mount for Saskia. The young lady and the young horse seemed to understand each other instinctively. He couldn't know the pains she had been put to the past few days to insure the success of this moment. He only knew that she rode very well, much better than he had expected.

Saskia was not so lost in admiration for Sunshine that she had no chance to observe her cousin and the superb way he managed the big roan. He was wearing a new fawn riding jacket and sat straight and tall in his saddle. She supposed there was much to find favor with in his appearance if one chose not to go beyond the externals.

They spoke little, neither wanting to fall into argument with the other but apparently incapable of chatting cordially just now. But they both enjoyed the short ride, giving the horses a chance to stretch their stride to its full length, and they returned to their aunt's house refreshed and as nearly in charity with each other as they ever were.

Five bustling days flew past Saskia. A dozen lists were made; a thousand details seen to. Now everything was approaching readiness. The family would arrive tomorrow, and Saskia stood in the front hall of Number Two Laura Place checking the final preparations. The first gowns had been delivered that morning. Most of the new servants were settled, and the new hangings were even now being put up in Mama's workroom. Movers in the front parlors were rearranging furnishings to Saskia's specifications, provisioners were trooping through with coals and wine, candles and tea. Even Aunt Hester had been amazed that so much had been accomplished so capably, so quickly.

Leaving things in the hands of Mr. Ware, the new and top-lofty butler—and whatever would he think of the madcap van Houtens?—she walked to Milsom Street for what she hoped would be the last in an interminable string of fittings with Mademoiselle Fleurette.

She was gone only a little over an hour so it was with surprise that she returned to find the gentle buzz of activity in the house turned into an uproar. A carrier's cart stood before it. In the open doorway Ware wore a *very* displeased expression. A childish whoop and a furious barking came from an upper window to assault her ears, and Saskia knew what had happened. The van Houtens had arrived, *a day early!* How very like them, who were never about when you wanted them, to appear now before you did! With a feeling of doom, she stepped into the hall.

The slate floor had disappeared under a litter of trunks, valises, portmanteaus, and bandboxes. Into one, the ample form of Mrs. Jansen was muttering imprecations in vehement Dutch.

"God in hemel! Alles overhoop! Nou, waar is mijn vlugzout gebleven?"

The furniture movers, still rearranging, merely stepped around her, toeing aside a trunk that stood in their way.

With a whoop that would have done justice to an American savage, Willem came sliding down the polished banister to land neatly at her feet. Mina, of course, followed immediately.

"Hallo, Sask!" they chorused. "Some house, this!"

"Saskia!" came a delightful cry as Beatrix, enchantingly disheveled, her golden curls all atumble, tripped in from the back garden. "Oh, Sask, did you see? There are tulips!"

Neil wandered in from the library, the ever-present tome under his arm. "I say, Sask, did you know there is no Dr. Johnson in the library?"

With a loud, happy bark, Rembrandt joined the melee. He bounded up to Saskia, his particular friend, nearly sending her tumbling in his exuberance.

Now Rembrandt, be it understood, was not your ordinary everyday house pet but a very superior bulldog of unquestioned nobility and a pedigree that made the Rowbridges look like the veriest upstarts. Just why, when given the pup as a birthday gift two years ago, the twins had immediately agreed to christen him Rembrandt, was abundantly clear. One look at his pug nose and his gnarled and intelligent countenance, and no other name was possible. He was an angelically ugly pup whose nose seemed to begin somewhere in the vicinity of his ears and looked as if it might overspread his entire face had it not been rudely jutted aside by a very *determined* chin.

He gave one more bark, a stern instruction to Saskia to deal with all these peasants, please!

She looked around her at her clamorous family with a growing smile. This house, for all its elegance, had seemed very empty, very foreign. Now, suddenly, it was *home*. She looked down at Rembrandt, the easiest of the group to deal with. He cocked his massive head, wagged the stump he so obviously wished were a tail but which could not, in all conscience, be said to deserve the name, and drooled, his endearing way of smiling.

"Odious dog!" she said kindly and gave one floppy ear a scratch. He sighed and sank to the ground, very nearly amputating one small female foot with his bulk. Saskia pulled her mangled extremity from under the canine mass, gave him a pat, and left him to snore in symphonic contentment.

She now turned her attention to Mrs. Jansen, who was handled with like efficiency. A few soothing words in quiet Dutch sent her happily off to the kitchens to assert her authority and gloat over the luxury of the house-keeper's room. The twins were given a coin and directed to a nearby sweet shop on Pulteney Bridge. Neil was sent back to the library to seek out a promised copy of Lord Mahon's *Treatise on Electricity*, and Trix ran up to inspect Saskia's new gowns. The movers finished and took themselves off. The provisioners drove away followed shortly by the carrier's cart. A sudden, unnatural calm descended on the hall, and Saskia sank into a chair.

During this little scene, the scowl on the butler's face had slowly been replaced by a look of grave admiration as he watched her efficient handling of everyone concerned. She looked up and gave him a wan smile. "I promise you they will settle in quite soon, Ware. They are not difficult. Truly they're not."

Unexpectedly, he smiled. "I'd forgotten how lively a house with children can be, miss. I was once a footman to the Marchioness of Brigo, you know. She had seven. It will be quite like old times."

"I'm relying on you, Ware, to see me through. Now . . ." She got up resolutely. "Where is my mother?"

"I believe the mistress has retired to the back sitting room, miss."

Of course. Mama had the homing instincts of a pigeon. Her very own writing room would pull her like a magnet.

Cornelia Crawley looked up from her new desk as her daughter entered. The drapery hangers were still busily at work and Mama, totally oblivious to their presence, had been scribbling rapidly with one of her new rightwing quills. And nary a sneeze! "Hello, my darling," she chirped. "How pleasant to see you. Do tell me, dearest. How much gunpowder do you suppose would be required for Magdalena to blow up Castle Almendoro rather thoroughly?"

"Mama, you are early," accused her daughter.

"No, are we? How odd. I can't recall ever being early for anything before. You look tired, darling. Ring for some tea from that nice Mr. Ware. Just the thing." She dipped her pen again. "Perhaps a half-dozen kegs, cleverly placed . . ."

Chapter Nine

The morning promenade in the Grand Pump Room was in full swing when the three van Houten ladies made their first visit next morning. There were few members of the *haut ton* in attendance—they no longer flocked to Bath in the huge numbers of half a century before—but the pretty room could count on all the Nabobs, Cits, India merchants, invalids, and half-pay officers with which the town was chock-a-block to fill it to overflowing every morning. The Pump Room was still the place to see and be seen.

Saskia feared it would tax her ingenuity to coax Mama away from the trials of Magdalena and into her duties as chaperone. So she was surprised at the alacrity with which her mother agreed to accompany them. Mrs. van Houten, when she emerged from her reveries to assume the guise of fond mother, was not half so vague as her daughter thought her. She understood quite well that this stay in Bath was a golden opportunity for all her children and especially for her two eldest daughters. She would do her best for them. With a sigh of resignation, but with a very good grace, she placed herself at their disposal.

As they stepped down from their new barouche Saskia gave a quick look at her two companions. Pride shot through her. They were all three in new dresses and all of a quality they'd not enjoyed in many years. Mama looked remarkably handsome in a walking dress of amethyst levantine topped with a spencer of dove-grey silk. Beside her Beatrix was a vision in sprig muslin with ribbons of the same warm gold as her hair and a pink glow of excitement. Even Saskia felt she was not such a mean bit in her Circassian dress of moss-green lustring. The sisters traded a grin as they stepped through the graceful double doors into the elegant room.

It was already buzzing with sounds emanating from tongues waggish and frivolous, grumbling and complaining, laughing and gossiping. As counterpoint to them all came the tinkling strains of the little orchestra hired to beguile the invalids into thinking that the hot Bath water did not taste *quite* so vile as they knew very well it did. At one end of the room, the statue of Beau Nash looked benignly out on the world he had created.

This was Saskia's third visit to the Pump Room. She had taken time away from the week's innumerable errands to join Lady Eccles on two occasions and be introduced to a number of her cronies. It was important to her plans for Beatrix that they meet as many respectable people as possible. Now she glanced anxiously around for familiar faces.

She spied a friend of her aunt's with relief, a Mrs. Crinshaw. The perfect person! Mama would love her. Aunt Hester called her a "silly twit of a thing, but with a good heart." She was certainly amiable. Her eyes were wide; her smile was wide; her head nodded in assent when anyone spoke to her. At Saskia's first meeting with her, the conversation had taken a typical form:

"And the house in Laura Place . . . ," said Saskia.

"Yes?" replied Mrs. Crinshaw.

". . . is much larger . . ."

"Yes."

". . . than we are used to, but . . ."

"Yes."

". . . I'm sure we shall be comfortable there."

"Oh yes!"

Mrs. Crinshaw was such a very *agreeable* woman. Attendant on Mrs. Crinshaw this morning was her granddaughter Letitia, a young girl just Beatrix's age. Saskia steered her two charges in their direction.

"Why, it is Miss van Houten!" twittered Mrs. Crinshaw. "How delightful! Yes, indeed. And your family, of which we have heard so much! You know my Letty of course." Curtsies were made and hands were shaken as the introductions were made.

Beatrix and Letitia Crinshaw hit it off at once, as Saskia had hoped they would. Letitia was very shy, but Trix, all unknowingly, hit on the very way to bring her out. Though far from plain, the girl had not Beatrix's claim to beauty and had been struck dumb with admiration at sight of the golden vision. And so when Beatrix instantly declared, "That is the *most* becoming hair style, Miss Crinshaw. Is it all the crack? Could you show me how to do it?" Gratification flooded the girl's face, and Beatrix van Houten had another devotee. The two of them had their heads together, whispering about all the things that seventeen-year-old girls find to whisper about.

The two older ladies seemed also to be at no loss for conversation. Mama was detailing the intricacies of plot devices and character development while Mrs. Crinshaw nodded her turban and exclaimed, "Oh, yes," and "I quite agree," and "I'm sure it is so."

As neither conversation required her attention, Saskia was at leisure to gaze about the room. Amid the bustle of her first week in Bath, she'd been surprised to find how much she enjoyed living in a town again. She'd spent a good part of her life in a noisy Amsterdam canal house, and she found country life basically flat. The quiet joys of the country might soothe the savage breast, but they were not her preferred amusements. But here were people aplenty to set her lively mind to working.

She had already come to recognize the faces of many of the visitors and residents of the town. Naturally she had indulged in her favorite game of assigning them all ridiculous names. She looked around the room now to see who else was present.

There, almost directly across from her was her Mrs. McPug who looked very much as though a magnificent frame of five feet ten had been squeezed down to about four feet eight, then wrapped in a puce satin sausage skin and spewed into the room. At the moment her little pug face was turned up in a smile and her chins were jiggling with laughter.

Beyond the round lady strutted Mr. Peacock, a rainbow-hued gentleman in a mulberry coat and shrimp-colored inexpressibles, a tight waistcoat in parsley green, the whole topped by a large cravat of jonquil mull. He obviously longed for a return to the days when gentlemen knew how to dress, before that upstart Brummell had started them all on the road to boring soberness.

And, oh yes, there was Miss Proboscis. She was strongly marked with a spinster's mien, behind a much larger quantity of nose than nature usually bestowed on an individual. She was very tall, and very thin, and was principally nose. All the rest seemed to belong to it. With a smile, Saskia let her eyes move on.

They soon lighted on a very old gentleman whom she had never seen before. She cast about in her mind for a name to fit him. Benjamin Franklin, perhaps, for he was quite bald, excepting only a longish grey fringe around the back just like the one she'd seen in a print of the famous American statesman. A young man solicitously handed him a glass of water, bending over his Bath chair and carefully tucking a rug about his feet.

Far from being pleased by this kind attention, the old man scowled and waved him away with a look of contempt. With a grimace he sipped at the rusty water. Perhaps she would christen him Sir Gordon Grumble.

Little more than a sip could have passed his lips when he gave a start. He was looking in Saskia's direction. His watery blue eyes caught there, then popped open to an alarming degree. He gasped and immediately fell to coughing violently, choking on the water. The attendant began vehemently slapping his back, which seemed to make the coughing worse, until the old man got control of himself sufficiently to wave the fellow off. When the paroxysm subsided at last, he looked up again. His look of disbelief had not evaporated.

He seemed to be looking at her, but that surely could not be. She turned to look about her, and realized that it was Trix and Letty Crinshaw who had caught his attention. He stared as if transfixed.

She was now used to gentlemen being bowled out by her sister's beauty, but she couldn't help but be diverted at seeing the familiar expression on a man old enough to be her grandfather, at the least. He stared another long moment then, without taking his eyes from Beatrix, motioned to the attendant. Saskia could not hear their words, but the exchange seemed to be a heated one. The young man looked up in alarm toward Beatrix, turned back to the old man, shook his head, then looked up again.

At this point the old man's voice grew louder and quite insistent.

"What the devil do I care! Bring me that girl!"

"Be reasonable, sir," the attendant replied in a lower voice. "I am not acquainted with the young lady."

"Must I do everything myself? What the devil do I pay you for if you can't be of any use to me?" With that he grabbed the front steering handle of his invalid chair and began vigorously pumping it up and down, propelling himself across the room in Beatrix's direction.

The young man, looking very ill-pleased with these goings-on, gave in and pushed him in the direction he wished to go. Soon the chair stood directly before Beatrix van Houten, who had finally taken some notice of the growing commotion and looked directly into the old man's face with those heavenly blue eyes of hers. Mouth agape, he stared back.

Trix was too kind, too new to society, and far too modest, to consider any reaction to such an impertinent stare other than a pleasant smile and a shy, "Hello. I do not think we have met, have we?"

"Who are you, girl?" was the man's surprising question.

Many beturbaned and befeathered heads were now turned in their direction. Silence had fallen on a significant portion of the room. Even the little orchestra chose that unfortunate moment to cease their playing.

Beatrix only smiled the more and gave the old man a very proper curtsey. "I am Beatrix van Houten, sir."

"Van Houten? Van Houten? *Rubbish!*" was his surprising answer.

Saskia really thought the time had come for some intervention on her sister's behalf. She looked frantically toward her mother, who had entirely missed the building drama and chatted blithely on to Mrs. Crinshaw. Saskia, taking hold of the bit herself, stepped toward the old man's chair.

"I am Miss van Houten, sir. Have you some business with my sister?" She tried to make her voice sound as imperious as possible, but the man seemed undaunted.

"I do, miss, and I'll thank you to let me get on with it!" he growled. He looked Saskia up and down. "Van Houten, you say? Well, *you* may call yourself what you will and welcome. But *this* girl," he continued with vehemence, pointing at Trix, "is a Weddington if ever I saw one! Now who the devil *are* you, girl?"

"Weddington? Did someone say Weddington?" asked Mama, snapping out of her reverie at last.

"I did," the old man replied, "though what the devil it has to do with *you*, madam, is beyond me."

"Weddington?" repeated Mrs. van Houten. "My mother was a Weddington. Before she was a Rowbridge, of course."

At these seemingly innocuous words, the old man's face turned an alarming shade of purple, and he half stood up out of his chair. "Rowbridge! *Rowbridge!*" he thundered.

"Why yes, sir," Mrs. van Houten went on serenely. "Susannah Weddington Rowbridge, may she rest in peace, poor thing."

Saskia had never before seen anyone who looked more likely to pop, and she viewed the old man with a mixture of amusement and alarm. His mouth worked soundlessly, as though words were too much for it. His breathing rasped noisily, and he trembled visibly. Then, as suddenly as his rage appeared, and as inexplicably, it seemed to drain away. He closed his mouth and his eyes and sank weakly into his chair. When the eyes opened again, they darted from Trix to Mama and back again, and finally he smiled. Well, not precisely a smile. More like the memory of a smile, from very long ago. His face seemed to be out of practice.

"Susannah," he sighed, feasting his watery old eyes on Trix. "My Susannah's grandchild." His voice dropped even further, till he was barely whispering. "And I never even knew."

"Your Susannah?" said Saskia, then before she could catch her unruly tongue she went on. "Good God! You must be the 'hateful father'!" Her hands flew to her mouth on a gasp, too late to pull back the uncivil words.

He turned to her. "That's right," he said, not pretending to mistake her meaning. "Samuel Weddington, the hateful father."

"I beg pardon, sir. I didn't . . . that is, I hope . . . oh, dear. Can it be possible, sir? Are you really Mama's . . . grandfather?"

"If her mother is the ungrateful chit who ran off with that curst rake of an Edward Rowbridge, I am."

"Sir!" cried Mama, in full glory. "I must protest! Papa was *not* a rake! At least, I expect he was," she modified, "but not after he married Mama. Most certainly *not!*"

"Much you know! And I suppose you'll be saying Susannah wasn't an ungrateful chit to run off with him just when I'd got a Marquis lined up for her."

Despite her best intentions, a bubble of laughter burst from Saskia. "I hardly think, Mr. Weddington, that any of us can agree with you there. If she hadn't done so, none of us would be here, you know."

"Very true, darling," said Mrs. van Houten. "And I shouldn't like that at all. So, you are my grandfather? I never had one, you know, so I expect it will be diverting."

"You think so, do you? And what did Susannah tell you about me?"

"Why, nothing at all. Indeed, I don't believe I ever heard her mention you." The words were lightly said, with no intention to wound, but no one could miss the look of pain that shot across the old man's tired old face. Beatrix certainly didn't miss it and deftly diverted his attention.

"Mama, that makes Mr. Weddington our *great*-grand-papa! How famous! How did you know who we were, sir?"

"Your face," he said.

"My face? But . . ."

"I've often told you, dearest," said Mrs. van Houten, "that you favor Mama. You have her eyes."

"Favor?" growled the old man. "She's the image of her. Of my Susannah."

"Saskia, only think!" said Trix. "Just a week ago we'd hardly any relatives at all, and now we are positively inundated with them. Isn't it a lark?"

"Well, it certainly is a change, I'll admit," said Saskia. "But you must think us shockingly uncivil, sir. Allow me to introduce our friends." She did so, but the man paid not the least attention, being quite unable to tear his eyes from Beatrix. In this he was not alone. The thin-faced young attendant, once over his embarrassment at his employer's behavior, stood staring at the girl like a hungry orphan at a sweet-shop window.

"And, Mr. Weddington," began Beatrix. "Oh, dear, I really cannot call you that. And Great-grandpapa is so very *long*. I know! We shall call you *Opa*. That's Dutch for Grandpapa!"

"*Opa?* Silly name!" His voice was gruff, but one could not help but see that the idea gratified him immensely.

"Well, what an incredible coincidence," said Saskia.

Mr. Weddington raised his bushy eyebrows in her direction. "Coincidence? Do you try to tell me you didn't know I was in Bath?"

"Of course we didn't know. We didn't even know you were alive," said Saskia. "Do you live here, sir?"

"I should think not! Don't see how anyone can stand the place. I'm a Londoner, born and bred, and I'll thank the doctors to get me back there."

"Have you come to drink the waters, then?" asked Saskia. "I hope you are not ill, sir?"

"Can't think why you should hope any such thing. And why the devil shouldn't I be ill. Been ill for years. I'm eighty-six, girl. I've earned it."

"But, *Opa*," said Beatrix. "You cannot mean you enjoy being ill. You are funning us."

"If it's a jokester you want, missy, you've come to the wrong man," was his gruff answer.

"I do hope it is nothing serious," Saskia said politely.

"Damned gout! Doctors pouring all that swill into me all day." He made a disparaging gesture toward the pump. "Bound to make a body sick. You ask me, a good bumper of strong ale'd do me better."

"Now, sir, you know . . ." began his attendant.

"Shut your trap, Hawkins. You're as bad as the rest of them."

Saskia frowned at the old man. He may be their great-grandfather, she thought, but he was shockingly uncivil. But she would not react as she would wish. She was a properly brought-up young lady.

"You must come and dine with us one day, sir," she said politely.

"Oh, must I? Never say must to me, my girl. I don't dine out."

"Well then, we shall come and visit you, *Opa*," said Beatrix. "Where are you lodging?"

"Walcot Street, the Pelican."

"The Pelican!" cried Mama, clapping her hands together in delight. "Dr. Johnson!"

"Eh?"

"The history of those walls! Boswell! Hory Walpole! I *must* visit!"

"Oh, yes!" chimed in Mrs. Crinshaw, who had, in any case, kept up a running stream of "yeses" ever since Mr. Weddington's approach. Miss Letitia was far too intimidated by the man's countenance to have uttered a word.

"Very well, then," said Beatrix. "The Pelican. When may we come, *Opa*? We have so much to talk to you about! So many questions to ask."

Mr. Weddington took a long look around at his new-found family, then gave them a perceptible nod as though he had decided some argument in his own mind. "You may come to lunch. Day after tomorrow."

She might have imagined it, but Saskia fancied she saw a tear forming in the corner of the old man's eye. He shut them abruptly.

"I am tired, Hawkins," he said. "Take me home."

Mr. Hawkins bowed to the ladies, and the old man was wheeled away. The ladies watched him go, quite struck with the coincidence of the whole thing.

"Well, Mama!" exclaimed Saskia as soon as Mr. Weddington was out of earshot. "Only fancy your grandfather Weddington still alive and here in Bath. He's awfully gruff and ill-mannered, isn't he?"

"Oh, no!" cried Beatrix. "I think he's sweet."

"Sweet?" said Saskia with a lifted brow. "I would hardly have chosen that word."

"No, I know you wouldn't. And I think he goes to great pains not to let people know that he is." Beatrix, for all her giddiness, could often surprise with her insight. "I think he has had a very unhappy life, and he is not well. We must be very kind to *Opa*."

"Oh, yes," clucked Mrs. Crinshaw. "Obviously unwell. And staying at the Pelican, too. Well, it is *perfectly* respectable, of course, but far from luxurious these days."

"But Aunt Hester said he was terribly rich, did she not?" asked Beatrix.

"Rich as Croesus was what she said," said Saskia. "But that was many years ago. And she also said he was a great friend of Grandfather Rowbridge, at least until Grandmama ran off with him. Perhaps he was a gamester too and lost his entire fortune in some despicable gaming hell."

"How romantic!" exclaimed Mama.

"Romantic?" asked Saskia. "I would rather have called it inconvenient."

Mama clapped her hands in romantic reverie. "Don't you see? He suffered such a shock when his only daughter ran away that he threw himself into dissipation, became quite reckless, and lost everything."

"It sounds suspiciously like one of your stories, Mama," said Beatrix with a little laugh. "And in this case it may be the truth. He certainly does not look overprosperous."

"Oh, dear!" said Saskia with a glance at the long-case clock reposing at the feet of Beau Nash. "Only look at the time. Aunt Hester will be calling in Laura Place shortly. I sent her word that you were arrived, and she is anxious to meet you. Come, Mama, Trix. We mustn't keep her waiting." She turned to Mrs. Crinshaw. "You will forgive us, ma'am?"

"Yes, yes. Oh, yes. Run along. But do say you will come to a small gathering I am giving on Wednesday. Nothing formal. A young people's party for Letty. Do come."

The invitation was eagerly accepted. The van Houtens had made their dive into the social world of Bath. Saskia herded them from the room.

Lady Eccles made the promised call of inspection, and she brought Derek Rowbridge with her. Neither was displeased with what they saw. In fact, Derek was struck quite speechless, rooted to the floor, at first sight of Beatrix van Houten. It was exactly the sort of reaction Saskia had come to expect from every gentleman first laying eyes on her sister. It amused her to see that the proud Mr. Rowbridge was as vulnerable as any of them.

When he recovered from his reverie sufficiently to acknowledge the other introductions, he set about making himself agreeable to his new relations. To Saskia's surprise, he did this very well. He had never been so agreeable to *her*. He even went so far as to convince Rembrandt to lick his hand with abandon.

The twins had been admonished on pain of the direst consequences to be on their best behavior for their aunt. They tried bravely, but their cousin's casual and teasing attitude proved a sore trial to them. Luckily, it turned out that their Aunt Hester was more charmed by the real flesh-and-blood children they were than by the perfectly mannered dolls they were striving to be for her benefit.

Derek's mathematical skill, necessary for any naval officer, set him firmly in the role of paragon in Neil's eyes, and Beatrix quite simply thought him the handsomest, most delightful gentleman she had ever encountered.

Once Lady Eccles accustomed herself to the idea of all those *children*, she was very ready to act as mentor and benefactress to them all. Plans were made for Trix and Mama to accompany her shopping on the following morning, much to their delight.

The whole family seemed to be in high spirits, looking forward to the coming adventure. All except Saskia.

That night found her alone in her pretty bedchamber, wrapped in a sumptuous dressing gown of softest silk, delicate satin ribbons tied at the throat. She was staring into the fire and brooding. Tomorrow marked the official beginning of the contest. She must set her mind to the problem of Rowbridge Manor.

She couldn't imagine why anyone would buy an estate, then simply shut it up and abandon it. And she didn't truly think the house, after so many years, could hold any clues. Yet she could think of no place else to begin. Perhaps, she not very sanguinely hoped, it would offer up some shred of information, a starting point, to lead her she knew not where.

So. She would visit Rowbridge Manor tomorrow. What she hoped to find, how she would even gain access, she hadn't the smallest notion. But since she hadn't another idea in her head, it seemed worth a try.

Derek Rowbridge sipped gratefully at a glass of fine brandy and stretched his long, well-formed legs to the fire. He looked down at his grinning face, reflected in the mirrorlike shine of his new Hessians. He brushed an infinitesimal speck of lint from the sleeve of his new coat, a Bath superfine of deep blue. Derek was quite enjoying the unaccustomed luxury of the life of a gentleman of leisure. It was, after all, the life he had been born to, then been cheated of by circumstances beyond his control.

But alas, the leisure must end, for there was a job he must do, or at least attempt, to repay his great-aunt for all this munificence. If he succeeded, it need never end.

Derek was a man of action, quick-thinking under stress. He could command men to follow him in battle, or react instantly amidst blazing guns and threatening seas. These were the enemies he understood: tides and winds, storms, guns, and Frenchmen. But in this new battle he felt out of his depth. The enemies were beyond his ken. A faceless landowner and a chit of a girl with a sharp tongue and a governess's lack of humor. Where to begin?

He stared into the fire intently, considering the question with the same cold calculation he used in pondering his opening play in a game of piquet which he could not afford to lose. There seemed to be only one logical place to begin, and that was with Rowbridge Manor. He had no idea what he would find there, or even what he hoped to find, but perhaps inspiration would strike at the proper moment. His luck seemed to be running.

So tomorrow he would mount Pasha and ride out to see what he could see.

Chapter Ten

Saskia was strangely touched as she turned Sunshine through the gates of Rowbridge Manor and began up the once famous "Oak Drive." The brisk ride from Bath had given her a more optimistic view of things than she'd had the night previous. She knew that a pair of elderly caretakers inhabited the house and looked after the grounds, but she expected to find it in a sad state of decay after so many years.

She was, therefore, pleasantly surprised when the house came into view. There was an undeniably lonely look to the great Tudor mansion. The rows of leaded windows were shuttered; no welcoming thread of smoke rose from the twisted brick chimneys. But it seemed to be in good repair. No broken panes let in the spring damp, and the shingled roof looked intact. It was still a lovely house, and Saskia could understand why her Aunt Hester wanted it.

She turned Sunshine toward the kitchens and tethered her in the shade of a giant elm, then approached the house with resolution. Her knock resonated through the kitchens. Then came a soft pattering of steps and a tinkly voice. "Yes, yes, an' it's me a-comin' fast as ever I can."

The door opened, and she found herself gazing down at a friendly-looking antique of a lady, small and terrier-like. She had a yelpy but not unpleasant voice, springy grey hair under a mobcap, and spirited blue eyes. She wore spectacles and carried a small, marble-covered volume in her hand.

At sight of her visitor, the woman bounced back from the door, smoothed her apron and exclaimed, "Oh, lawks, miss! I do beg pardon for speakin' so. I thought as how it must be Mary Manners a-comin' to fetch back her mistress's book, an' I ha'n't finished with it yet. But come in, come in, do." She ushered Saskia into a comfortable and spotless kitchen, then peered up at the girl closely. "Do I know you?"

Saskia gave a charming laugh. "No, I'm afraid you don't."

"Oh, that's nought to be afraid of. There's many a body I don't know, I s'pose."

"I'm sure that's true. And I'm sorry to have dropped out of nowhere in this odiously unexpected fashion. Are you Mrs. Gleason?"

"That I am. Well, at least I'm *Miss* Gleason. Why is it a housekeeper's always Mrs., even when she's Miss? Never did understand that. I wouldn't *mind* being Mrs., though not Gleason, in course," she finished with a girlish giggle.

Saskia looked puzzled. "But I was told there was a couple here. Is there no Mr. Gleason?"

"Oh, aye, to be sure. We are a couple, I s'pose. Gleason's my brother, you know." Without asking if her guest was tired or thirsty, Mrs. Gleason was already putting the kettle to the boil. Saskia thrashed about in her mind for what to say next. She set down her crop, removed her gauntleted gloves, and idly picked up the book Mrs. Gleason had laid on a table. Her instant smile showed that the skies had opened and manna from heaven poured down upon her head. It was a copy of *The Deadly Ruins of Grammonti*, by Cornelia Crawley.

Mrs. Gleason was one of Mama's fans, and Saskia, with blinding brilliance, had her approach.

"You're a reader, Mrs. Gleason."

"Oh, lawks, yes, miss. Me and Mary Manners, that's Mrs. Carlton's nurse, we be the great readers of the neighborhood. Now if Sukey Cotton or that Shifton woman can read so much as a receipt, it's more'n I ever knew. But *my* mama made sure I could read the Bible, which in course I still do reg'lar. But I like a good story now an' again, y'know. 'Specially the romantical ones."

"You're a fan of Miss Crawley's?"

Mrs. Gleason clapped her hands in delight. "Ohhhh! In't she jest the best? Her words are so, well, so *real*. I don't know when I had such a good cry as for those poor orphans in *Castle Vedrino*. And shudder? My, my, my. Gleason had to fix me a nice cuppa tea 'afore I could close my eyes *that* night." She handed her guest a nice "cuppa" tea.

"Yes, it is very scary," said Saskia with a twinkle. "Miss Crawley nearly changed the plot for fear her readers would go into spasms. She told me so herself."

The sparkling blue eyes opened into pools of astonishment. "Never say you *know* Miss Crawley! Really? I mean to talk to an' all?"

"Well, yes. I'm afraid I speak to her quite frequently. She's my mother, you see."

"Cornelia Crawley? *Almera's Revenge! The Marquis of Shadows! That* Cornelia Crawley?"

"The very one," laughed Saskia. "I am Miss van Houten. Crawley is Mama's *nom de plume*, you see."

"Well, I never! Cornelia Crawley. Why the tales she can tell! I never seen the like. Now tell me, what became of poor Master Tom from *Dark Abbey*? Did he get to sea at last?"

Saskia's eyes danced with mischief. "Of course he did. Who could imagine Tom in that stuffy old school." She lowered her voice to a conspiratorial whisper. "He ran away, you see."

The old blue eyes widened again; the wrinkled mouth

pulled into a perfect circle, and Mrs. Gleason let out a soft, "Ohhhhh, I am glad."

With a belated realization of the proprieties, she made a curtsey and said, "Pleased to meet ya, miss, I'm sure. 'An only wait till Mary Manners hears! Won't she be green? The daughter of Miss Crawley right here in the house!" Overcome, she sank into a chair to collect herself and sipped gratefully at her tea. Saskia did the same.

She fetched about in her mind for what to say next. "Perhaps you understand why I am here, Mrs. Gleason?"

She received a blank stare. "Well," she went on, improvising madly, "Mama has a truly wonderful idea for a book. More, well, more *English*, you know. Set in a big country house rather like this one. We'd heard—the way one does hear things you know—that the Manor might be just what she has in mind. She has sent me to discover what I can about it. She likes to have real places and people to base her stories on. Perhaps that's why they are so real. Do you think I could look around, make some notes, just to get the feel of it, you see?"

"Mercy! Why, it'd be an honor, miss, I'm sure. Imagine! *Our* house in one o' Miss Crawley's stories."

"I'd want to see all the principal rooms." She was getting into the spirit of the game. "And are there attics? We could not have a Cornelia Crawley novel without attics, perferably with cobwebs like ropes."

"Oh, there be attics, miss, lawks yes!"

"And of course we would need a housekeeper in the story." She pulled a small notebook from her pocket, wondering at her foresight in bringing it. "Now let's see, your eyes are blue, are they not?"

Mrs. Gleason looked faint with delight. After patiently waiting through several more "Mercies!" and "lawkses!" and other pertinent exclamations, Saskia found herself being shown through a green baize door into the house to which her grandmother had come as a bride.

She might have stepped into another century.

One might assume—and without being wrong—that
Mr. Gleason was pottering about the grounds while his
sister was ooohing and aahing over Saskia in the kitchen.
He was, in fact, tinkering in the stable and had not seen
her arrive. Shortly thereafter, as he strolled through the
yard, he did see another rider approaching up the lane.
This was an unusual occurrence, and the more so as this
rider was clearly a gentleman. The horse he rode was a
fine polished roan, well set up and a good sixteen hands,
if Gleason was any judge, which he knew well he was.
Hadn't been a gentleman out to the Manor in he
couldn't remember how long.

Now the fellow got closer, there was a familiar look
about him. Couldn't say just what it was—didn't know
him or anything like—but damme if the fellow didn't
have something of the old master about him. But there,
no good speculating about what he wanted when here
was the gentleman getting off his horse and obviously
about to *tell* what he wanted.

"Good morning," said the gentleman. "I'm looking for
Mr. Gleason."

"Aye, an' you've found him," came the answer.

"How do you do. I'm Derek Rowbridge." Mr. Gleason
belatedly touched his forelock, then gingerly took the
man's proffered hand.

"Aye. An' that explains it, then."

"I beg your pardon?"

"Beggin' *yer* pardon, sir, but it's the nose. The Rowbridge nose. You'll be Master Richard's boy, I'm thinkin'."

Derek looked surprised, but answered smoothly, "I
am. Did you know my father then?"

"Aye, sir. Put him on his first pony, I did. 'Course, I
were just an undergroom then and him a nipperkin, but
Master Richard an' I, we were friends."

Derek liked the man instinctively, and he smiled.

"Aye, an' you've the Old Master's smile too. You be a
true Rowbridge, right enough."

Derek couldn't know it yet, but he had just received
the highest encomium the man could give. It might

have been more than forty years since a Rowbridge had lived at the Manor. It might be that his pay came from some upstart name of Banks. But John Gleason knew who his *real* masters were. Derek might have been the prodigal son, returned at last.

Unfortunately, such affection helped Derek not at all in his quest. The questions he put to Gleason netted little more information that he'd already had from Lady Eccles.

"And no one has lived in the house in all these years?" he asked.

"Nary a soul, 'cept me an' Bess. Don't seem right, neither. House like that. Meant to be lived in. Now I think on it, there was one fella, a Nabob, come out to have a look. Right after the accident, it were. Said he might be wantin' to buy it. But nothin' came of it. Looked at the drawing room and the library, plopped his hat back on his bald head, and took hisself off. Weren't what he had in mind, I reckon."

"The house was for sale?"

"Didn't say it was. Never has been. But he seemed to think he could have it all the same. Didn't seem the sort used to hearing too many 'nos,' if you take my meaning."

"What was his name?"

"Can't say I ever heard it. Or if I did, it's clean gone. More'n forty years ago, y'know."

"Might I have a look at the house? I'd like to see the place where my father was born."

"Aye, an' so ye shall. I'll not say no to Master Richard's boy, whatever's said."

They turned toward the house.

The chill air of uninhabited space struck Saskia in the Great Hall. The sparse furniture was swathed in Holland covers; no welcoming fire crackled in the enormous fireplace. Little light penetrated the heavily shuttered windows, but the stained glass over the door broke the sunlight into solemn rainbows, giving the Hall the unreal look of a painting. Her half-boots clicked on the slate floor as she followed Mrs. Gleason to the drawing room. It was dark, a bit musty-smelling. Ghost shadows lurked in invisible corners; the weird shapes of draped furniture seemed to object to the intrusion of life. They reflected only cold emptiness, refusing to give any sign of the laughter, tears, and human living they'd witnessed.

"Tsk, tsk," clucked Mrs. Gleason. "Can't see a thing in here." She walked with a brisk, squeaky step to the windows and threw open the shutters. Light flooded the room, evaporating the ghosts in the corners to nothing more than motes of dust, dancing in the sunbeams. Covers were whisked from chairs and tables. Settees and cabinets became only furniture again, waiting patiently for whatever services might be required of them.

Saskia felt she'd stepped into a museum. The furniture was of the heavy, opulent style favored before Old Mad George became King. There was oak and walnut, linen-fold paneling, and velvet, rather than the satinwood and beech, silk and muslin to which her modern eye was accustomed.

Mrs. Gleason skittered about, sending a stream of chatter over Saskia's head. ". . . and the Mistress saw her morning callers here. Her favorite room it was. Now you'll want to see the library. *That* were the Master's room, God rest his soul."

Saskia snapped to attention. "Mrs. Gleason, do you mean that you were here when the house was still occupied?"

"Oh, lawks, yes, miss. 'Twas my first position when I went out to service. In course, I were just a housemaid then. Lord, but it were a good few years ago. Me an' Gleason were asked to stay on and care for the place. We were young an' strong then, an' we came as a pair, y'see. Even an empty house big as this one takes a day's work to keep it from wrack and ruin."

"Apparently Mr. Banks wants it well cared for."

Something suspiciously like a "humph" passed Mrs. Gleason's pursed lips; her minuscule bosom heaved as much as ever it could. "Well, as to that, miss, I wouldn't say 'well cared for' myself. It's a shame is what it is. Me an' Gleason does our best, but it's more'n two folks can do. As to Mr. Banks, I couldn't say, never having set eyes on the man. I get my pay reg'lar from Mr. Dawes, an' he lets me have Rose Malley ever now an' again for the heavy airing."

"Mr. Dawes?"

"The agent. Sour ol' thing, he is. He comes out reg'lar to have a look-see. It's a comfortable life, miss. I'd serve a mistress right well if I had one, but I'm jest as pleased to be my own, I'll not deny."

They turned toward the library.

Mr. Gleason led Derek through the kitchen and up two flights of back stairs to the nursery floor. "Ye'll be wantin' to see Master Richard's room. A good lad were Master Richard."

Derek let slip a smile at hearing his robust and rakish father referred to in this manner and stepped into the room. He was far from sentimental, but his smile grew, his truly charming smile, as he saw his father's hobbyhorse, forlorn in a corner. A set of toy soldiers in old-fashioned uniforms marched across the mantel, their boots buried in dust. The windows were unshuttered, the calico curtains a pale dead grey. But they had been a bright happy blue once. It was not unlike Derek's own nursery at Willowhurst.

It had been so long since he'd thought of his father with anything but resentment that Derek surprised himself as memories of laughter flooded his mind. He was riding on Papa's shoulders crying "Giddyap!" as they galloped round the room. He was rocking with laughter as he and Papa, stark naked, jumped into the pond at Willowhurst, dunking each other with abandon.

He coughed to clear the lump that had suddenly appeared in his throat and turned away.

"Ye'll be wantin' to see the Old Master's room, I don't doubt. It be jest below."

Saskia stepped into the library. Dark oak paneling and bookcases covered the walls; Morroccan bindings gave a patina of age. A large well-upholstered wing chair, its leather arms aged to a soft glow, sat before the grate, wondering, perhaps, why the master was so long away. It was a thoroughly comfortable room, and Saskia felt a stirring of kinship with her long-dead grandfather.

One thing dominated the room. It was a portrait, and it held pride of place over the fireplace. It had obviously been lovingly hung only in the year of Edward Rowbridge's death.

When she saw the portrait, Saskia froze. For here, in a picture hat and blue ribbons and with an elfin smile, was her sister Beatrix. The same China-blue dancing eyes, the same golden curls, had been caught by the hand of a master.

"She were a pretty thing, was Milady," said Mrs. Gleason. "Painted by Mr. Gainsborough, it was. And not a penny would he take for it. Said it was treat enough just to paint her. Oh, a great favorite with everyone, she was."

Saskia looked more closely at the painting. *Susannah Rowbridge, 1775* read the caption. Saskia had never seen a likeness of her grandmother. At least she thought she hadn't. In truth, she had seen one nearly every day for the past seventeen years in the face of her sister. The resemblance was unearthly. She immediately and completely understood Mr. Weddington's reaction in the Pump Room.

"What was she like?" she almost whispered.

"Oh, she were a treat. Always happy and laughing. And kind? Why the stableboy himself could count on a visit from Milady if he took sick. With that soft, pretty voice of hers, and the smile in her eyes. Until the end, that is. I disbelieve I ever seen a body change so as she did when the Master were killed. The life jest went out of her," she sighed.

"And my . . . Mr. Rowbridge?"

Mrs. Gleason gave a girlish giggle. "Oh, he were a lively buck, *he* was. If he weren't a one for catching a body on the stairs!" she added with a hint of blush. "Mind now, there weren't none o' that after Milady come. Lawks! If ever a man was potty for anyone, he was for her. Worried 'bout her all the time he did, towards the end. Seems to me he mighta worried a bit more 'bout hisself. Had to go get his neck broke, an' then where was she, poor thing?"

Saskia pulled her eyes from the painting and began an inspection of the room. She calmly slid open a desk drawer, astonished at her boldness. Mrs. Gleason didn't seem to mind. But whatever she hoped to find, it wasn't there. Quills, a wafer box, some engraved visiting cards. But not a trace of a paper, ledger, or journal. She opened other drawers. No letters, no documents, no records of any kind. She didn't know how high her hopes had been until they fell flat.

As though reading her mind Mrs. Gleason said, "You'll get little of the Master in here, for all it were his favorite room. You can almost feel him still upstairs, with all his things about, but not here. Mr. Dawes, he come an' took all the papers an' things away soon as Milady left. Didn't touch nothin' else. Well, come along upstairs an' you'll see for yourself."

Derek stood in his grandfather's bedroom, but the lump in his throat did not return. He had never known his grandfather, never ridden on his shoulders or laughed with him. The emotional response was set aside and the keen analytical powers took over, searching for a clue, anything, that might lead Derek to the mysterious Mr. Banks.

The room was as perfectly preserved as the nursery. Some furniture was draped with covers, but the heavily carved bed, with its chocolate brocade hangings, stood proudly uncovered and dominating the room. Brushes and razors were still laid out on a shaving stand; old-

fashioned coats and knee breeches, embroidered waist-
coats and lace-trimmed shirts still hung in the wardrobe.

"But this is incredible!" Derek exclaimed. "Was nothing sold or taken away by this fellow Banks?"

"Nothin's been touched, sir, 'ceptin' only the papers.
Orders. Don't make no sense to me. But we done what
we was told. Seal it an' leave it. That's what we was
told, an' that's what we done."

"The papers?" asked Derek with a sinking feeling.

"Aye. Took 'em off straightaway, all tied up with red
ribbons. Even took the Missus's account books."

"Banks did that? Did he say why?"

"Never seen no Banks. It were Dawes what come out.
Ain't nobody laid an eye on any Mr. Banks. Not even
Dawes, I reckon."

"Dawes?"

"Agent. Got hisself an office in Bath. Cabbage-head, if
you ask me." He sighed heavily. "Fair breaks my heart,
it does. The Master, he loved this ol' house. One week it
were full o' livin'. Next week it were dead."

Derek wandered about the room. He slid open drawers
peered under covers and in cupboards. "Tell me about
him, about my grandfather," he said.

The ladies headed up the back stairs, saving the main
bedrooms for later. Saskia pulled her notebook from her
pocket to please Mrs. Gleason, but the only notes she
made were: *Banks, Dawes, portrait, papers, WHY???*

"She were a thrifty housekeeper too, was Milady.
Knew what a thing cost. Right surprised us all, her
comin' from money an' all. But there, she had to know,
didn't she, livin' here. Never a penny to spare. Shameful,
I call it!"

Mrs. Gleason chattered on inconsequentially while
Saskia poked her nose into cupboards and corners, looking for something, anything, that might help her. There
was nothing.

"Well, sir," said Mr. Gleason, "then he broke his neck

an' that were the end o' that. Shouldn'ta been ridin' that colt. Weren't properly broke an' so I told him. 'Twere a wager, I reckon. Always were a bettin' man, the Master."

"I know," said Derek grimly as they descended the grand staircase and headed for the library. "It runs in the family."

"Mind, there weren't hardly none o' that after the Missus come, no sir, 'ceptin' only at the end. Seemed like he needed money real bad at the end. Try most anything to get it."

The bits of information were catalogued and stored in Derek's well-ordered mind, but they didn't seem to add up to much. He looked keenly around, not wanting to miss anything. But what was he even looking for? He found nothing.

Her grandmother's room was charming, thought Saskia.

"Pretty, ain't it, miss? Jest like her. Partial to yellow, she was." The old lady could still sniff away a tear for her mistress after all these years.

"It is a charming room."

Mr. Gleason coughed. "An' would you be wantin' to see the cellars, sir? There still be some fine old brandy set down. French, it is. The Master liked a good drink."

"Thank you, Gleason, but not today. If you'll save it, I'll come another time."

"Oh, I'll save it, right enough. You ask me, it belongs to you."

With a grateful farewell and a promise to bring her mama soon—"Really, miss? Mercy! Lawks! My, my, my"—Saskia walked slowly to where Sunshine nibbled placidly at some fresh spring grass. She mounted with the help of a dead tree stump and headed around to the lane, dwelling on the information the morning had gained her. Snippets. Memories. Gossip. Was there, buried somewhere in Mrs. Gleason's chatter, the vaguest beginnings of a solution?

Derek thanked Mr. Gleason warmly and stepped through the French doors on the stable side of the house. They marveled together over Pasha, then he mounted and turned toward the lane, trying to make something out of the nothing he had just seen and heard.

He came up short at sight of another rider coming around the side of the house. He recovered quickly from his surprise.

"Cousin Saskia!" His sharp voice brought her from her thoughts as nothing else could have done.

"Cousin Derek!" She instantly bit back the sharp remark that sprang to her tongue at sight of him. "How do you do? It seems we both felt in need of a ride today."

He looked around for a sign of the groom that must surely have accompanied her. He saw none. "Cousin! Do you tell me that you rode out here alone?"

"I wasn't aware that I had told you anything," she replied. "But yes. I came alone. Why should I not?"

"Would you have allowed your sister to do so?"

"Of course not! The cases are entirely different. Trix is very young."

"Whereas you are a positive dowager!" He was not a natural satirist; the words came out wooden. "You have not ridden in years and are, moreover, on a mount to which you are not accustomed."

"Oh, Sunshine and I understand each other very well." She stroked the mare's golden neck. "*Niet waar, Zoonschijn?*"

"Well, you will not ride home alone. I shall accompany you."

"There is not the least need, I assure you."

"I am going back myself, in any case."

"Oh, very well!" she said irritably. "I daresay Mrs. Jansen will have tea ready when we get to Laura Place. You may as well join us."

He gave her a stiff nod. "I thank you for the very gracious invitation."

She colored up. What was it about him that made her so shockingly uncivil? She changed her tack. "Mina will be ecstatic. You are quite first oars with her, you know."

"She is a likable child. So is Willem, though sadly in need of a strong hand."

"I have done my best with them," was her cold reply.

Now it was his turn to flush with embarrassment. "I did not mean . . . I referred only to the lack of a man in the household. I think you have done admirably with them, considering the circumstances. I meant no offense."

"Oh, I know you did not, and I am sorry for ripping up at you. We seem always to be trying to snap each other's heads off, don't we?"

"Well, we are rivals."

"Yes, but must we be enemies as well? Come, Cousin. Cry friends?"

She stopped her horse and put out her hand.

"Friends," he said. As he shook the hand he noticed how well she was looking today. She had lost her governess appearance entirely, and the deep russet of her new riding habit gave warm highlights to her hair and eyes. Her jacket was severely cut, like the old black habit, but its Polish frogging and gold braid gave it a great deal of dash. There was a soft frill of lace edging the snowy cravat wrapped high up her long neck. She looked, well, handsome in it. Yes, that was just the word.

"Do you know the strangest thing has happened!" she said, pulling him from his admiration. "Mama's grandfather has turned up alive and in Bath!"

"What? You mean . . ."

"Yes," she laughed. "The hateful father."

"But . . . oh, dear. One more person for you to deal with. I shall begin to feel guilty for my lack of encumbrances soon."

She laughed again, and he gave an answering smile. He really was looking well this morning, she noted. His corbeau-colored riding coat and top boots did him justice. In fact, when the black scowl left his face, he was quite a handsome gentleman.

"Oh no," she said. "I intend to fob him off onto Trix. She's delighted with the idea. She will bully him into health. And Aunt Hester has provided us with so many servants that I need never worry about leaving the twins at home. I mean to be sure that you don't get the upper hand on me, Cousin Derek."

"What did you think of the house?"

"Lovely. I can see why Aunt Hester wants it."

"Yes. It is exquisite."

Conversation lagged, each giving a sidelong look at the other. Had he found something, Saskia wondered. What did she discover, Derek asked himself. Am I losing already, they both mused.

The rest of the ride passed in uneventful chatter as they treaded warily around the edges of the only topic that interested them. Their speculations continued unabated. They might have cried friends, but they were a long way from trusting each other.

Chapter Eleven

The entire van Houten clan set out for the Pelican for their appointed luncheon with Mr. Weddington. After a great deal of jostling and muttering as they all six tried to squeeze into the barouche, they finally settled, making a merry, lively party.

"Now you must not be rowdy," Saskia adjured the twins. "Great-grandpapa is a very elderly gentleman and not well."

"Older even than Great-aunt Hester?" asked Mina, certain that such a thing was not possible.

"Yes, darling. Older even than that," she answered with an amused smile.

"I hope there'll be *snoepjes*," said Willem, using his favorite Dutch word for sweets. "Jannie won't give us enough even now we can afford piles and piles of them."

"That's because she cares about you far more than you deserve," his sister reprimanded.

"We called on *Opa* yesterday after our shopping," said Beatrix, "and he gave us wine and macaroons. Poor *Opa*. I'm afraid Aunt Hester was very hard on him." Then she giggled. "I don't think he really minded, though. He just gave back as good as he got. After that they got on famously."

"I think," said Mrs. van Houten, "that I must put them both in my next book. Do you all pay attention, my darlings, to remind me later of all their eccentricities."

Neil did not join in the discussion, having his nose, as usual, buried in a book. "I do hope, Neil," said Saskia, "that you don't mean to have your face in that volume all through lunch. It would be most insulting to Great-grandpapa."

"Really, Sask!" came the offended reply,. "I'm not a total boor, y'know. I hope I know better than to be so uncivil."

"Yes, dear," she said wryly. "I hope you do." Neil disappeared back into the depths of his book.

The barouche turned into Walcot Street and pulled up before the once-famous and now dwindling hostelry. They were greeted by Hawkins, Mr. Weddington's attendant. The poor young man had a marked tendency to stop breathing whenever his eyes strayed to Beatrix, as they frequently did. His thin, pale face grew alarmingly red. Trix was a picture today in one of the new Kendal bonnets that were all the rage in honor of the engagement of the Princess Charlotte. Its blue ribbons, just the color of her eyes, were tied in a large, jaunty bow at her left ear. Saskia glowed with pride to look at her while Mr. Hawkins gulped at the air.

Mr. Weddington awaited them in his private parlor, well wrapped up in blankets and rugs against any stray drafts. The room was comfortable and spotlessly clean, but the curtains had faded, the carpet showed its age, and the low beamed ceiling was smudged with the smoke of years. It reinforced Saskia's conviction that her great-grandfather's once enormous fortune had evaporated almost entirely.

Mrs. van Houten beamed. "This could be the very room in which Dr. Johnson and Mr. Boswell discussed the course of history," she proclaimed, exactly as she had done the previous day. She walked slowly about, gently touching walls and furniture as though the ghost of the famed lexicographer could be transmitted into her fingertips.

Saskia introduced the younger members of the family. Mina's eyes grew huge with wonder as she made her curtsey. She'd never imagined anyone could be quite so old or quite so intimidating. Willem and Neil both gave proper bows and shook the old man's hand, Neil even going so far as to say, "How do you do, sir," with perfect civility.

"*Opa!*" cried Beatrix. "How well you are looking today! Have you had some of the *kandeel* Jannie sent you? She swears by it as a strengthener."

"If you mean that Dutch swill, no I didn't. Nor do I intend to! I'll not muck up my insides with such heathen stuff. Good English porter is what I need!"

"Tsk, tsk, tsk," tsked Hawkins, tucking the old man's rug more firmly about his knees.

"Don't you cluck at me, man," growled Weddington. "And stop fussing!" He swatted at the fellow as if he were a pesky fly. "Get away, do! Leave us to our lunch. I'll ring if we want you, though I can't think why we would."

"Now, sir . . ." began Hawkins.

"Out!"

"It's all right, Mr. Hawkins," soothed Beatrix. "We will take good care of *Opa*. Why don't you go out and enjoy the sunshine?" The obvious dismissal was softened by a smile so dazzling the sunshine could not hope to compete. Reluctantly, Hawkins ducked his long body through the low doorway and left.

"He'll fidget me to death, one day!"

"Yes, I think he might, *Opa*," said Beatrix. "But he's gone now, and we can be comfortable."

"Comfortable! Humph!"

"I'm told you met our Aunt Eccles yesterday, sir," Saskia intervened. "What did you make of her?"

"Uppity female, with her arrogant Rowbridge nose!"

"Oh, dear," said Saskia, fooling no one with her mock gravity. "I'm told I have the Rowbridge nose too."

"And you'd be well advised not to stick it where it doesn't belong, miss," he retorted.

"Now, *Opa*," said Beatrix. "Just because Aunt Hester wouldn't let you bully her. You know very well that you admired her excessively."

"Well," he hedged, "I do like a woman with spirit."

"You didn't seem to think much of it in your daughter, sir," reminded Saskia.

"She ceased to be my daughter the day she ran off with that rogue!" he thundered.

"Oh, stuff!" said Beatrix. "If that were so, we couldn't be your great-grandchildren, and you know you shouldn't like that a bit."

"Well who asked you to be? I've managed well enough without you."

"It doesn't look to me as though you have," retorted Beatrix.

Saskia was relieved at the entrance of a pair of waiters just then to divert their attention. The meal was not lavish—the Pelican was known for serving a good, plain ordinary—but it was nicely chosen and well prepared. There was a tasty soup, cold chicken and roast beef, a mound of fresh ripe fruits, and a plate full of sticky Bath buns with curls of butter and pots of marmalade. For Mr. Weddington the waiter brought a bowl of thin gruel and a pot of herb tea, neither very appetizing in appearance.

One look at her grandfather's grimace decided Beatrix. She imperiously sent the gruel away. "However are you to feel better with only such stuff to eat, *Opa*? You need something hearty to strengthen you. Here. This will do you much better." She served him up a generous portion of the rare beef. He accepted with a surprisingly sheepish smile. It was obvious that he was destined to be ruled by Beatrix henceforth.

"That's right, darling," said Mama encouragingly. "And do help Grandpapa to some strawberries."

"May I pour you some of this claret, sir?" asked Neil. "It is quite tolerable." How very grown-up he sounds, thought Saskia with a wry grin. The family party had taken on a surprisingly comfortable atmosphere. Even the children had not been forgotten.

"Look, Mama!" cried Willem. "Sugarplums!" The word came out intelligible but sadly muffled as he stuffed the treat into his mouth. His example was quickly followed by his twin sister, and their *Opa* instantly became a good deal less formidable. "Thank you, *Opa!*" they mumbled through sticky lips.

By now everyone felt very mellow, not least Mr. Weddington who was feeling better than he had in months, years even. Hawkins was rung for and directed to accompany the twins to Molland's, in Milsom Street, for ices. He was given no opportunity to remonstrate with his employer over the uneaten gruel and the suspicious beef bones on his plate. A small sticky hand was placed in each of his long-fingered knobby ones, and he was shooed from the room.

Neil started to reach for one of the few remaining sugarplums, then seemed to recollect his budding adulthood. His maturity was still too fragile to stand up to sugarplums. Saskia saw the aborted movement and successfully stifled a giggle. She wasn't the only one to notice. Mr. Weddington, odd as it may seem, had once been young himself. He peered at his great-grandson from under shaggy brows, then reached for the bowl of sweets. "Haven't had one of these in years!" He bit into one with relish. "Ahhhhhh. Have one, young man. They're quite tolerable."

At that Saskia did laugh heartily along with everyone else, even Neil. They all indulged in the sugarplums and felt themselves very clever.

Mr. Weddington leaned back in his chair and patted his unusually full stomach contentedly. "So, puss," he said to Beatrix. "All set to take the town by storm, are you?"

"Oh yes, *Opa*," she laughed. "Won't it be fun? We've already been invited for several picnics and rides and we are going to Letty Crinshaw's party on Wednesday.

And we are to attend the assembly in the Upper Rooms this week. It's all so exciting! And," she added with a twinkle, "I've quite decided that I wish to have all Bath at my feet."

"Imagine you'll do it, too. My Susannah did, and you're her double."

"She certainly is, sir," said Saskia. "I could hardly credit it until I saw Mr. Gainsborough's portrait of Grandmama. The resemblance *is* remarkable."

His eyes, which had begun to droop in after-lunch somnolence, snapped open. "You've seen that, have you? Where?"

"Why, at Rowbridge Manor. Have *you* seen it?"

"Oh, I've seen it. Years ago, it was. It don't do her justice. They should have got Reynolds for it."

"Or Mr. Romney," said Mama. "Why only look what he did for Lady Hamilton. *The Seamstress, Circe, The Spinner!* Why he must have painted her thirty times at least, and she wasn't half so pretty as Mama."

"Or half so respectable, from what I understand," added Saskia dryly.

"Well, that is true. Her liaison with Lord Nelson. Not quite the thing. But *such* a romantic story. I wish I'd written it."

"Romance! Humph! Look where romance got Susannah. Wife to a rogue, a widow with a baby before she was twenty. She could have been the Marchioness of Hough."

"She often told me," said Mrs. van Houten, "she wouldn't have traded her year with Papa for all the diamonds in England. Such a tragedy he died so young. Saskia, darling, you must take me out to the Manor to see Mama's portrait. I wish to commune with it."

"And just how'd you come to be in the library at Rowbridge Manor, miss?" he asked Saskia.

"Well, that is rather a long story, sir. You see . . ."

It was a long story, and Saskia became so involved in explaining all about the contest and Mr. Banks and what she had come to think of as the Mystery of Rowbridge

Manor, that she paid little attention to the number of very interesting expressions that crossed Mr. Weddington's face as he listened. He said little beyond the occasional "Oh, did she?" and "You don't say?" and, as Saskia wound her explanation to an end, he muttered a softly intoned, "Well, I'll be damned!"

He digested the story a moment when she fell silent, then gave an odd smile. "If it ain't just like a Rowbridge to think up such a stunt." He turned to Mama. "I'm surprised you allowed it, Cornelia." Saskia noticed his use of Mama's first name.

"Whyever should I not?" answered Mama. "In fact, I'm going to follow all the details closely. I've quite decided to make a novel out of it. I feel I'm ready to tackle a comedy."

"Mama!" cried Saskia. "It's no joke! I only wish it were."

"Damned right it's no joke, my girl," said Mr. Weddington. "I know to the penny what Hester Eccles is worth. When you win this one you'll be set for life, all of you."

"Well, *Opa*, I'm sure that would be very comfortable, but I'm not at all certain I will win."

"You'll win, all right," he pronounced.

"I don't seem to be making much headway."

"Rubbish! No Rowbridge is going to beat a Weddington!"

"But I'm not a Weddington, *Opa*," said Saskia truthfully. "At least no more than I am a Rowbridge."

"Well that blasted cousin of yours ain't got a drop of Weddington blood in his veins, and that's what'll land him in the basket."

"Oh, Sask'll win, sir," said Neil. "But it's the van Houten blood that'll make the difference."

"How I wish I had the confidence you all seem to have," said Saskia. "I will do my best, but Cousin Derek does have one important advantage over me."

"Oh?" said Mama.

"No," said Neil.

"What?" growled Mr. Weddington. "What's a Rowbridge got that you don't, I'd like to know?"

"He is a man," Saskia stated simply.

"Oh," sighed Mama.

"Yes," said Beatrix. "I see what you mean."

"What has that to say to anything?" asked Mr. Weddington.

"Quite simple, *Opa*. As a gentleman, Cousin Derek can poke about to his heart's content, prying wherever he chooses. No one will think any the worse of him. But I am a Young Lady of Quality." She began to recite a litany of the unwritten, but no less rigid, rules of behavior pertaining to that class. "A Young Lady may not walk about in public places unescorted, even in broad daylight. A Young Lady may not call upon a gentleman at his place of business, even if she *has* business with him. A Young Lady may not speak to a gentleman to whom she has not been properly introduced, even when she positively *must*. And she may not ask indelicate questions or appear to know anything at all about Those Things that a Young Lady Does Not Know About! It's all very tedious and bothersome, besides being remarkably unfair."

"Being a woman never stopped Hester Eccles from doing anything she wanted!" said Mr. Weddington. "You're her great-niece. Why shouldn't you do the same?"

"Now what's this, *Opa*? Do I detect a hint of admiration for Aunt Hester in your voice? And am I now to rely on my Rowbridge blood to see me through?" she teased, her eyes dancing with fun. "But it won't do. Aunt Hester was married to a lord, which does ease things a little. And besides, I've not the slightest wish to share in her reputation, much as I might admire her. She is accepted now because she is more than seventy and more than a little odd. But what is seen in her as eccentricity would in me be thought fast."

"You wouldn't like that, Sask," cautioned Neil.

"No, dear, I shouldn't think I would," she answered.

"Generally speaking, I enjoy being respectable, though I *will* go riding or walking where and when I please, and quite alone if I wish, despite what Derek Rowbridge says!" Mr. Weddington was eyeing her speculatively, deep in thought, but she didn't notice. "I can but do my poor best. I think my next step must be to call on Mr. Dawes. Though how I am to do so, I can't imagine. We have grown so busy already. And I'm not even sure he will see me." She laughed. "Perhaps I ought to go in a veil!"

"Dawes?" asked Mr. Weddington, his furry brows shooting up.

"He is the Bath agent for our mysterious Mr. Banks. I don't quite see what he can, or will, tell me, but I must do *something*. I'll go see him tomorrow."

"I'll bet Aunt Hester has a veil you can wear," said Beatrix. "Something wonderfully *Eastern* with gold fringes and all-over sequins!"

"Oh, dear!" Saskia laughed. "I shouldn't dare show my face in such a thing."

"That's the idea, silly," answered Trix. "Not to show your face."

"There must be an easier way to call on a man of business without ruining my reputation."

"Widow's weeds," stated Neil. "One of those heavy black veils. No one'll suspect."

Mr. Weddington watched this nonsensical conversation with growing amusement and the beginning of an idea. Mrs. van Houten, on the other hand, wasn't listening at all.

"Saltpeter!" she exclaimed suddenly and inexplicably.

"I beg your pardon, Mama?"

"Saltpeter," she repeated. "For the gunpowder. The very thing. Why did I not think of it before? Come, my darlings, I must get back to my work at once." She bustled about gathering up parasols, shawls, and reticules.

"But, Mama, the twins!" said Beatrix.

"What the devil is the woman talking about? Saltpeter?" asked Mr. Weddington.

"Magdalena," explained Saskia, with a sigh. "Mama has had an Idea."

Mrs. van Houten—or rather, Cornelia Crawley—was herding her children out the door. "You will see to the twins, won't you, Grandpapa? Just point them toward Laura Place and give them a push. Come, come, my dears. The Muse does not wait, you know."

They barely had time to say their good-byes before they found themselves in the yard, Mama clucking at the ostler to hurry. Mama could be surprisingly forceful when the need was urgent.

As Mr. Weddington watched them go, a slow smile cracked his face, seeped up into his eyes, and grew until his old face was pink with the pleasure of it. It had been a long, a very long, time since anyone had shown him any affection, since he had allowed anyone to do so. Now here was a girl with Susannah's face, planting a kiss on his old bald head, just as she had used to do. Here was a fine young man who shook hands with the gravity only an eighteen-year-old could muster. Here were laughing children calling him *Opa*—silly name, but he liked it—and a young woman with mischief behind her facade of sense.

He finished his glass of wine, savoring its richness. He was feeling better than he had in years. He'd go out tomorrow, he decided, and take the air, buy some presents for his great-grandchildren. And there were one or two calls he might make while he was at it. Well pleased with himself, he reached again for the bottle of claret.

Chapter Twelve

As it turned out, Mrs. van Houten rode back to Laura Place in solitary splendor, communing with her Muse. The others decided to enjoy the bright sunshine by walking, taking the long route by way of Milsom Street. There was a particularly wonderful pair of gloves in Dandrey's that Trix was dying to show Saskia, and Neil had succumbed to the lure of Duffield's Library. It wasn't the Bodleian, but it did have books and newspapers and all the latest journals. Mr. Duffield was destined to become *very* familiar with young Mr. van Houten's face.

"I can't think," said Beatrix as they strolled along, "that *Opa* is truly comfortable in that horrid place."

"Don't let Mama hear you calling it horrid!" replied Saskia with a laugh. "It's positively dripping with history and therefore with romance."

"Shouldn't be surprised if it does drip," agreed Neil. "Every time it rains."

"Of course I don't mean it isn't quite respectable," said Beatrix. "But he has only Mr. Hawkins to look after him, you know. And I *don't* think Mr. Hawkins knows how to make him feel comfortable."

Neil agreed. "With that long Friday-face of his, more

117

likely to send him into a decline. What a *gloom* the fellow is!"

"Exactly!" cried Trix. "And that is why I think we should invite *Opa* to stay with us in Laura Place."

"Stay with us? You mean live with us?" asked Saskia.

"Of course. We've ever so much room. Jannie will see that he is excellently fed, and I will make him laugh. He is sure to be better then."

"Perhaps he might not wish to live with us. He is used to being on his own, you know, having his own way."

"He may have it just as well in Laura Place." Saskia knew full well that he would have no such thing. The poor man would be ruled by Trix, and by Jannie, from the moment he set foot in the door. But that might, in fact, be just what he needed. He seemed better already than he had that first morning in the Pump Room.

"Do say we may ask him, Saskia."

"It's hardly up to me, dearest. You must ask Mama."

"Pooh! You know very well Mama will agree to whatever you decide."

"She always does," Neil concurred. His tone of resignation made Saskia stare. How tall and handsome he'd grown this past year, and how proud she felt to walk down the street with him.

"Well, then," she said. "You must ask Neil, Trix. As the man of the family, it ought to be his decision."

He stared at her in astonishment, wondering guiltily if she had read his mind. He had recently begun to resent her hand on his bridle, and here she was calling him a man and deferring to his judgment. The image of himself as grown-up was of fairly recent date, and he was enormously flattered to have it endorsed by his formidable sister. "Well, uh, that is . . ." He hesitated, being new to the making of decisions. "You must, uh, do as you think best, Sask. Running the house is woman's work, after all." The responsibilities of manhood did not yet fit quite so snugly as the image.

"Well, if you are sure you have no objection, Neil,"

she answered demurely. "Very well, we shall invite him. But he may not wish to come, you know."

"Oh, he will," replied Beatrix confidently.

"Where do you suppose he could have seen the painting?" Saskia asked after a bit. "Of Grandmama. One can't quite imagine Grandfather Rowbridge inviting him to the unveiling."

"Gainsborough exhibited at the Royal Academy," said Neil. "He could have seen it there, maybe."

"Is it very beautiful?" asked Trix.

"Yes," said her sister. "It is very lovely. Just like you. Is that what you wished to hear?"

"Of course not!" she retorted, then a blush overspread her pretty features. "Oh dear. I suppose it is what I wanted to hear, for you know I'm so nervous. I haven't been to balls and parties and such. What if I shouldn't know how to act? Or if no one should ask me to dance? I'll die of embarrassment, I think."

"Well, love," said Saskia gently, "I don't think you need worry overmuch. Just be yourself and have fun. It's all I want for you." She was lying, of course. She wanted a great deal more than that for her beautiful sister. She wanted it all. All the comfort, the admiration, the pretty clothes and grand houses, all the security that comes with being well established in the world. And she would get it! In just the few days they had been here Trix had already aroused a flattering degree of notice from several young officers and gentlemen and at least one viscount. Saskia would not let her hopes soar too high too quickly, but she wouldn't give up her dream of seeing Trix comfortably settled with a good, kind, *wealthy* husband.

The threesome soon reached Duffield's Library and Neil wandered off to lose himself amid the dusty tomes. The sisters tripped happily up the fashionable shopping street, dodging Bath chairs and young girls in search of ribbons. They nodded to acquaintances, laughed at the more outrageous bonnets adorning elderly heads, and received more than a few goggle-eyed stares from gentlemen having a first glimspe of Beatrix. She, modest thing that she was, seemed unaware of their admiration.

"Do you think," she asked Saskia, "that Cousin Derek will be at the assembly this week? I don't think I should be quite so nervous then. And perhaps he would ask me to stand up with him."

"Do you like him so much, then?"

"Oh, yes! Is he not the *kindest* man, Sask? And so handsome! I daresay every girl there will envy me if he does ask me to dance."

"Kind? I don't know that I would have chosen the word myself. But he is certain to dance with you. It would be grossly uncivil not to, and he is far too proud to be uncivil in public." As she spoke, she realized that this very reason would cause her cousin to dance with her as well. Her stomach gave a strange leap at that moment, but she attributed it to the sight of the Bath buns in a nearby shop window.

"I can't imagine Cousin Derek being uncivil to anyone," continued Beatrix. "He is far too gentlemanly." Saskia gave her a hard sidelong look, but made no further comment.

"Wouldn't it be a lark if Cousin Derek were to fall in love with one of us?" said Trix with a laugh. "It would be the perfect solution, for then we should all be rich!"

"Really, Trix," answered Saskia with unusual warmth, "what a perfectly bird-witted notion!" She turned firmly away. "Do look at that hat! What a quiz!"

They dallied for more than an hour, breathing in the heady perfume from a scent shop, shouting over the clatter and rumble of carriages, carts, and drays on the cobbled street. Then it was time to return home. Saskia, having successfully convinced Trix that lemon-yellow gloves with orange gauntlets and green embroidery were not *quite* the thing for a young lady in her first season and having pulled Neil from the pages of the *New Journal of the Physical Sciences*, headed them all down the hill.

It was just at the bottom of the street that they encountered their cousin. He was in conversation with an unfamiliar gentleman and a very young lady in a very large poke bonnet.

"Cousin Derek!" cried Beatrix in delight.

"Good afternoon!" He greeted them heartily. Saskia was surprised at his evident good humor. What a nice smile he has, she reflected. He should let it show more often. But then, gentlemen always smiled at the sight of Trix. She returned the greeting and the smile.

How warm and brown her eyes look against that bronze green she has on, thought Derek, looking at Saskia. She should wear it more often. He spoke again. "You've not met Captain Durrant as yet, have you? He saw the old *Fair Lady* through many a bombardment and pulled me out of the drink more than once." His affection for his commanding officer was evident as he made these introductions.

"And this is my daughter," said the Captain, beaming proudly. "Melissa. Ever since her mother died fifteen years ago, she's what brings me home to England."

Bows and curtsies and handshakes abounded. Miss Melissa was about sixteen, with long dark lashes and a pretty blush for Neil, who was obviously the most splendid young man she'd ever seen. To his sister's amazement he blushed back, admiration bright in his eyes. It was the first time his admiration was not directed toward something bound in Morocco and edged with gilt.

Captain Durrant was a sturdily built gentleman of about forty with a face toughened by wind and bronzed by sun, but still handsome. His dark hair was touched with grey at the temples, his handshake was firm, and his eyes smiled. Saskia liked him at once.

"Do you remain long in Bath, Captain Durrant?" she asked.

"Only till the end of the month. Visiting my little girl, here." Melissa blushed prettily as he chucked her chin. "Lives here with my sister, she does. I'm going back to sea."

Pure joy was reflected in his face at the notion of striding a deck once more. "I've just been given a ship. A frigate, she is. One hundred sixty-two feet and all beauty. Fitting up at Portsmouth now. We head out in five or six weeks."

"But with the war over where will you go?" asked Beatrix.

"West Indies. Jamaica, Bermuda, all that lot. I'd hoped to persuade Rowbridge here to come along. I need the best first lieutenant I can get, and he's it. But he has other concerns. Turned into a regular lubber, he has," he said with an affectionate laugh. "Now I've seen what pretty cousins he has, I understand his reluctance to spend months with my old face!"

"If the timing weren't so bad, sir, I'd go like a shot, and well you know it," said Derek. "But there's something I must take care of here. If things work out the way I hope, I'll never sail again, sir. At least not for the Navy. But if they don't, you may look for me to turn up in Jamaica on the first boat."

The Durrants were lodging in Argyle Street, so it was natural for them all to fall into one party. Somehow— Saskia didn't know quite how—they divided themselves almost exactly into three pairs. Beatrix was chattering gaily to Derek, admiring him with her melting blue eyes, and receiving his admiration in return. Neil and Miss Durrant brought up the rear, not speaking much, but smiling a great deal. Saskia and Captain Durrant led the procession.

"Do tell me about your ship, Captain," said Saskia with interest. "A frigate, you say? That's a three-master, is it not, and full-rigged? How many guns does she carry?"

"Thirty-six."

"On a single gun deck? Or is she double?"

He looked at her with admiration. "Now how is it that a pretty young lady knows so much about ships?"

She laughed her warm, soft laugh. "Well, Papa dabbled for a while in shipbuilding. Not very successfully, I'm afraid—poor Papa wasn't successful at much of anything, except loving us all to death—but he did take me to the yards with him once, in Amsterdam. And the architect there explained all manner of things to me, one or two of which I even understood! Mostly I remember how much I wanted to get on the biggest ship there and sail to all the wonderful places I've never seen."

"Well, I've seen most of them only to learn you're better off here. But Amsterdam, now there's a beautiful city! I'm proud to be an Englishman, and always will be, but the Dutch, they do know how to build a city. Water! There's the key."

"Oh, yes!" She smiled broadly. "It is lovely, isn't it? You are one of the few people I've met in England who has actually seen it. Waking up to the sound of ducks on the canal! Trees reflected in the water, especially in the autumn. And all the bustle of the Damrak, with ships unloading from all over the world, and shoppers, and children, and old market women all mixed up together." She sighed. "Sometimes I miss it dreadfully."

"Now that peace has returned to the earth, perhaps you will visit."

"Yes, perhaps."

They were nearly to the Durrants' door when the twins came skipping up from the direction of Laura Place.

"Sask, you'll never guess," cried Willem, a grimace of extreme distaste marring his little Dutch face.

"Haven't you two been home yet? Jannie will be worried."

"Oh, but Sask . . ." began Mina.

"Where are your manners?" she exclaimed. "Make your bows to Captain Durrant before I die of embarrassment. These disreputable children are my brother and sister, Captain. Willem and Wilhelmina."

"I wouldn't go inside if I were you, Sask," said Willem in a voice of doom. "Visitors!"

"Oh dear! Then we must hurry. Who is it?"

"Mr. Kneighley." He wrinkled up his nose at the name. Saskia's heart sank.

"*And* his mother," added Mina. Saskia groaned.

"*And* his sister!" the twins chorused. Saskia sighed.

"I might have known," she said forlornly.

"Not bad news I hope, Cousin," said Derek.

"Well, not tragic exactly, but hardly what I should call pleasant. Do you remember, Cousin Derek, that morning we were speaking of *Pride and Prejudice?*"

"Of course."

"Well, my Mr. Collins has come to Bath."

"The prosy rector?"

"Precisely."

"Oh," he said with a smile that was truly sympathetic. "Oh dear." The others looked on, mystified.

"Well, I must go and greet them. Come, Trix, Neil."

"Shall we see you at the assembly, Miss van Houten?" asked Captain Durrant. "My sister is pushing Melly out of the nest this season and has insisted that I accompany them."

"Oh yes!" chirped Beatrix. "We shall be there. I can hardly wait."

"Till then," said the Captain with a tip of his hat. Melissa gave a blushing curtsey to them all and a soulful smile to Neil, and they entered their house.

"May I escort you, Cousin?" asked Derek. "I should like to pay my respects to your mother and confess a dark desire to meet your Mr. Collins."

"His name ain't Collins," said Neil. "It's Kneighley. And what the devil should bring him to Bath is more than I know!"

"Come with us, by all means," said Saskia. "You may tell me whether I am right in the characterization."

"Poor Mr. Kneighley," sighed Trix. "I'm sure one really *ought* to like him, or at least respect him. He is such a *worthy* man."

"Which is what makes it so particularly difficult to admire him, is it not?" said Derek with great perspicacity.

"Exactly!" she answered. "How well you understand everything, Cousin Derek."

They had reached Laura Place. Saskia took a deep breath, squared her shoulders, and entered the house. Voices drifted from the sitting room. The deep, ponderous tones of the rector of Eynshant could be clearly distinguished.

"Naturally I should not wish to be thought unmindful of my filial duties." Saskia gave an involuntary shudder. "Of course, in a large sense, my family is comprised of the whole of my parish flock. My children. My brothers before the Maker. Yet I could not reconcile it with my conscience to neglect the temporal needs of those whose blood I am privileged to share. It was necessary for Mama to come to Bath, and I could not consider allowing her to make the trip unescorted by her only son, with her health in such a fragile state. I was, at length, persuaded that Pitchley would serve the faithful sufficiently well during my absence. I would scarce have considered leaving for so much as a day had that not been the case, as I'm sure you are aware, ma'am."

"Quite, sir," came the faint reply.

"Poor Mama," whispered Saskia. "We must rescue her." She stepped into the fire. "Here we are at last, Mama. Did you think we had fallen into the river? Why Mrs. Kneighley! What a pleasant surprise. And Mr. Kneighley. How do you do, sir? And you have brought your charming sister. How pleasant. Have you rung for tea, Mama? Trix, do go and ask Jannie to send up some of her lovely *speculaas*."

Mr. Kneighley had risen gravely to his feet to take her hand. But his eye was on Derek, whom he studied with scarcely concealed curiosity and concern. "This is Mr. Rowbridge," she explained. "Our cousin."

"Cousin? I was not aware that you were possessed of any English cousins, my dear Miss van Houten," said Mr. Kneighley.

"Nor were we," she answered with a forced laugh. "It seems our Great-aunt Hester is fond of surprises."

Derek offered the clerical gentleman his hand. "How do you do Mr. Coll . . . uh, Kneighley." Saskia choked on a stifled giggle. How odious he was, she thought, to make her laugh. And look, his eyes were twinkling! She shot him an accusing glare, but it was intercepted by Ware with the tea tray. She busied herself with the cups and plates. "What has brought you to Bath?" she inquired of the rector's mother. "I hope you are not unwell, ma'am."

"Alas," sighed Mrs. Kneighley from the depths of her layers of shawls. "My constitution has ever been frail, you know, my dear. It is the reason I so particularly wish dear Delbert to be settled with a wife. Soon I shan't be able to take care of him myself as I should wish. And he is the kindest son. The tiniest complaint from me and nothing would do for him but to bundle us all off to Bath at the first opportunity."

Anyone with less personal knowledge of Mrs. Kneighley than Saskia had might have accepted this at face value, for the lady fit the image perfectly. She was *wilted*. Her shoulders drooped with carefully studied grace; the pale hand that lifted the delicate teacup seemed scarce able to support the burden. She sighed deeply and frequently. The effect was heightened by the flowing crape with which she was lavishly draped, the color of wilted roses. A wan little smile was meant to—and sometimes even did—convince the viewer how bravely she stood up to the vicissitudes and ignominies fate chose to heap upon her poor head. A regular daughter of Job, thought Saskia uncharitably.

Mrs. Kneighley's breathy monologue continued. "And then there is my sweet Griselda, poor child. She was so anxious for a little frivolity. But then what girl isn't? I hear Bath can be very gay. Do you find it so, my dear?"

As the "poor child" of a daughter to whom she referred was fully thirty years of age, was unfailingly critical of "frivolity," and was scowling ominously at her mother, Saskia had little trouble divining the true reason for this inconvenient visit to Bath. And it was with great difficulty that she hid her annoyance.

They had come to spy on her, and she knew quite well it was Mrs. Kneighley's doing. Delbert Kneighley, in his arrogance, would never entertain the tiniest fear that Saskia might be tempted by the pleasures and the gentlemen of Bath. His mother knew better. Under that drooping exterior lived a will that refused to be crossed. She had decided that Saskia van Houten would make a suitable daughter-in-law, and that was that. Now, with a wealthy aunt in the background, she was more convinced than ever. She would brook no interference with her plans, and she had come to Bath to see that there was none. What a mother-in-law the woman would make!

Mr. Kneighley was conversing stiffly with Derek. A more pointed contrast between two gentlemen could scarce be imagined. The weasel and the wolf, she thought with a stifled giggle. No, that was unfair. Despite his new sartorial splendor, there was nothing wolfish about Derek. He was more of a cold fish.

She turned to Mrs. Kneighley. "Yes, we find Bath pleasant, ma'am. We already have a numerous acquaintance and have received a flattering number of invitations."

"Indeed?" she replied with something less than her usual languidness.

"I have just been saying the same to Mr. Kneighley, Cousin," said Derek. "We were speaking of the assembly. He and Miss Kneighley will surely wish to join in the 'frivolity.'"

"Oh, I scarcely think . . . ," she began, glaring daggers at him. "You forget, Cousin Derek, that Mr. Kneighley is a man of the church. I am sure he does not care for dancing."

"You do me an injustice, my dear Miss van Houten," said Mr. Kneighley. "Though not, of course, putting myself in the way of occasions of dancing as would, naturally, be sadly improper for a clergyman to do, still

I consider the ability to dance creditably to be an accomplishment without which I would deem myself sadly lacking as a completely rounded social individual. There are those societal duties of which none of us may acquit ourselves. I fancy I am able to 'sport a toe' on the floor for a respectable country dance without disgrace either to myself or to the lady I have the felicity to claim as my partner."

"Quite," said Derek with a wry smile.

The others were left with nothing whatever to say on the subject.

The visit went on interminably. Rembrandt took exception to Mr. Kneighley's right foot and the rector's frantic attempts to beat him off were useless. Derek disengaged the bulldog with a single firm word. His reward was a scowl from the rector.

Neil was reminded to continue with the Ovid translation he had finished days before. Beatrix was gently chastised for her finery and reminded of the sin of vanity. The twins, putting in a belated appearance, were adjured not to give their sister any trouble and to read a sermon nightly. It was only by the sternest of looks from Saskia that Willem was kept from retorting in a very rude manner.

And, most odious of all, Mr. Kneighley begged as his right the opening dance with Saskia at the assembly. She could not refuse without being positively uncivil, and some of the joy of anticipation went out of the evening.

"And may I count on the first dance with her beautiful sister?" Derek asked Beatrix.

"Oh, you know I'm not, Cousin Derek," she demurred. "But I had hoped you would ask me."

Mrs. Kneighley leaned toward Saskia's ear. "A budding romance? Quite proper, I should think. A frivolous young girl like our Beatrix should settle early."

"What nonsense!" Saskia answered, surprising herself with her sharpness. She hurried to soften her words. "I'm sure you are mistaken, ma'am. Trix is far too young to be fixing her interest just yet, and our cousin is not at all the sort of gentleman for her."

"A girl's heart does not always follow her head. They have not all got your good sense in these matters, my dear."

Yes, thought Saskia fiercely. Good sense is all-important in such things. And Mr. Kneighley represented good sense. He was bidding Mama a ponderous good-bye, to her vast relief. At last he and his ladies were gone. Derek took his leave as well, and Saskia walked him to the hall.

"Well, Cousin," said Derek, "your characterization cannot be faulted. Mr. Collins to the life."

The mood for such trifling was dead in Saskia. "Yes, but Mr. Collins was a very worthy man after all. I'm sure I shall like being a Mrs. Collins when we are married."

"Married!" he exclaimed. "Surely not! Even you could not deal with such a clown."

"*Even* I? How dare you! What do you know of me? I shall marry whom I please!" And why ever am I saying these horrid things to him, she thought, when I *don't* please to be married to Mr. Kneighley. "He is far more of a gentleman than you have ever shown yourself to be. And he is not a clown!" But he *is*, her mind shouted.

"You are quite right, Cousin. It is no business of mine. Obviously the two of you are perfectly suited!" He pounded his beaver onto his auburn locks, bade her a stiff good day, and stalked out.

Chapter Thirteen

Hester Eccles hadn't enjoyed herself so much since the Padishah of Turkey was courting her. To be sure, the scale of the current entertainment could hardly compare with that raree show. It had entailed gifts of a dozen fresh-killed oxen daily and gilded peacock's eggs borne by black Nubians. Coffee had been strewn on the road before her house each morning, and janissaries guarded her door each night. Yes indeed, that had been quite something. Too bad the Padishah himself had been such a disagreeable man, forever cutting people's tongues out and such. She'd had to hire another bodyguard to protect herself from *him*.

This little Bath diversion she'd concocted was tame by comparison, but then she was a good deal older now and no longer up to such extravagance. Derek and Saskia were entertaining her very well. They might even get Rowbridge Manor for her, though they were making precious little progress. But there was time and to spare, and watching them circle around each other like a pair of wary pups was diversion enough for the present. That match looked to turn out better than she had dared to hope.

All the bustle of visiting and shopping and introducing Cornelia and the girls about had made her feel quite young again. Beatrix was a stunner, of course, and hardly worth investing great effort in. The girl would look lovely in a Hessian sack! But the older girl, now there was more of a challenge.

Lady Eccles had been almost distressed by her first sight of Saskia. Frowning at her cousin, she had looked so stern, pinched even, and older than her years, with mousy hair and an equally mousy gown. But she was divinely tall, with an elegant figure, and she did have those remarkable Rowbridge eyes.

Dressing Saskia had taken considerable thought, but it had produced the desired results. She could carry off smart colors and styles more dashing than most of the Bath misses littering the town. She had good taste to match her good sense, and her confidence grew with her attractiveness. Actually, she had something more than her sister's undeniable prettiness. She was handsome.

And then there was the nephew. Distressingly sober for a Rowbridge, but a fine young man nonetheless. Wherever could all that *responsibility* have come from? But Lady Eccles was pleased with him. She had always considered the Navy to be a profession that required a man to be handsome, elegant, and agreeable. She'd seen straight off that he was the first. He'd become the second as soon as he had rigged himself out in style. Now she was learning that he could be the last when it suited him. And it seemed to suit him more often lately.

She smiled a pleased smile and pulled deeply on her hookah, savoring the pungent smoke and letting it drift about her head. She would drink her goat's milk, then set out for Laura Place. The girls could accompany her to the Pump Room this morning.

Before she could reach for the gong to summon Rahjim, he slid silently into the room. "Pardon, Ladyship, but visitor, he will not go away."

"Visitor? Who can be calling on me at this hour?"

"A Mr. Banks, Ladyship."

Her head came up; her eyebrows shot up; finally the

corners of her mouth curved up into a delicious smile. "Ahhhh," she sighed with great satisfaction. "Show Mr. Banks in, Rahjim." She straightened herself to her full majesty, towering over the room from atop her howdah and fixed her eye on the door.

The gentleman entered in Rahjim's wake. He was very old, and he leaned heavily on a blackthorn stick, but he was no suppliant at her throne. He fixed an eye steely as her own on Lady Eccles. There was, however, a glimmer of a smile in their depths, a smile the lady returned.

"Ah, well, I suppose I ought to have known," she said.

"If you could just put me in touch with Mr. Banks," said Derek Rowbridge to Mr. Dawes in the agent's offices in Westgate Street.

Mr. Dawes scowled all over his scrawny face, pulling his thin grey eyebrows down to a ludicrous degree and straightening to his full five feet. He was not at his best this morning. His normal routine had been upset, and Mr. Dawes was a man who set great store by routine. Heaven alone knew why he should, for a more boring daily round could scarce be imagined.

He had—quite suddenly it seemed—become an elderly man, and new business was not coming his way. His day consisted of sorting through a thin supply of mail, arranging it into neat piles as though it had some importance, then moving an unimpressive number of papers and documents from one side of his desk to the other. He would painstakingly sharpen a pen to sign some paper with a flourish it did not merit.

Once or twice a day he would exchange pleasantries or grumbles with his equally boring and very inept clerk. The tenor of the exchange was dependent on the quality of the breakfast set before Mr. Dawes by his sister, who did duty as his housekeeper. This morning the eggs had been dry, the ham greasy, and the sirloin gone. The hapless clerk had been thoroughly grumbled at.

Now Mr. Dawes was thrown off his stride altogether. First there had been that young woman striding unanticipated and unannounced into an office that, to Mr. Dawes's certain knowledge, had seen no female presence in half a century. An impertinent young woman, she'd been too, with a foreign name but demanding as any Englishwoman, asking him all sorts of irrelevant and unbecoming questions about Rowbridge Manor, questions to which he had no answers. He had got rid of her with a rudeness he disliked.

Now here came this smooth-looking gentleman, gloating in the name of Rowbridge, smug in his youth and his health, and wanting to be told what the agent could not tell him because he did not know. So he bluffed.

"No, no, no, quite impossible, my good sir. Quite impossible, indeed. Simply out of the question," he blustered.

"Would you mind telling me why it is out of the question, Mr. Dawes?" Derek asked coolly.

The cheek of the fellow, thought the agent. Coming in here, calling himself a Rowbridge, and making these unseemly demands. The grey eyebrows worked excitedly; the eyes raked Mr. Rowbridge from head to foot. But it was no good. It was distressingly clear that the young upstart was not to be put out of countenance. Mr. Dawes gave up.

"Because I do not know Mr. Banks," he admitted. "I have never set eyes on him, and that is the truth."

Disappointment cut deep in Derek. He tried a few more questions, but it was clear they would lead him nowhere. He reluctantly took his leave of the unhappy agent.

Moments after Derek had left, the clerk tapped at Mr. Dawes's door. "Beg pardon, sir," he said, "but there's a gentleman in the street wishing to speak with you personally."

"Well, who is it? Why doesn't he come up? I do not conduct my business in the public thoroughfare!"

"It's a Mr. Banks, sir. He refuses to come up. He said

. . . well, he said you could damn well come to him, sir."

"Banks? Did you say Banks?"

"Yes, sir. Banks, sir." The poor clerk was wondering what evil deed he had committed to have earned his current position.

Much as he might dislike the idea, Mr. Dawes was in no position to keep Mr. Banks waiting. He provided a goodly portion of Mr. Dawes's income. He descended to the street.

"So you're Dawes," growled the very elderly, very bald man from the depths of a sedan chair. He studied the agent outrageously, sighed importantly, and added, "I don't suppose I should have expected anything more."

"May I serve you in some way, Mr. Banks?" the agent asked stiffly.

"D'you think I'd have put myself to the misery of seeing your face if you couldn't? I've got a job for you, and you'll do it and keep your mouth shut about me into the bargain." He reached deep into his layers of coats and pulled out a pair of sealed letters. "You had some visitors today." It was not a question.

"I did, sir. They were asking about Rowbridge Manor."

"I know what they were asking about. I want these notes sent to them. Get that turkey-cock of yours to carry them round at once. And tell him not to mention me!" He put the letters into Mr. Dawes's hand, signaled to his chairmen, and was carried away before the agent could protest.

When the protest did come, Mr. Dawes found himself alone in the street, spluttering at the air. He handed the notes to his "turkey-cock" of a clerk with curt orders to see them delivered at once, then set off for the Bull and Boar and the consolation of a pint.

A rare peace prevailed in the household in Laura Place. Trix was out riding with Melissa Durrant, Letty Crinshaw, and a score of others. Neil had surprised his sisters by offering to accompany them. Willem was shut up in the schoolroom with the friendly new tutor whom Derek had suggested, struggling manfully with his equations. Mina was earnestly, if unmusically, practicing one of Mr. Clementi's sonatinas, agonizing over the tricky Italian fingering. Saskia had tried every ploy imaginable to get Mina to practice, to no avail. Then Derek idly suggested one day that a young lady who couldn't play creditably was not to be bothered with. Now Mina practiced daily.

Mama was at work in her study; Jannie was at work in her kitchen. And Saskia was brooding.

She was no closer to winning this blasted contest than she had been the day she arrived in Bath. And that Dawes fellow this morning! Intolerable little mushroom! Treating her like an errant schoolgirl. She had been uncivil to him, but oh, how he had deserved it!

She sat curled up in an unladylike fashion in a big comfortable chair in the front parlor, pondering her next move. She had lost some of her eagerness for the contest, though she wasn't sure why. Why could Aunt Hester not simply divide her fortune between them and be done with it? If Saskia lost, the van Houtens would be back with nothing. But if she won, her cousin would have nothing. The thought had inspired her at first. Now she found it an unpleasant, guilt-producing notion.

Ware broke in on her thoughts with a letter on a silver salver. Probably yet another invitation. Their numbers had increased almost to a torrent.

But it was not an invitation.

My dear Miss van Houten,

Since our meeting this morning, I have had communication with the owner of Rowbridge Manor. Mr. Banks has confessed a willingness to listen to your proposition regarding the property. He will send a representative to discuss it with you. You will meet this representative at precisely three o'clock this afternoon in Sydney Gardens. Enter the labyrinth, take the second turning to the left, and walk to the end of the alley. Wait in the *cul-de-sac*. And come alone.

Your humble servant,
Osgood T. Dawes, agent

Well! This was progress to be sure, if more than a little high-handed. She felt certain this odious little man would not have ordered her about in such a way had he been dealing with her cousin. But of course she would answer the summons, rudely put or not. A meeting with Mr. Banks! Or with his representative, which came to the same thing. Dare she hope she had won? She ran up to change for the fateful meeting.

Derek Rowbridge threw the letter onto a table in disgust. The cheek of that Dawes fellow, ordering him about as if he were a schoolboy! And he a Rowbridge! He had half a mind to ignore this imperious summons altogether. But of course he would do no such thing. That *would* be the height of foolishness. This was his chance. Perhaps the contest would end this very day, with himself the victor.

He sobered at the thought. What would become of the van Houtens when their fling in Bath was over? He had grown fond of the twins. Neil was bright, a challenge to talk to. And Beatrix, it was a joy just to look at her.

Well, there was time and to spare to worry about them. He must speak to Banks's man. He set out for Sydney Gardens.

Saskia glanced at her lapel watch as she approached the labyrinth. Quarter to three. Her eagerness and her unladylike stride had brought her here quickly. She scanned the faces of everyone nearby, chiefly small children and their nannies. An elderly woman in a shawl sat on a bench, eyes closed and face turned to the sun's warmth. A giggly housemaid strolled by arm in arm with her beau, a footman by the look of his rainbow-hued attire.

She paced back and forth, nervously killing time. Every so often a squeal of delight or a grumble of frustration drifted over the high hedges of the maze. "Here. I'm over here!" "No, no. Left. Go to the *left!*" and "Another damned dead-end." Saskia smiled.

Today could mean the beginning of a whole new future for the van Houtens. Neil would be off to Oxford, Willem to Eton. Mina would have a good governess. She wouldn't like it, but she needed taming, and Saskia would find someone young, bright, and gay, someone Mina could like.

And for Beatrix! A season in London. Maybe even Almack's! More gowns, all of the finest, to show her off. She would snare a baronet at the least. Maybe even an earl. How lovely she would look in a countess's coronet and ermine.

Saskia turned and retraced her steps, pacing back toward the entrance to the maze. Her pretty daydreaming was rudely shattered as she saw a familiar figure approach.

"Cousin Saskia! What the deuce ... ?"

There stood Derek Rowbridge glaring at her, though why he should be glaring so grimly she couldn't imagine. She felt a blush begin up her neck. What was happening to her? She never blushed! It must be guilt. Yes, she was feeling guilty because her cousin was about to lose the contest.

But how inconvenient. She glanced at her watch again. It lacked but five minutes of three. She must get rid of him.

It was clear she was not alone in her discomfiture. Derek was knocked off his stride at sight of her standing there so primly on this particular spot at this particular time. What the deuce was the girl about, and why couldn't she have chosen the bowling green or the shrubbery for her afternoon commune with nature?

He made an effort to appear calm. The poor girl didn't know, couldn't even suspect, that she was about to lose the contest. The thought gave him pain. What would become of her, he wondered. Back to Eynshant, he supposed, probably to a marriage to that stick of a Kneighley, poor thing. She really deserved better. Perhaps when he was certain of his aunt's fortune he would find some discreet way to help the van Houtens. They were family, after all.

"You've chosen a lovely day for your stroll in the gardens," he commented pleasantly.

"Yes, lovely," she answered, wondering how she could get rid of him. "You had the same thought yourself, it seems."

"Yes. Just out for a bit of air, you know. I find the gardens refreshing."

"Oh, yes. Very refreshing."

How long will she stand there, he wondered. Can I hint her away? "Did your sister accompany you today? I don't see her about. Perhaps she has wandered off to see the tulips?"

Of course he would ask about Trix, she thought. He had been paying her a marked degree of attention lately. And Trix didn't seem to mind a bit. "Oh, no. She is riding with friends today. I enjoy coming here quite by myself. It is peaceful, and I can think." And please take the hint and go away, do!

He caught the hint, but he had no intention of going away. "I can understand the desire to wander about on one's own, letting one's thoughts meander at will. Pray do not think you must stay here chatting on my account, Cousin. You'll like to see the waterfalls, no doubt." Now take yourself off, girl. It's three o'clock!

The sound of a church bell chiming the hour drifted over the lawns. A middle-aged gentleman approached the maze. Could that be the man? No, here came a little boy running. "Take me on your shoulders, Papa!" he cried. An elderly man in a big hat had taken a seat on a nearby bench and seemed to be dozing in the sun. But the doze could be a sham. Suppose he, too, were waiting for a meeting in the maze?

So occupied were they both in searching about that neither was aware of the obvious agitation of the other. And neither did they notice a sedan chair stopped some little distance away. The curtains were drawn shut, but a pale old eye squinted through a slit, and a mischievous smile cracked the old face within.

Blast! Saskia told herself with an uncharacteristic lack of delicacy. Derek looked as though he'd taken root on the spot. Well, if she couldn't get rid of him civilly, she must be uncivil. "I am so glad you understand my desire to be alone, Cousin, but as I was here first, I shall stay! And *pray* don't feel you must bear me company!"

The little minx, he thought. Now what do I do? Clearly to stay now was impossible. "Very well, Cousin. I leave you to your musings. Good day!" He walked briskly away, stopping as soon as he was out of sight around a corner. Then he peeked back. Surely she would go now that she had won her point. Stubborn, tedious girl!

No sooner had his broad back disappeared around the corner than Saskia plunged into the maze, her steps hurrying over the gravel. Second turning to the left, yes here it was. Now walk to the end of the alley. Yes, here was the *cul-de-sac*. Now wait. There was no one about, and she fervently hoped that Mr. Banks's representative, not finding her here at precisely three, had not left. But no, no one had left the maze in the last quarter of an hour. Of that she was certain. She waited.

Nothing happened for the longest time, and her agitation grew almost unbearable. She fancied she could hear her heart beating louder and louder in her ears. But wait. Silly girl! It wasn't her heart at all. It was footsteps, and they were approaching. The crunch of boots on gravel grew louder, the step firm and brisk. A man's step, and he must be much younger than Saskia had expected. But the steps did not turn into her alley. They were passing by, walking along the other side of the hedge. Disappointment flooded her. But then the steps, so determined in their approach, stopped dead. The man could be no more than a yard away from her, directly opposite to where she stood, with only the high hedge between them.

She realized she'd been holding her breath and let it out on a sigh. The gravel crunched as the man turned toward the sound. There were two beats of silence, then Saskia heard a harsh whisper.

"I've been sent by Dawes."

It was him! What a relief. She hadn't missed him after all. But why was he whispering? "Yes, yes. I've been expecting you," she whispered back.

Odd, he thought. It's a woman. He hadn't expected that and didn't much like the idea of doing business with a woman. But he was in no position to argue the matter. "You've come to talk about Rowbridge Manor?" he asked.

"Yes, of course," she answered. "To discuss the sale of it."

"You understand it is not for myself I speak. I am merely hoping to expedite matters for the parties involved."

"That is my position as well, sir. Of course I do not know what terms would be acceptable. But I do know that my party is most anxious to complete the arrangements." And so am I, she added to herself.

"Indeed? Well then, there should be no difficulty in bringing matters to a happy conclusion." Very happy indeed, he thought.

"It is quite a beautiful house. Do you not think so?" She felt ridiculous whispering such inanities to an unseen gentleman through a hedge, but she would play the game out anyway he chose.

"Very beautiful." Now what is her game, he wondered. Trying to drive up the price, no doubt. Well, he didn't care a fig what it cost his aunt, and apparently neither did she. "It is easy to understand anyone's desire to purchase it."

"Oh, yes!" Was she sounding too eager? She had never been much of a bargainer. Well, it wasn't her money. Not yet, anyway. "Do you not think, sir, that we might better conclude the matter face to face? I am beginning to feel quite foolish."

"Of course." He felt a fool himself. Very odd business, this. "If you will walk along this alleyway, I shall do the same."

The gravel crunched again, loudly on his side, more lightly on hers. The alleys seemed much longer than they had only a few moments before. But finally a figure emerged from each and . . .

"Cousin!" cried Saskia, leaning heavily into the thorns of the hedge.

"What the devil . . . ," exclaimed Derek, as thoroughly taken aback as she. Two mouths hung agape. Two faces grew dark with the pure thunder of indignation. They both regained the power of speech at the same moment.

"If this is your idea of a joke . . . ," began Derek.

"I really had thought better of you . . ." began Saskia.

"Did you send me that note?" they both demanded in one voice.

Silence fell, a silence during which each glared at the other. Then, slowly, the truth began to sink in. This was the most ridiculous situation! Saskia's eyes were the first to be touched by a sign of amusement. The little yellow flecks in her eyes began to dance. One corner of Derek's mouth began to twitch with laughter. A giggle escaped Saskia. Derek let out a guffaw. Before long they were holding their sides, shaking with full-bodied laughter till the tears streamed from their eyes.

"Oh! Oh, dear!" Saskia finally managed to gasp. "How very foolish we must look!"

"Well," Derek managed to say between giggles, "we

did manage to 'bring matters to a happy conclusion.' "
And he was off again.

"Oh, don't, Derek, please!" Saskia cried. "I can't laugh anymore. Please don't make me!" With that she sat on the ground—Derek had already given in to gravity—and roared some more.

It was several minutes before they were sufficiently in control to consider just who had brought them to this.

"That odious Mr. Dawes," said Saskia. "It must have been his idea. He sent the notes."

"I shouldn't have thought the fellow had enough brains to think up such a stunt. But you can be sure that he will have some fancy explaining to do to me."

"To *us*, Cousin Derek. Don't you dare go see him without me!"

"Come then." He rose and brushed off his buckskins, reached out for her hand, and pulled her lightly to her feet. "We'll see him at once." They headed toward the exit.

Unfortunately, during their fit of laughter they had managed to get themselves completely turned about and had lost all sense of direction. They were soon deep in the maze with no idea whatever of which way was out.

"Another damned dead-end," muttered Derek.

"No, no. It's left. Go to the left!" said Saskia.

They were hopelessly lost, and Saskia half expected a minotaur to appear at any moment and gobble them up. It would seem a fitting end to this very unusual day.

"All right. Now let's just think this through calmly," said Derek. "There is obviously a very simple, direct way out."

"Wait! I've remembered something. I read once that if one always keeps one's left hand on the hedge, following wherever it goes, one must eventually come out at the other end. Shall we try?"

And so they made their way out, with only a little more grumbling, a few chuckles, and some thorn pricks. When they emerged at last, they were laughing, they were arm in arm, and they were more in charity with each other than they had ever been.

They did not see the sedan chair nearby move off shortly after their emergence. Inside was a very satisfied old man, chuckling to himself.

Chapter Fourteen

It had been a very long time since Saskia van Houten had had the leisure to look forward to, shop for, and linger over her toilette for a ball. There had been one small assembly in Whitney last season to which she had taken Beatrix, but it was scarce worth the name. Saskia had spent most of the evening trying to keep the Squire's son away from her sister, the rest of the time propped on the sidelines with the chaperones, tapping a foot or a fan in time to the whiny music poured out by the sadly inadequate little orchestra.

But tonight was an entirely different matter. This was a Bath Assembly, and Saskia was attending as a Young Lady and not as a chaperone. Aunt Hester was to accompany them, thus assuring them of a warm reception, and Saskia had given in to her excitement.

She felt she deserved it. She had planned to have a quiet day in preparation for the evening, but it seemed that nothing much turned out as she planned it lately. In fact, today had been trying in the extreme. She only hoped she wouldn't collapse with fatigue in the middle of the cotillion. She had traipsed all over town the whole of the day, and her feet hurt.

Her visit with Derek to see the odious Mr. Dawes the

previous afternoon had not been noticeably productive—the agent was not inclined to be helpful—but they had gleaned one vital piece of information. Mr. Banks was in Bath. That was the positive side of things. The negative was that Mr. Banks knew all about them, their search for him, and their aunt's desire to buy Rowbridge Manor. And apparently he wasn't interested, or why pull such a silly stunt on them as that farce in the labyrinth? They each and separately decided to find him and convince him to change his mind before the other could do so.

Consequently, Saskia had visited virtually every hotel and lodging house in Bath this day—and there was a ridiculously large number of them, she learned—in search of the old man. She had sent Neil to the Guildhall to peruse the list of rate-payers in the city, hoping to turn up his name. There were fourteen homeowners by the name of Banks in Bath, and she saw them all. None of them bore the slightest resemblance to her man. All the questions asked along the way lead her nowhere.

And Saskia knew that she had not been alone in her enquiries. At several stops she had been preceded only moments before by Derek Rowbridge. She had little doubt that at others he followed her just as closely. It was a miracle they hadn't bumped smack into each other.

But they would meet this evening. He might even dance with her. She wasn't at all certain how she felt at the prospect. But suddenly she didn't feel quite as tired as she had.

She picked up the fine Norwich silk shawl, of gossamer green shot with gold, that her Aunt Hester had positively insisted she have, and which she was certain had cost every penny of fifty guineas. It was but the finishing touch to an elegant, softly draped gown of water-green crape cut on classical lines that left bare a rather large expanse of white bosom. It was quite the most daring gown Saskia had ever imagined, much less worn, and she suffered a twinge of doubt at the wisdom of giving in to her aunt's blandishments. But oh, it was lovely, and it made her feel like quite a different person. She very much *liked* feeling like a different person. She had long suspected that Saskia van Houten, with all her grave responsibility and her much-vaunted common sense, had become a dead bore. Tonight she didn't feel the least bit boring.

The gown brushed gently across the toes of the lightest of Grecian sandals; a fine gold cord was wrapped thrice about the high waist. A small aigrette of green plumes, tipped with gold, adorned her head. Her hair had been burnished by her maid's brushing to a rich mahogany, ready to glow in the candlelight of the Assembly Room's massive chandeliers.

She gazed at the image reflected in the pier glass. One quick, tiny frown chased across her eyes as she wondered again if perhaps the total effect wasn't just a bit *too* daring for Bath. But she had never felt so pretty, so desirable, in her life. She would savor the unaccustomed sensation while she could.

She picked up her gold filagree reticule and glided gracefully from the room.

Down came the chin, inch by tiny inch, pushing the cravat into perfect folds. Derek Rowbridge was pleased with the result and managed a grin for Pike, his new valet. Pike did not grin back, merely reaching out to tweak a fold into lying yet more perfectly. Being of a totally unprepossessing aspect himself—pale hair, bland features, and average height—Pike took great pride in his chosen profession. No one ever noticed him. Therefore, his delight was in seeing to it that his master was noticed.

He knew very well that this master would have been satisfied with something considerably less grand than the showy confection adorning his back, for the gentleman had a lamentably casual attitude toward adorning his person. True, his fine physique could show off a coat well, and his strong legs showed to advantage in either pantaloons or knee breeches. But he had developed some remarkably bad habits and ideas about being *comfortable* in his years aboard those horrid, smelly, damp ships of his.

Tonight, though, the results of Pike's efforts were not wholly to be despised. The dark blue, long-tailed coat set on the broad shoulders without so much as a suggestion of a wrinkle. The white marcella waistcoat and satin breeches were precisely right.

The valet would have been surprised had he been privy to his master's thoughts as he gazed into the cheval glass. Casual about his dress Derek may have seemed, but the attitude had in large part been brought about by his perennially empty pockets. But this—this polished young gentleman gazing back at him—this was more like it. It passed through his mind that he and his Cousin Beatrix would make a pleasant sight for the opening dance. Not that many of the onlookers would have an eye for him when she was in the room. What a beauty the girl was! And surprisingly sweet, too. Not the least like her sister.

He had to smile at thought of Saskia, remembering the absurd scene they had played out yesterday in Sydney Gardens and wondering if she was as worn out from this ridiculously unproductive day as he was. He hadn't seen her today, but he knew precisely where she'd been and what she'd been doing. Their paths had been crossing and recrossing all day.

So exhausted was he that he'd nearly given up thought of attending the assembly—the York House's best featherbed looked terribly inviting—but he promised Durrant that he would be there. He had asked his Cousin Beatrix for the first dance. And he admitted to himself that he really did wish to go though he wasn't sure why. There had been an edge of excitement in him all day, as though tonight were to be of great moment.

He wondered idly how Saskia van Houten would appear at her first Bath Assembly. She had lately been looking a good deal less spinsterish, even if she still looked always very neat and proper. Perhaps she would wear that bronze-green shade again, which gave her eyes so much life. Oh, well, it wasn't as though he gave a fig what she wore, for a more disagreeable girl he'd never met. He sent for a carriage and set out up the hill to the Upper Rooms.

Every head in the octagon room turned as Lady Eccles and her two nieces entered the Upper Rooms. With the stars in her eyes rivaling the glittering candles in the great chandelier, Beatrix van Houten was a sight to take any man's breath away. In a cloud of periwinkle-blue muslin and violet ribbons, a wreath of violets and white primroses in her hair, she looked like some fairy spirit. Saskia glowed with pride in her sister, not even noticing that more than one of the admiring glances were directed not at Beatrix but at her. With a slow, stately progress occasioned as much by Aunt Hester's regal temperament as by her infirmity, the three of them made their entrance into the ballroom.

They were besieged as soon as they stepped through the double doors. So many friends and acquaintances had been made since their coming to Bath. Greetings, compliments, and requests for dances came from all sides. Saskia, beaming her hellos, scanned the room. She wondered if Captain Durrant had come. He would make a pleasant partner.

Her roving eye landed not on the pleasant face of the Captain, however. It was the distinctly unpleasant visage of Delbert Kneighley that interrupted her gaze. He was making a determined approach toward her to claim the first dance. A sigh escaped her; there was no getting out of it. She prayed that his unbending sense of propriety would stop him from asking her for a second dance, but she placed no great reliance on it. His mother would have poured him full of quite specific instructions regarding the wooing of Miss van Houten.

Thank goodness that Mrs. Kneighley's zeal to get her only son a wife had stopped short of attending the festivities herself. As emissary she had sent her daughter to supervise operations. Miss Griselda Kneighley was most obviously less than pleased with her mother's decision. She'd trussed herself up in stiff black levantine, unrelieved by so much as a frill of lace, and propped herself in a straight-backed chair below the orchestra from which vantage point she could survey the room with ill-concealed disdain.

Miss Kneighley had a trick of incessantly opening and shutting her eyelids, the speed of which exercise depended on the precise degree of her agitation. One could judge the level to a nicety, if one but had a good pocket watch, by carefully counting the number of bats per minute. It was clear that at the present moment she was very agitated indeed.

Mr. Kneighley shouldered his way through the crowds of admirers to reach Saskia. To her immense surprise and chagrin, he executed a jerky, flourishing bow over her hand, nearly pulling her off her feet in the process, and planted on it a noisy kiss. His mama must be alarmed indeed to countenance such extreme action. He had certainly never thought of it on his own. So full of himself was he that he didn't notice the smirks of amusement touching the lips of the other attendant swains.

Flushing a deep red—it seemed she was blushing an awful lot lately—she introduced Mr. Kneighley to her aunt, to whom the rector made a bow so low and so slow that all conversation in the group ceased until he could bring himself upright again.

Lady Eccles gave him two fingers to shake and studied him frankly, rudely even. He prattled on about "what an honor . . ." and, "been looking forward to . . ." and so on. She returned no answering smile.

"Kneighley," she said when he had finished. "Yes. I believe I have heard the name somewhere or other."

To complete Saskia's discomfiture, Derek Rowbridge chose that moment to make his entrance. He looked magnificent, she noted. He headed straight for Beatrix, over whose hand he bowed with a casual grace to touch it with the lightest of kisses, a teasing look in his eye. The comparison between the two gentlemen could not be avoided, and the poor rector definitely did not come out on the plus side of the conclusion.

"So, Rowbridge!" said Lady Eccles as she offered him her cheek to kiss.

"So, Aunt Hester!" he returned with a grin.

"Pert!" She laughed. "Who dressed you? Never seen you look so well before."

"My valet will be pleased to hear it, ma'am. You, as always, are magnificent." She was, too, in a gold turban studded with enormous rubies, an intricate gold-and-black shawl wrapped around her shoulders. He turned to study his two cousins, genuine admiration writ large in his eyes. Trix was an absolute treat, of course, but it was Saskia whom he studied with surprise. How could he have ever thought her "governessy"? That gown had most certainly never graced a schoolroom, and it was clear that water-green became her even better than bronze. He smiled warmly and wondered why she was looking so uncomfortable.

He turned back to Beatrix. "Quite breathtaking, Trix. I see I was clever to get my request for a dance in early."

She dimpled up at him prettily while her bevy of suitors complained. "Taking unfair advantage, Rowbridge," said one. "Leave it the Navy," complained a young army corporal, and "You'll not get the jump on us a second time, old man," exclaimed a third.

"I'm so awfully glad you did ask me, Cousin Derek," said Beatrix softly. "I shan't be nervous with *you*." Any man in the room would have gladly given an hour of his life for the smile she bestowed on him. It was not lost on Saskia, and, inexplicably, a little of the joy went out of the evening.

Mr. Kneighley made a grave bow to Derek. "Good evening, Mr. Rowbridge. Kind of you to lend the child your countenance. Such inexperienced young ladies as ours are natural prey to ballroom beaux. But we shall not leave them unprotected, shall we?" He turned his weaselly smile on Saskia. "My dear Miss van Houten. You are looking quite, uh, fashionable." If he was shocked by her gown—and she could see to her great delight that he was—he was not quite fool enough to say so. He knew that young ladies must be humored in such matters. And then, she had no man to guide her judgment and shape her taste. After they were married, he would see that such mistakes were not allowed to happen. Such a gown would be sadly improper for a clergyman's wife!

"Shall we join the set, my dear?" He belatedly remembered one of his mother's lessons in wooing. Young ladies must be charmed with romantical allusions and fine speeches, she had said. Well, Delbert Kneighley was nothing if not a fine speaker. "The floor awaits, and I feel Terpsichore, in her benevolence, will smile kindly on the efforts of us, her would-be servants. 'The golden lyre to which the dancer's step listens' beckons us. Come, my dear."

Saskia placed her gloved hand in his and walked onto the floor, not knowing whether to laugh or to die of embarrassment. Behind her she thought she heard a distinct "Humph!" from the direction of her aunt.

Terpsichore might tend to look kindly on her would-be servants, but after one glance she had obviously decided to have nothing whatever to do with Delbert Kneighley. Convinced that his partner would enjoy a show of spirit, he threw himself into the dance, intently moving in entirely the wrong direction so confidently and unambiguously that three shoes rosettes, one satin slipper, and a pair of pinchbeck buckles were rendered useless and any number of toes badly bruised before he could be got turned around again. And still, while apologizing to his victims with cold civility, he so thoroughly proclaimed by his demeanor that he was right and all the rest of the set wrong in their moves as to be ludicrous in the extreme. Saskia had never been so mortified.

After what seemed like hours, the dance ground to a

close, but Mr. Kneighley, instead of returning Saskia to her aunt, steered her in the direction of his sister. The stiff black presence was immobile as they approached except for the rapidly snapping eyes. Mr. Kneighley faded off to fetch some lemonade.

"Good evening, Miss Kneighley. I hope you are enjoying the assembly," said Saskia with civility.

The eyes speeded up. When Miss Kneighley spoke, her voice came out high and thin, the lips set so tightly together they scarce moved enough for the thin, icy line of voice to push its way past them. "As I believe you are aware, Miss van Houten, I do not approve of dancing. It smacks of heathenism and shouts of immorality." Saskia had never known it was possible to speak without moving one's face, and she stared fascinated by the phenomenon.

"Yet you are here, ma'am," she said at last.

"It is not by choice, I assure you! I was told to attend, just as I was told to be gracious to you. I attempt at all times to be obedient to the wishes of my sainted mother, as I hope you are aware, but I fear I am no good at prevarication."

"You do not approve of me, do you, Miss Kneighley?"

"Of course I do not! You are not at all suited to be married to my brother, Miss van Houten. Why only look at that gown! Scandalous! Delbert has no need of you, nor of any other wife."

"Doesn't every man need a wife?"

"Every man needs a housekeeper, Miss van Houten! *I* am an excellent housekeeper."

Oh dear, thought Saskia. Poor Griselda Kneighley is actually jealous of me. It was a diverting thought, considering the limited appeal of the gentleman in question. Saskia could only offer a meek, "I'm sure you are."

It looked as though another attack was building—Miss Kneighley's eyes were going furiously now—but luckily, Captain Durrant sailed up just then to save Saskia from the further slings and arrows of her particular outrageous fortune. He had come to beg a dance, and he was speedily and gratefully accepted.

"Tell me, Captain," she said as they took their places on the floor. "Have you rescued many drowning sailors in your years at sea?"

"One or two, Miss van Houten. Why do you ask?"

"Because I was just about to go down for the third time in the flood of her disapproval."

"Poor thing. I'm glad I was at hand." He gave her a twinkling smile. "Was your entire life flashing before your eyes?"

"No. Does that really happen, do you think?"

"It does indeed."

"You sound as if you spoke from experience, Captain."

"I do. If it hadn't been for Derek Rowbridge pulling me out, I wouldn't now be dancing with his so charming cousin."

"My cousin saved you?"

"That he did. In the Mediterranean. We were in heavy action against a French frigate that was trying to run the blockade. A cannon-burst took off most of the quarterdeck and knocked me clear over the taffrail. Broke both legs and took the wind out of me. I was sinking like a hundredweight of cargo. Derek was after me before I knew where I was, even though he'd taken a ball in the shoulder himself. Pulled me out more dead than alive, he did."

Saskia gave an involuntary gasp. "He was wounded?" Her eyes flew to her cousin, dancing with Melissa Durrant. She had never pictured him amidst the thunder of battle, shells exploding all around him. It was a dreadful picture.

"He certainly was," continued the Captain. "But he just threw his arm in a sling and took command of my ship all the same. I was as good as dead, completely useless. He brought her, and me, home safe. Finest man I've ever known, Derek Rowbridge."

Her eyes still on her cousin, smiling at his partner as

though he'd never had a worry, she tried to reconcile this new information with her personal knowledge of him. He was rude, arrogant, bad-tempered. And he was a hero.

Chapter Fifteen

As the evening wore on, Saskia was pleased to find herself moving from one partner to another. It didn't appear as if she would sit out a single dance. A delightful notion, but there was a strange little hurt that her cousin had not asked her to stand up with him.

She found her eyes wandering to him more and more as the evening wore on. He made no move in her direction, though several times she surprised him looking at her. He danced very little, but did manage to gain three dances with Trix, quite a feat with such a bevy of suitors surrounding the girl. Saskia heard them laughing now. She took herself to task for not warning Trix that she must on no account dance with the same gentleman more than twice. Perhaps it was acceptable when one was related to the gentleman—Aunt Hester must have countenanced it—but Saskia could not like it all the same.

"The quadrille," came Mr. Kneighley's voice, interrupting her thoughts. Saskia jumped at the sound. "The queen of modern dances I conceive it to be, requiring grace and agility and a stateliness proper to the elegance of our time. Shall we attempt it, Miss van Houten?"

The quadrille! Saskia moaned inwardly. That most

devilishly difficult of dances, calculated to make all but the most skilled and graceful look bumbling and awkward. And Mr. Kneighley was most definitely neither skilled nor graceful. Had she truly been so evil as to earn this punishment? She looked frantically about for some escape; her pleading eyes turned to her aunt.

"She would be delighted to stand up with you, Mr. Kneighley," said Lady Eccles with unbelievable perversity.

It was then that Saskia noticed that her cousin had approached and stood behind their aunt's chair. He looked at Saskia, then at Mr. Kneighley. One side of his mouth turned up; it was not a smile. Saskia felt herself flush, favored Lady Eccles with a glare, and followed Mr. Kneighley onto the floor.

Lady Eccles turned a pleased smile to her nephew. "Quite a hit the girls have made tonight."

"Did you think they would not?" he asked.

"Well anyone with eyes in his head would know that Beatrix would take. But Saskia's success is a pleasant surprise, I'll admit."

"Yes," he said slowly. "You have done well by her, Aunt. She looks wonderful."

The sharp old eyes slid sideways to study his face, but her tone remained light. "Yes, thank goodness. It will make my task the easier."

"Task?"

"Yes. You see, I have decided to find the girl a husband."

He snapped his attention from his cousin on the floor to his aunt at his side. He looked as though he had been slapped. "Not Kneighley, surely?"

"Kneighley? Don't be ridiculous. The fellow's a complete twit." The rector was dismissed with a wave of her hand. "He will be got rid of easily enough."

"And yet you practically forced her to dance with him."

"Oh, yes. For the moment he is serving a useful purpose."

"Purpose? What purpose?"

But Lady Eccles had apparently decided that enough had been said for now. The ruby-studded turban bobbed lightly in time to the music; one foot tapped out the beat. Derek might have ceased to exist, for all the answer he got.

"Servant, ma'am," he finally muttered and wandered off to join his captain across the room.

Lady Eccles watched him go, still humming the quadrille, a slow smile of satisfaction creasing her face.

Captain Durrant greeted his lieutenant with warmth. "Want to thank you for standing up with Melly," he said. "She's nervous, you know."

"My pleasure, sir. She's a charming girl."

"Yes, she's a pretty little brig." The Captain beamed. "Too young to be sailing such high seas, though, in my opinion. Only sixteen. Smooth fellows making up to her. She don't seem to notice 'em much, though. I'll give her that. If you ask me, it's that young cousin of yours she's got an eye for. More her speed."

"Neil?" asked Derek. "No need to worry, then, sir. He's all right. Young, of course, and far too serious, but a good lad."

"I can see he is. Raised pretty much by his sister, wasn't he? Now there's a fine girl."

"Saskia?" he asked, then paused a long moment. "Yes," he said slowly. "Yes, she is."

"Bright, capable, but nothing sour or stiff in her. Only look at how well she's handling that booby she's dancing with. He wouldn't know a poop from a yardarm. But she's steering him well to leeward of the others."

Derek watched the dancing couple for a moment, noting the twinkle of amusement that Saskia, despite her embarrassment, had been unable to suppress. "Yes," he said. "I see."

"That girl'd make a fine first mate for any captain's home. That she would."

Derek whipped his eyes back to his captain, wondering just how much was implied in the words, and wondering why he should care so much. Saskia van Houten and Captain Durrant would make a fine, handsome couple. A memory focused in Derek's mind, the feeling of the icy sea closing over his head as he struggled for life, his captain's and his own. He had to force himself to breathe.

He stared at Saskia, bright beautiful Saskia, gliding gracefully about the floor, and suddenly, blindingly, came the recognition of something he had no desire to recognize. No! No, it was not possible! He *could* not be in love with this uppity girl! She was pert, proud, and managing. She didn't even like him. And what's more, she was his rival, threatening the rosy future he had dared to envisage. He would not consider it!

Giving his head a firm shake, he excused himself to Captain Durrant and headed for the card room, hoping fervently that someone, anyone, would give him a stiff drink.

The quadrille went on forever, it seemed to Saskia. She hadn't worked so hard on a dance floor in years. Keeping Delbert Kneighley from coming a cropper was full-time labor. By the time it finally ground to an end she was getting the headache. At least she need not dance with him anymore tonight, nor ever again if she could possibly help it.

Almost without thinking, she searched the faces lining the room for her cousin as she made her way back to her aunt. But there was no sign of him. Had he gone? Surely he would not leave without bidding his aunt good night.

"I wonder if Cousin Derek will dance with Trix again tonight," she said as nonchalantly as she could.

"I'll see that he doesn't," replied Lady Eccles with a nod. She watched Saskia look around the room with a great deal of satisfaction. "I believe he's gone into the card room. Perhaps he doesn't intend dancing anymore this evening."

"Do you think not?" asked Saskia quickly. Too quickly.

Her reaction was not lost on her Aunt Hester, who

added, equally nonchalantly, "But perhaps I am wrong. Ah, there he is now and seemingly looking about for a partner."

Derek stood in the door of the card room, and he was, indeed, sweeping the room with his eyes, apparently in search of someone. He had an odd look on his handsome face. Grim and, well, *determined*, thought Saskia. Yes, that was the word. His eyes paused briefly as they touched her, and she gave him her warmest smile. But he made no move toward her. His scowl only deepened, and his eyes passed on. She felt as if she'd been slapped.

When he found the object of his search and began a resolute approach toward it, Saskia couldn't help herself turning to stare at his goal. Griselda Kneighley! Why on earth was he making for her? He'd never ask her to dance, surely! And besides, she'd never accept. But it was most certainly Griselda Kneighley, in all her proper blackness, for whom he was headed. He favored her with his charming smile and shook her hand, then took a seat beside her. The two were soon deep in animated discussion, Miss Kneighley's fluttering eyes wandering now and then in Saskia's direction with a frown or a nod.

The odd conversational pairing soon became a trio as Mr. Kneighley joined in, and the discussion continued throughout the next dance. Saskia, partnered by a dashing young major in scarlet regimentals, had little attention to spare for her partner, and nearly strained her neck in an attempt to keep her cousin in view as she negotiated the figures of the dance.

Then he disappeared into the card room once more.

Soon the evening was nearly over, the clock creeping up on eleven—Bath was definitely *not* London—and there was but one dance remaining. And Derek Rowbridge asked Saskia van Houten for the honor of partnering her in it.

As soon as they took their places on the floor, he was looking ever so grim, almost as though he were angry at her. She couldn't for the world think why he should be, but then he never seemed to need a reason. As the music rose and fell and they slid gracefully through the moves, his eyes never left her face. She was beginning to feel uneasy at this scrutiny and was near to making a sharp remark when she noticed that it was not anger in his face. He looked sad somehow.

"Well, Cousin," she said brightly in an attempt to lighten the atmosphere to match the bright music. "I have been trying to think what you and the Kneighleys could have found to talk about so earnestly all this time. I shouldn't think you had very much in common with either of them."

"Wouldn't you? Do we not have you in common, Cousin Saskia?"

"Me? But whatever could you have to say to one another about me?"

"Is it not common to discuss mutual friends at social gatherings? I quite thought it was all Society ever did."

She was glad to see that some of his seriousness had left him, and she replied in a bantering tone, "And are you going to tell me what you were saying?"

"Probably not. You are far too proud already."

At this she laughed outright. "Oh, come, Cousin Derek. You'll not gammon me into thinking *you* were singing my praises. Nor, I am sure, was Griselda Kneighley. She is not at all in favor of me."

"No, she is not," he said with a little smile.

"Now Mr. Kneighley, he might put in a kind word in my behalf, but you were most likely filling him with all manner of horrid and ungentlemanly things about me."

"Most likely."

"Wretch!" She laughed back at him. "I'm sure you were. But he won't believe you, you know. Difficult as it may be to believe, Mr. Kneighley *likes* me."

"Really?" By now his smile had grown and spread to his eyes. "But then we both know the man is a fool."

"Oh! You are odious!" She wished she could stamp her foot, but it didn't fit with the steps of the dance. She took a pet and decided to say no more. They danced awhile in silence.

He was not be deflected from the subject, however. "You really must not marry him, you know," he said very quietly.

"Why must I not?" she snapped. "I must marry someone, I suppose. Mr. Kneighley is a very solid, respectable man." She couldn't think why she was defending Delbert Kneighley to her cousin as she no longer had the least intention of marrying him—she'd known that for some days—but she couldn't help herself.

"Oh, yes," Derek went on. "There isn't a particle of harm in him that I can see, beyond his unbearable foolishness. But that doesn't make his society any the more agreeable or his conversation any the less insipid. You'd die of boredom in less than a month, if you didn't kill him first."

Despite her best efforts a bubble of laughter escaped her. "It's true. And I don't imagine I should find it very comfortable to be hanged for his murder."

"You can do far better, you know."

"But I don't know any such thing."

"Don't be a fool, girl. Only look at all the fellows who've been after you tonight. Durrant, for instance."

"Oh, the Captain has been so kind. Thank you for introducing us to him, Cousin Derek," she answered with enthusiasm.

He wished he had never set eyes on Ned Durrant. "And only look at all your other suitors. You haven't missed a single dance."

Who would have imagined he would notice that, she thought. "Yes. Isn't it diverting? There are certainly benefits to being the sister of the prettiest girl in the room. Trix couldn't dance with all of them, so they settled for me."

"I should hardly call it 'settling'," he said quietly. "You look extremely lovely tonight, Saskia."

She turned a deep becoming pink, whether from pleasure or embarrassment she didn't know herself.

"Thank you, Derek," she murmured, then hurried to change the subject. "Do you not think Trix is radiant tonight?"

"When is she not?" he replied. "I doubt that I have ever seen a more beautiful girl than Beatrix. Sometimes I'm almost afraid to look at her lest a closer inspection reveal some flaw. But when I am drawn to do so, it is only to find her more perfect than before. It is quite astonishing."

So ardent were the words that Saskia failed to note the lack of warmth in his tone. He spoke dispassionately, as one might describe a particularly fine statue. His eyes held none of the fire they contained when they looked on Saskia herself.

But she was not looking at him. She did not see his expression. She heard only the excessive admiration for her sister, recalled his laughter as he danced with her, remembered how handsome they had looked together. Suddenly the long day seemed to catch up with her. She felt very, very tired.

Chapter Sixteen

The rain began early next morning. The sky seemed to have suddenly discovered its error in granting several days of exceptionally fine weather, and decided to correct it with a vengeance. No soft drizzle this, no gentle spring rain to caress the daffodils and coax the new leaves to spread to its touch. This was the deluge.

The sky opened to pour torrents of stinging water on anyone and anything foolish enough to venture out of doors. Blossoms were knocked from the trees; tender young shoots just venturing out to test the spring air were pummeled back into the ground for their presumption; and all sane people, and most of the not-so-sane, kept their noses firmly behind their own doors and close to their own fires.

Though some might question the absolute sanity of at least part of the van Houten establishment, even they kept themselves close confined in the luxury of the house in Laura Place. They were capable of entertaining themselves nicely, the result of long practice and a genuine liking for each other's company. And the recent addition to the household of Mr. Weddington—he hadn't taken too much convincing at Beatrix's hands—had added a new element.

163

Derek Rowbridge was not so lucky. Confined within the walls of the York House he was soon in a sorry state. The hotel was painfully thin of company, and he was driven to distracting himself with bottles of brandy and long, involved games of one-handed piquet. Might as well polish his skill at cards, he reasoned. At the rate this damned contest was progressing, he would soon find himself back in the clubs of St. James's Street playing for shilling points and praying for luck.

But one cannot play cards forever. Derek was left with far too much time for brooding, and brood he did. He soon had to openly admit to himself what he had reluctantly glimpsed and tried to brush away on the night of the assembly. He was madly, crazily in love with Saskia van Houten. And he was terrified.

He gazed deep into the fire, trying to burn her vision from his mind, but she seemed to smile back from the flames. He took a long pull at his brandy and noticed how its color was like the amber sparks in her eyes when she was angry. He gave in to a painful little smile as he remembered their first meeting, such a short time ago really, in the Castle Inn. How those wonderful eyes of hers had flashed! She had made it abundantly clear that she found nothing in him to admire and much to dislike. He had little reason to think she had changed her mind.

It was true that she didn't seem quite so disapproving lately as she had been that first day. She smiled more frequently when she looked at him. And it seemed she looked at him more often. But she also turned that same wonderful smile on many of her acquaintances, most especially Derek's closest friend. Captain Edward Durrant and Saskia van Houten made a strikingly handsome couple, he thought, tossing back his brandy and reaching for the bottle. How well-matched they were. Their practical temperaments were perfectly suited. Saskia knew about ships, and she loved the sea. Durrant had always wanted a large family and bemoaned the fact that he had but one child.

And Durrant had begun talking about marriage. What was it he said the other night about Saskia? Something about what a fine first mate she'd make. Well, he was right there. Derek couldn't imagine any woman who would make a finer wife that Saskia, once you got used to her sharp tongue and her managing ways. He tried to scowl at the image of her in his mind, but he didn't quite pull it off.

What if he were to offer for her himself? If she didn't laugh him right out of the room—as she would most probably do—what sort of reaction could he reasonably expect? That she would accept him was out of the question. He had absolutely nothing to offer a wife. No money, no profession, no future, nothing but a large drawer full of bills with no receipts to them.

And this ridiculous contest! He felt fairly confident that she was doing no better that he was—they kept running into each other when they weren't busy running into blank walls—and it was beginning to look very much as though there would be some very wealthy charities in Turkey one day.

And what of her wishes? Even supposing she loved him—wishful thinking beyond foolishness—she quite simply could not afford to marry a pauper. She had a large family to whom she felt a great responsibility. Durrant, though not precisely wealthy, had a comfortable income and would have no objection at all to taking on the lot of them.

And then there was Aunt Hester. She had decided to find Saskia a husband. Derek knew instinctively that when Hester Eccles set her mind to accomplishing something, that something was speedily accomplished.

And, if all other efforts failed, there was always that twit of a Kneighley waiting in the wings. She would marry him. Even the Delbert Kneighleys of this world had more to offer than he. The realization brought his fist and his brandy glass crashing to the table, showering amber droplets of liquid in all directions.

"Blast!" he exclaimed, mopping ineffectively at his

coat. This was ridiculous! He was actually sitting here getting himself stinking drunk over a sharp-tongued chit of a girl who thought of him with contempt when she bothered to think of him at all. How smugly pleased she would be if she could see him now. Well, he would not allow this to continue. The rain be damned! He would take himself out for a good meal and seek out some convivial company. He would go enjoy his status, however temporary, as a gentleman of leisure. He would put Saskia van Houten firmly from his mind.

Pounding his beaver fiercely onto his head and grabbing his many-shouldered cape, he almost dashed from the room. He absently accepted the umbrella proffered by an astonished footman at the front door of the York House and struck out into the flood.

Ten minutes later, dripping and steaming, he was ensconced beside the fire in the Bull and Boar. He sat quite alone, not touching the plateful of roast beef and Yorkshire pudding on his table, and completely ignoring the happy chorus of voices all around him. A glass of brandy was in his hand; a bottle stood on the table. He proceeded to brood a great deal and get very drunk indeed.

On the first day of one of the worst rainstorms in the history of Bath, Saskia had been quite cheerful. She had always loved rain. One couldn't grow up in Holland without developing a certain affinity for wet weather. And if one lived in England it was helpful if one didn't actually hate it. She was also a bit relieved to see the downpour that first morning. She certainly couldn't be expected to traipse all over town in search of the elusive Mr. Banks in such weather, and since she hadn't the slightest notion what to try next, she was glad not to have to try anything, and not even to feel guilty about it.

She set about catching up on the household chores that had been sadly neglected. She brought her accounts up to date, and played jackstraws with the twins. She kneaded bread with Mrs. Jansen, and listened attentively while Mama bounced plot ideas off her.

But by the third day of rain even Saskia was beginning to feel worn down. The twins grew fidgety at their enforced inactivity. Jannie's rheumatism and *Opa's* gout began acting up. Even poor Rembrandt, dejected at being cooped up so long indoors, drooped by the fire, resentment and boredom mingled on his wonderfully ugly pug face.

Only Trix retained her always sunny disposition as she twittered about the house, bullying *Opa* into eating his dinner, fahioning a bonnet for Mama, or coaxing Neil away from his books for an hour or so now and then.

Saskia couldn't account for her low spirits. They had had no visitors at all, due to the storm, but that had never bothered her before. She was at a loss to put a name to an emotion she had never experienced before. She didn't know that one could feel lonely in the midst of a large and loving family, the loneliness that longs for the company of a specific other. She only knew that she felt tired, and dispirited, and totally unlike herself.

It was that third afternoon that Beatrix found her sister at the window seat in the front parlor, staring blankly out onto the grey drenched street while rivulets chased each other down the panes of glass. An open book lay in her lap. Rembrandt snored loudly at her feet; Mr. Weddington snored softly in a chair by the fire, one foot raised on a cushion.

Beatrix walked silently to the window and sat beside her sister. "Has he been asleep long?" she whispered.

"What?" Saskia looked at her with a start. "Oh. No, not long. I was reading to him, and he drifted off."

Beatrix was alarmed at the fatigue in her sister's face. Saskia was their rock, their anchor. Trix had never seen her in such low spirits.

"Are you feeling well, Sask? You look so tired."

"What?" she said again, seeming to concentrate on Beatrix with an effort. "Oh, yes. Yes, of course. I am perfectly all right, darling," she said with forced brightness.

"It is just this odious rain. It seems like it will never stop, doesn't it? Perhaps we ought to have Neil design us an ark."

Beatrix returned the smile and tried to maintain the light mood. "And who shall we invite aboard our ark? There is a nice female terrier across the way that Rembrandt has taken a marked interest in. And Melissa has two kittens."

With a brave show of spirit, Saskia entered into the game. "Willem caught a pair of frogs last week up by the canal, and I expect Jannie will want her rabbits along. And of course the doctor must come along to look after *Opa*."

"Oh, no he shan't!" Trix wrinkled up her nose. "He is a horrid doctor and makes *Opa* feel more ill than ever. I shall take care of him myself."

At that Saskia laughed, quietly so as not to wake *Opa*. "Well then we can give his berth to Melissa. We must have Captain Durrant, of course, to pilot us."

"And Cousin Derek for first lieutenant!"

Saskia's laugh faded and she turned a blank face to the window again. "Do you like Cousin Derek so very much, Trix?"

"Oh yes! Yes, I do. I don't know how I would have got through the assembly without all his encouragement. And he is so very handsome, is he not? He quite cast all the other gentlemen there into the shade."

"He said much the same thing about you. He admires you very much, you know."

"Well, I am glad he does. He is so particularly the type of gentleman one would wish to attract, don't you think?"

There was a pause before Saskia answered. "Yes," she sighed. "Yes, I do."

A tiny frown furrowed Beatrix's brow. She had never seen her strong, self-sufficient sister in such a mood. There was something terribly wrong. She must try to find out what. But her thoughts were diverted by a stir-

ring and grunting from across the room. Mr. Weddington had returned to the world from the depths of his
nap.

"*Opa!*" said Beatrix. "You are awake. How nice. Did
you have a comfortable nap?"

"No, I did not!" he grumbled. "Damned rain! Damned
cold! Damned gout!"

"Oh, dear," she clucked sympathetically. "You are
uncomfortable, aren't you? I'll get you some of Jannie's
ginger powder and a nice cup of tea. Then you will feel
more the thing."

"Tea, humph! What I need is for that damned fool of
a doctor to come and bleed me."

"That you do not, *Opa!* Bleeding indeed! What an an-
tiquated notion. You shall have no such thing."

"Don't you bully me, my girl. I've been having my
blood let these seventy years and more."

"Quite. And I'll wager you've been uncomfortable for
fifty of them."

"Sixty!"

"Well, there you are, then. There will be no more
bloodletting in this house. You need to grow stronger,
not weaker."

He stared defiance at her a moment, then broke into a
grin. It occurred to him that he was smiling quite a lot
lately. And here he'd thought he had forgotten how.
"What a baggage you are," he teased as he reached up
to pinch her cheek. "Lord preserve the husband that
gets loaded with you, puss."

"He will be a lucky man to have me, *Opa*, just as you
are. Now I'll go and get your tea. Tomorrow when you
are feeling stronger, we shall have a nice *hutspot*. Jannie
does it so well, and you know how you like it." His pale
eyes looked up at her and got a twinkle in return. "Perhaps," she said with a grin, "a glass of port would do
you better than tea. Yes, most definitely port." She
dropped a kiss on his freckled pate and skipped from
the room.

He watched her go with the softest of smiles. "Just like my Susannah."

Saskia didn't comment because she hadn't heard. She was staring at the watery street once more, lost in the maze of her own thoughts.

Chapter Seventeen

On the morning of the fourth day the sun peeked through the clouds at last. Birds reappeared from wherever they had been hiding to chirp tentatively. Nursemaids made cautious forays out of doors, one eye on their rambunctious charges, the other on the still watery sky. Dogs, including good old Rembrandt, barked and romped and splashed in puddles. A romping, splashing bulldog is quite a sight to behold.

A general sigh of relief rippled through the town, but Saskia was still in low spirits, wandering aimlessly about and speaking little.

Then, at midafternoon, there came a knock at the door. Ware was soon ushering Derek Rowbridge into the parlor. Suddenly Saskia saw the window sparkling with sunbeams and heard the sounds of spring ringing in the air. He was offering her his most enchanting, most devastating smile, and she wondered for a moment if she was becoming ill. She really was feeling very peculiar.

It was Beatrix who jumped up clapping her hands to greet him. "Cousin Derek!" she cried. "How glad we are that you have come. You wouldn't believe how dreary we have been with no visitors."

He smiled down at her and squeezed her hand. "I

cannot believe that anyplace that claims your company could be dreary, Trix. I think you carry the sunshine with you wherever you go," he said. "Rembrandt! You unholy brute. Get down!"

The lonely bulldog had jumped up from his somnolent attitude on the floor at first sight of his friend Derek and begun scampering about at his feet. Since a scampering bulldog is very like a thundering herd, he was most definitely not to be ignored. A fond scratch on the chin and a playful jostle, plus a firm refusal to do more, soon reduced the scampering to a mere wriggle as he attempted to wag his invisible tail.

At last Derek was free to return his attention to Saskia. His eyes feasted on her, all trim and smart in an afternoon dress of that peculiar shade of grey that the English called "Paris smoke" and the French referred to as "London fog". It was cut high in the throat and long in the sleeve, but there was nothing the least prudish about it. She had a vaguely startled look on her face.

"We have missed seeing you, Cousin Derek," she said in a voice of deceptive calm. "Do have some tea. It is still quite hot." With a graceful gesture, she filled a dainty Wedgewood cup.

"Derek! Cousin Derek!" whooped Willem as the door flew open and the boy threw himself into the room. "I was sure that was your roan!"

"Cousin Derek!" chorused his feminine shadow. "Will you listen to me play? I promise I have been practicing ever so hard."

"I'm sure you have," he said kindly. "I look forward to hearing the results of your endeavors, *after* I have had my tea."

"Mina," said Trix. "However did you come to get so much mud on your new muslin? You had better run and change before Jannie sees it and has palpitations."

Mina wrinkled up her nose. She had had sufficient experience of Jannie's "palpitations". "You won't leave will you, Cousin Derek? Promise?"

"Not unless I am ordered out. Now go upstairs, Miss

Hoyden, and make yourself fit for company. You might run a comb through your hair while you are at it," he added, tweaking at her ribbons.

With a giggle Mina ran off.

"We've been on the greatest lark," exclaimed Willem. "There're ever so many frogs up by the canal. I thought perhaps they'd drown in all that rain, but we caught dozens of them."

"Dozens?" said Derek. "I shudder to think what you have in mind to do with them." Willem's only answer was a mischievous grin. "I must pray I've not been chosen one of your victims. Where've you stashed them?"

"In Jannie's bathtub," said Willem triumphantly.

"Willem!" cried Beatrix. "Go and get them out at once! Do you want to ruin us all? Take them out into the garden."

"But they'll get away! And besides, they need water." He was already beginning to look defiant as only he could do.

Derek intervened with quiet force. "Go, Willem. There is certain to be a washtub or some such thing outside. Put an inch or so of water in it and tie a bit of cheesecloth over the top so they won't jump out. Now go." Willem went.

"Hallo, sir," said Neil, bumping past Willem in the doorway. "I hoped when I saw the sun that you'd come today. I've run across a math problem that's devilish tricky. Thought maybe you'd take a look at it for me if you're free."

"I'd be happy to, Neil, though you're near to leaving me in the shade when it comes to mathematics."

"Thank you, sir. Devilish good of you, sir," said Neil with obvious admiration and gratification.

"Later, Neil," said Trix. "Come have your tea."

Saskia had been strangely silent throughout this easy family scene. She sat looking at Derek, her head cocked to one side rather like Rembrandt when he was trying to understand something. How well Derek handled them all, she was thinking, and how much they all seemed to like and respect him. He was so easy and natural with them. Why then was he so often curt and short-tempered with her? She supposed it must be because they were rivals, if unlikely ones. She did, after all, represent a possible impediment to his financial freedom. Of course, he threatened her in the same way, and she didn't hate him.

She pulled herself up short. She had once hated him, hadn't she? Or at least disliked him intensely. When had she stopped, she wondered, for she was sure she no longer felt the same. She wasn't sure what she did feel, but it was far removed from hatred. She gave a deep sigh.

The sound drew Beatrix's attention to her sister, sitting there gazing at Derek. To Trix's surprise she saw that every trace of the fatigue and despair that had been there but a quarter of an hour ago had disappeared. Saskia's face held a rosy glow, and her eyes had regained their usual animation. She seemed to be paying rapt attention to Derek and Neil's intricate mathematical conversation, and Trix was struck with a happy realization. Saskia and Derek? Why, what a lark! she thought. How delightful. There was no one she would rather have for a brother-in-law. And how *right* they were together. I wonder when they will realize it, she asked herself. Perhaps I will have to help them do so. We shall see.

The afternoon drifted away in a thoroughly comfortable manner. Derek was invited to dine *en famille*, and he gladly accepted. He played a ruthless and enjoyable game of piquet with Mr. Weddington, and had a compliment for Jannie's *poffertjes* that made her round Dutch cheeks glow. He seemed a natural part of the household.

The pleasant chamber music of the afternoon clanged to a discordant cadenza with the arrival on the scene of Delbert Kneighley. Saskia thought she heard thunder in the far distance, but it might as easily have been the rumble of doom she always felt now at sight of him.

How could she have considered for as much as a moment that she could marry him? "How do you do, Mr. Kneighley," she said, plastering on a frigid smile to replace the warm one she'd worn all afternoon.

"Ahhhh! A family party, I see," he oozed, nodding to Derek. "At sight of the first break in the clouds, I rushed forth into the steaming streets to join you."

"You should not have put yourself out to call in such uncertain weather, sir," said Saskia.

"Ah, but I knew you would expect me, my dear Miss van Houten. Of course, one would not look for a mere acquaintance to call on such a day, for I am tolerably certain we shall have more wet weather before we are through. And with the river flooded clear to the High Street already. Tsk, tsk, tsk. Quite shocking. But I hope I know better than to think of myself as a 'mere acquaintance' with you, my dear Miss van Houten. We need stand on no ceremony with each other."

As Mr. Kneighley seldom stood on anything else, Saskia hardly knew what to say. "Then perhaps you would prefer to sit, Mr. Kneighley," she offered, gesturing to the nearby—but not too nearby—settee.

"Ahhh, you are a wit, Miss van Houten," he teased, waggling a finger in her direction, and prying his narrow lips up into something he thought was a smile. "But I hoped perhaps we might take a turn in the garden while Helios grants us the last warmth of his golden rays."

Oh dear, thought Saskia, I am always in trouble when he begins spouting mythological allusions. It was then that she noticed, with growing alarm, that he was wearing his Sunday rector outfit of glossy black breeches and stockings which crinkled somewhat less that his weekday ones. She saw what was coming and, though dreading it, thought she had best get it over with. The sooner she was rid of Mr. Kneighley the happier she would be.

"Very well, Mr. Kneighley," she said with resignation. With a nod to the others—and a haughty sniff for Derek who had the temerity to smirk—she led him from the room.

The scene that now took place in the back garden was an almost exact repetition of Mr. Kneighley's first proposal of marriage at Eynshant. Apparently he had decided that his earlier eloquence could not be improved upon. Today, though, there was, as added feature, the fact that when he came to kneel it was into a puddle and when he jumped up from his dripping knees it was to back into a particularly vicious rose thorn. Saskia had to give him credit. He scarce missed a beat in his memorized speech, the extra "ooooh!" serving only as punctuation.

She was afraid to open her mouth to speak her denial for fear she would burst out laughing, so she had, perforce, to allow him to continue to the end. With a valiant struggle she composed herself enough to utter the appropriate phrases with which a Young Lady of Quality was taught to gently rebuff a suitor. He beamed at the words "sensible of the honor you do me," for he considered it a very great honor indeed. But when she got to "cannot accept your kind offer" he seemed not to have heard.

"Ah, I am so happy my dear. So happy. And when shall the glorious day be?" Apparently Mr. Kneighley was so thoroughly expecting to hear her acceptance that hear it he did, quite despite the fact that she had not said it or anything like.

"The glorious day will *not* be, Mr. Kneighley. You see, I do not love you."

"Ah, yes. Love, glorious love," he mused, opening his hands to the sky. "Like Daphnis and Chloe, our love shall remain ever perfect."

Saskia stared. "You cannot have heard me, Mr. Kneighley. I said I *cannot* marry you." She pulled away the hand he had snatched, and he froze in the very act of trying to kiss it, his thin lips pursed to the air.

"Cannot? Did you say cannot?" he asked. "No, no. Of course you did not. How absurd." He reached for her hand again. His mama had been quite adamant on the point of hand-kissing.

"Delbert Kneighley!" she exclaimed, stamping her foot and snatching her hand back again, pulling him off balance in the process. Into the puddle he sat with a plop.

He looked up at her dazed. "Whatever are you about, Miss van Houten? These are my best breeches!"

"I am sorry, Mr. Kneighley. I truly am. But if your dunking clears your head enough to make you believe that I cannot and will not marry you, I shall be grateful to it!"

This time he heard. But he still didn't quite believe. He pulled himself to his feet, the water dribbling down to puddle in his best shoes.

"Cannot? Cannot! Miss van Houten, have you taken leave of your senses? Of course you are to marry me. It was decided long ago. You have dragged me out into this vicious weather and caused me to ruin my best breeches so you could tell me this?"

Desperate to stop his flow and convince him that she meant what she said Saskia pulled out the first idea that sprang into her mind. "Mr. Kneighley!" she exclaimed in tragic accents. "I cannot marry. *I love another!*" She didn't think Mrs. Siddons herself could have given the line a better reading.

Belief was sinking in at last. He was amazed. He was astonished. But mostly he was angry. "Another? *Another?*" he sputtered. "But . . . but . . . Vixen! Heartless temptress! Leading me on. Flaunting yourself about Bath when you were promised to me! Griselda was right!" His face had turned an alarming shade of purple as his fury increased, and Saskia was reminded very much of the tantrums Willem used to have when he was about four. As he sputtered on, rapidly losing control, his words became unimportant and mostly incoherent, but Saskia could clearly make out "Jezebel" and "Delilah". Finally the poor man was reduced to stamping and jumping with rage, splashing yet more mud all over his best Sunday breeches. Saskia slid out of range and surveyed him with chagrin.

Suddenly, in the middle of a jump, Mr. Kneighley just

stayed in the air, his muddy feet and scrawny legs kicking an angry dance. Derek Rowbridge had hoisted him up by the back of the collar.

"That is quite enough! You forget yourself, sir!" Mr. Kneighley was unceremoniously removed from the premises. The last Saskia heard from him was a babbling, "Mama will have something to say to this!"

Saskia didn't know whether to sink with embarrassment or to go off into whoops of laughter. Mr. Kneighley often produced such a dichotomy of emotions in her. She rather thought she would opt for laughter. She felt sure Derek would join her in it; he seemed to share her sense of the ridiculous.

But when he returned from "escorting" Mr. Kneighley from the premises, he was not laughing. Saskia wondered how much of the silly scene he had overheard before his timely intervention, and she cast her mind back over it in an attempt to recall exactly what had been said. She couldn't think what could have made him look so grim. Was that anger in his face? What could he possibly have to be angry about, she asked herself. Or was it contempt? That would be more in his style. But then, when he turned more directly toward her, did it not look just a bit like sadness, well disguised?

Whatever it was, by the time he reached her it had changed into a sardonic smirk.

"An elevating scene, Cousin," he said coolly.

"Well, yes. Mr. Kneighley was certainly elevated." She giggled in spite of herself. "Handsomely done, sir, I must say. I do thank you for coming to my rescue. I was all at sea."

"I can't imagine you at sea," he said, then paused. "Not figuratively at least." She looked up, puzzled, and their eyes held for a moment. "Come. Mina was about to treat us to some Clementi."

"No treat, I fear," she said, accompanying him toward the house. "We must hope that Mina develops into the beauty she promises to be. I fear her musical talents will not carry her far."

"Unkind! Perhaps she just needs more practice."

"Oh, no. Ever since discovering that *you* liked young ladies who play the piano, we have been subjected to her agonized pounding day and night. Mr. Clementi would not thank you, I think."

"Well, Mina will have other charms."

"Yes, thank goodness. And she does try so very hard. You will be kind when she plays for us, won't you, Cousin Derek?"

He stopped and flashed angry eyes at her. "You always expect the worst from me, don't you Saskia?"

"Why, no! Of course I don't. I didn't mean . . ."

"Oh, never mind. I know," he said impatiently. "Come. Mina is waiting. And you needn't worry. I will be kind."

Chapter Eighteen

It was soon dinnertime and Jannie, who liked Derek very well indeed, set to with a will, her rheumatism entirely forgotten, to produce a real Dutch country dinner in his honor. That meant rich, hearty fare and plenty of it.

"Ah, Mrs. Jansen," he sighed as she carried in the thick, steaming *erwtensoep*, heady with split peas and rookworst. "What a welcome change from hotel fare. Even the renowned kitchens of the York House grow tedious. But this, this is *food!*"

Jannie beamed; everyone else laughed. The children set themselves to teach Derek the proper pronunciation of the wonderful things he was eating, and he discovered that wrapping his tongue around the broad *a*'s and soft gutturals was much more difficult than putting it to the delicious things the names represented.

There was dark, grainy *roggebrood*, spread thickly with sweet butter, and served with raw herring and *paling*, those delicately smoked eels from the Zuider Zee. Thick slices of rare and juicy *rosbief* were set off with hot potato salad, well-spiced and tart with vinegar. And the cheeses! Creamy white Edamer, red-rimmed *Goudse kaas* with cumin seeds, and soft *smeerkaas* spiced with garlic and herbs.

And just when Derek was patting his bulging stomach and complaining of the tight fit of his trousers, the desserts arrived. After playful protests, he allowed Jannie to spoon out a huge bowlful of creamy, coffee-scented *hopjesvla*, and he delighted in the frothy *Haagsebluf*, the berry-flavored meringue that disappeared in his mouth like a cloud on a summer's day.

The aura of good cheer set well on the whole family, but Saskia couldn't help noticing that Derek avoided her eyes as much as possible and she was hurt by it. When he did chance to catch her gaze, a tiny scowl would flit across his face and he would turn quickly away, to tease Mama or to flirt outrageously with Trix.

The whole family retreated to the drawing room directly after the meal, the gentlemen following close in the wake of the ladies. No one dawdled on Wednesdays, for Wednesday evening was always "Mama's Reading Circle."

"Reading Circle?" said Derek when informed by Trix of the treat in store.

"Oh, yes," replied Trix. "You see, Mama likes to try out her story ideas and characters and such before she is fully committed. So every Wednesday we get to read what she has written. She even promises to listen to our reactions and advice, though she doesn't promise to follow it."

"I look forward to it. You know, I have never before known a real-life authoress."

"It's too bad it isn't Saskia's turn to read. She is always terribly dramatic and has us all on the edges of our chairs. I'm afraid you will have to put up with me."

He grinned. "I think I can stand it."

Saskia, who was pouring out the coffee, overheard only the end of this little exchange as they approached her. The smile they shared was not lost on her either. It looked more and more as though her cousin was to become her brother-in-law, and she wondered why she felt so little joy at the prospect. He was precisely the sort of man she would wish for Trix (having apparently forgotten that but a short while ago she would not have wished him on anyone, even her worst enemy). He was now seen to be strong and kind and, yes, even gentle. If he won the contest, there would be no problems about money. And if she won it—hopeless wish!—she would be able to give Trix a large dowry. There seemed to be nothing standing in their way, provided one of them could come up with the answer. If neither did, then everyone lost out. Saskia caught herself sighing.

"Sit by me, Cousin Derek," cried Mina as she scrambled onto a settee. "Please?"

"If you promise not to drop macaroon crumbs and jam tart all over my coat," he answered with a smile and sat beside her. She gazed up at him rather worshipfully.

"Do you need another cushion, *Opa?*" said Trix.

"I do wish you would settle down, Willem," said Mama. "You are making me seasick with all your bobbing about."

"No, Rembrandt!" said Neil sternly. "You may not chew on my shoe! At least not while it is on my foot. Lie down!"

"Well, then," said Saskia as the bustle began to die away. "Is everyone settled?" Quiet descended on the room, but for the shuffling of the manuscript pages in Mama's hands.

The festivities officially began with Mama, as Miss Cornelia Crawley, reciting the words she recited every Wednesday evening. "Now you must all understand that this is only a first draft. There is still much work to do. I am counting on your comments and suggestions." She handed the pages to Trix. "As you will recall we left Magdalena a prisoner in Castle Almendoro, she having failed rather abysmally in her attempts to destroy it, poor thing. The Count is away, but she fears his return at any moment. Very well, Beatrix," she said with great dignity. "You may begin."

With a little cough and a deep breath, Trix began to read.

"The candle had burned very low now and sputtered and flickered in the draft from the huge fireplace, but still Magdalena's pen flew across the page of the diary. She must write it all down, every word, every horrid deed, so the world would know of the Count's infamy. And she must never let him know about this precious, this damning diary.

"The wind whistled in the chimney; a screech owl pierced the night sky with his cry, as he prepared to attack some small, warm animal. A shudder went through Magdalena at the sound, so like the vicious laugh of the Count, and she pulled her shawl closer about her."

As Trix's voice read on, sliding lightly over the words that told Magdalena's story, Saskia found her eyes wandering around the group. *Opa* in his wing chair was already beginning to nod. Rembrandt nodded at his feet. Neil listened analytically, forming editorial comments in his mind, while the twins leaned forward, rapt expressions on their little matched faces, both of them caught up in the "and then?" aspects of the story.

When Saskia's eyes lighted on Derek it was to surprise him gazing at her, with a glimmer of the same expression as was on the twins' faces. He seemed embarrassed to be caught at it, and they both looked quickly away, making a visible effort to concentrate on Beatrix's voice.

"As she scratched out the words, Magdalena's eyes lighted on the reassuring sight of the long, slender letter opener she had found in the desk. Its polished silver blade glinted in the flickering candlelight and the large ruby on its handle glowed like blood. When the Count finally returned, as return he would, she would have the means with which to protect herself. How stupid he had been to allow her the use of the library. It would be his undoing. One way or another Magdalena would see to it."

The story unfolded; the diary told its tale; but for all the excitement of Magdalena's travails, Derek was having trouble concentrating on the words. His mind kept wandering back to his cousin. And to the contest. Blast the silly thing! If it weren't for this crazy whim of Aunt Hester's he would throw caution to the wind and declare his love for his cousin. He would have nothing to lose and such a treasure to gain!

But there was the contest. And if he declared himself now his motives would be suspect. Simple logic, combined with the fact that she had never entirely trusted him, would lead her to assume that he was simply removing the opposition by enlisting it into his own camp. Not a bad idea, of course, if he didn't care so very much. How much more effective they could be if they were working together toward a goal that would satisfy them both.

But it was no good. She was certain to jealously guard this one and only chance to provide for the large family for which she felt so responsible. He had had glimpses of that steely determination that was so central to her character. She would never give in to defeat, or to him.

Her eyes caught his upon her once again. They both started and looked quickly back to Trix.

"A new sound crept into the library faint and far away but rapidly growing louder and more ominous. Magdalena's eyes flew up from the diary in which she wrote. Hoofbeats, approaching fast! It was the Count!

"She closed the diary with a hasty snap. She must hide it, hide it thoroughly and completely where he would never look for it. Her eyes chased wildly about the room, then she made a rapid decision and ran to one of the long rows of dark-bound, mildewed books.

She slid the slim volume of the diary onto a high shelf, between the others very like it in appearance.

"The hoofbeats stopped. Spurred boots crunched on gravel. Magdalena hastened back to the desk. Her hand hesitated momentarily, trembling, as she reached for the long deadly letter opener which would defend her honor. Then she grasped it firmly and carefully slid it into the long, tight sleeve of her gown.

"With her back to the wall, she turned to face the door. Outside the owl screeched once more. The candle sputtered and went out."

Trix stopped reading and looked up. "Well?" cried Willem in an agony of suspense. "What happens next?"

Cornelia Crawley turned to her youngest son. "I don't know, darling."

"But, Mama!" laughed Trix. "How could you stop at such a point and leave us all hanging? It isn't fair."

"It is quite simple, darling. Magdalena has not yet told me what happens next. I have given her a heart and a mind and a will of her own. And now I must let her tell her story. I am merely her amanuensis." Then she added with a twinkle, "And besides, one should always leave one's readers eager to hear more. Now tell me what you think."

The chorus of acclaim was general, "wonderful," "dramatic," and "descriptive" being the various reactions. Mina's response was an eloquent shudder, a very high accolade indeed.

The authoress turned to her eldest son. "Well, Cornelius?"

Very nice, Mama. But you might consider substituting 'vulnerable' for 'warm' in the 'small, warm animal' the screech owl is pursuing. Vulnerable as Magdalena is vulnerable."

Mama twinkled in approval. "Quite right. I am so glad you thought of that, darling. It is precisely the right touch."

"Mama?" said Trix. "Why does she hide the diary out in the open like that, right there in the library? Isn't she afraid the Count will easily find it?"

"Oh, no, darling. For you must know that the very best hiding spot for anything is in the most obvious place, preferably in plain sight. No one ever thinks of looking there, you see. What better place could there be for hiding a diary than in a library full of other books? It just disappears."

"Oh, yes. I see," said Trix.

Saskia saw too and felt immensely stupid that she had not thought of it before, specifically when she stood surrounded by shelves of books in the library at Rowbridge Manor. Suppose there was a diary hidden on those shelves. It might just provide the answer to what she had come to call The Mystery of Rowbridge Manor.

Her eyes flew to her cousin. He was still looking at her but rather differently now, as though trying to see into her mind. She could see at once that their minds, as they so often seemed to do, were marching in step along the very same path. He knew her thoughts; she could see it clearly. And he knew she could see it. In that instant they each decided that a careful search of Edward Rowbridge's library must be made, and as quickly as possible.

They felt that the moment that could decide their futures was very near, that the contest would soon be over.

The evening drew to an end. The words had all been read, the coffee had all been drunk, and Derek prepared to take his leave. Even the usually starchy Ware had grown solicitous. "I've brought up a muffler, sir," he said familiarly. "The wind's come up, and it's just started in to rain again."

"Thank you, Ware," said Derek, graciously accepting the heavy knit scarf.

Jannie bustled up from the kitchens to speed him on his way. She would never trust a hotel—and particularly not an *English* hotel—to know what a gentleman liked, so she had wrapped up a parcel of smoked ham, herring, and cold chicken with some of her sweet *koekjes* and saw them safely tucked into one of the enormous pockets of his cloak.

"*Wel te rusten, Mijnheer*," she gushed good-night. "*Slaap lekker.*"

He was waved off up the street until he disappeared into the drizzle. Saskia watched him go with her mind in a sad jumble, thoughts, worries, and speculations tumbling over each other with abandon. She was glad to escape to her room.

She was soon curled up in the big cozy chair that had become so particularly her own, staring into the fragrantly burning juniper logs as they snapped, hissed, popped, and the blue and yellow flames licked at the wood. Staring into dancing flames had always helped her to order her thoughts. Heaven knew they needed ordering now.

She sat a long time. The candle, as it had done for Magdalena, sputtered and went out, leaving her bathed in the golden glow of the fire. Thoughts chased each other through her mind like the flames chasing each other across the logs, but they couldn't seem to catch up with each other, linking up into a logical, discoverable pattern.

Only one thing emerged clearly. She felt certain that the secret of bringing to an end this contest that had become so odious to her would be found somewhere within the walls of Rowbridge Manor. She would find that secret.

She laughed softly at herself as the glowing pile of embers collapsed with a crack, sending a shower of sparks up the chimney. Really, this was impossible! It was very late, and she must get some sleep if she was to ride to the Manor in the morning. She would *not* let Mr. Derek Rowbridge or this blasted contest disturb her highly valued ability to sleep under any and all conditions.

She climbed into the big bed with firm resolution,

pulled the curtains close around her with a snap, and settled under the smooth comforter. She closed her eyes very determinedly only to lay awake for most of the remainder of the night.

Chapter Nineteen

The sun made another valiant attempt next morning to dry out the soggy town, and many Bathonians began to hope that the storm was indeed over. The alarming height of the river, which had caused swans to be seen swimming in the Abbey Churchyard, began to recede slightly. The shopkeepers along High Street set about assessing the damage to their wares. As the flooding of the Avon was, at the very least, an annual occurrence, they had not been taken completely unaware. They had cleverly moved most of their goods onto the highest shelves so that what resulted was more in the nature of a nuisance than a catastrophe. Not that that made the cleaning up any the less dirty or the grumbling any the less forceful, but things began returning to normal.

All this is not to say that the sky now presented an expanse of azure unmarred by so much as a cloud. In fact, the morning was still heavily overcast, the air sultry with a threatening stillness about it. Everyone crossed his fingers and hoped for the best.

Saskia, despite her nearly sleepless night, was up and about early dressed in an olive-green riding habit and with an air of anticipation in the way she attacked her

189

breakfast. As she laid thin slices of ham and roast beef and thick slices of creamy cheese onto butter-spread bread and gulped her coffee, Mrs. Jansen appeared with the final requirement for a complete Dutch breakfast, a perfect three-minute egg. At sight of Saskia's attire she checked herself in the doorway, a scowl replacing her robust smile.

"*Meisje Je gaat niet uit!*" she cried.

"Of course I am going out," replied Saskia. "Why should I not?"

"*De regen!*"

"But it isn't raining now that I can see," said Saskia between bites. "And I for one do not think that it will. Besides, I have business at the Manor that will not wait, rain or no rain. You can see for yourself that the heavy storm has passed. If it does rain a little I shall get a bit wet, that's all. It shan't hurt me. My skin is waterproof, you know."

Mrs. Jansen, who had a morbid fear of any sort of chill or fever—Mr. Jansen having been carried off by one twenty years before—propped herself mulishly before the door as Saskia rose from her chair, brushing crumbs from her skirt.

"*Je moet niet!*" she stated, her full arms crossed over her fuller bosom.

"Mrs. Jansen!" said Saskia in exasperation. "*Ik ga!* I am going! Right now." Mrs. Jansen had heard that tone before. Reluctantly she moved aside to let Saskia pass from the room.

"Good morning, Ware," she said to the butler as she drew on her gloves in the front hall.

"You are going riding, miss?" he asked, the slightest edge of concern in his carefully schooled voice. "The sky is still looking rather unsettled miss, if I might venture to say so."

"Not you too! Really, I am beginning to feel myself back in the nursery with a whole gaggle of nannies about me."

"I am persuaded, miss, that Mr. Rowbridge would advise you to stay in."

"Mr. Rowbridge. What, pray, has Mr. Rowbridge to say to the matter? I am hardly my cousin's ward, you know. My actions do not concern him in the least."

His frown of concern was immediately replaced by his more usual and fully professional blank visage. "Of course, miss. As you say, miss," he intoned in an icy voice.

She gave her jaunty hat, prettily adorned with a dove-grey veil and a curled ostrich plume, a final adjustment. "Good day, Ware. I shall be back in time for tea." And without waiting for a reply, which in any case Ware was too well trained to offer, she sailed from the room in a passable imitation of her Aunt Hester.

Sunshine was waiting for her, fidgeting a bit in her eagerness. "Yes, my poor darling," said Saskia in a soothing voice. "I know. You have been having a hard time of it, haven't you, all cooped up for days and days. So have I, but we shall have a good run to shake the fidgets out of us both."

The young groom threw her up into the saddle, then moved to mount his own chestnut. Saskia stopped him. "I shan't need you today, Jack."

"But Mr. Rowbridge, he said as how I weren't to let you go riding off alone anymore, miss."

She bristled up in her saddle, her spine very straight. "Oh, did he?" she asked in an icily calm voice, her eyes sparkling dangerously. He would do anything to hold her back, even to setting her own servants to spying on her! "Tell me something, Jack. Whom do you consider your employer to be? Mr. Rowbridge or my mother?"

"Well, properly speaking, miss, it be your mother, in course, but . . ."

"Thank you, Jack. In future you will take your orders from my mother or from me. Mr. Rowbridge has *nothing* to say to the matter. And I will not be followed! Good day." She spurred Sunshine into a trot and headed down Great Pulteney Street toward Sydney Gardens and the open country beyond.

The clattering of her horse's hooves on the stones served to amplify her anger as she rode through the town. That odious man, giving orders to *her* servants, trying to run *her* life. Nosy! Back-handed! Insufferable! She would take such treatment from no one! And he had called her managing!

The irony of the whole thing was that during her long hours of wakefulness Saskia had come to a decision. She no longer had any desire to compete with her cousin for Aunt Hester's fortune. She decided to propose a collaboration. Obviously they could be far more effective if they would only pool their resources, work together toward a solution, and share the reward. It was obvious that Aunt Hester had enough money for all. Saskia had actually looked forward to the opportunity of working in tandem with her cousin instead of as his adversary. She had intended to offer up as a sort of peace offering anything she might discover at the Manor today.

Now she chided herself for her foolishness. She had not thought him so unscrupulous. Bribing her servants! Obviously he would stop at nothing to beat her. Well, she would tell him nothing, no hint, of anything she might find. She would use it any way she could. *She* would win this contest, and Derek Rowbridge could go to the devil with her very good wishes!

The open country when she reached it presented a slightly bedraggled appearance. The battering it had taken these past few days was evident in broken branches and seas of mud. But the rock outcroppings glistened in their cleanness, and the grassy hills glowed an emerald green.

As Saskia spurred Sunshine first into a canter and then into a long, rolling gallop some of her first flush of annoyance dissipated in the excitement and freedom of the ride. A little more of its heat was cooled by the first raindrops. They were not many, but they were large and each fell with a noisy plop. The wind started up, cutting easily through Saskia's light jacket, and she slowed enough to reach up and jam her hat further onto her head.

She had often ridden in the rain and never minded a little wetting, so she gave no thought to turning back toward Bath. But when she was slightly more than half-way to the Manor, the rain began to fall harder and colder. The wool of her habit could no longer shed it effectively, and it seeped through the fabric to chill her skin. She was beginning to feel distinctly uncomfortable and did not relish the notion of hearing the "I told you so's" of Mrs. Jansen.

"*Kom nou, Zoonschijn. Weg!*" She urged the mare into a longer stride, and they fairly flew over the hills. The young horse seemed to understand her Dutch perfectly and was as anxious as she to reach shelter.

The full fury of the storm broke over her head with a blinding flash of lightning and a boom of thunder that sounded like the end of the world. The ground trembled with it.

Sunshine took violent exception to this nonsense—she had after all, been born in hot, *dry* desert climes—and she reared up, screaming at the way the earth was crashing all about her. Her front hooves pawed at the thick, watery air, but miraculously Saskia kept her seat. Down came the hooves and off went Sunshine in a positive fury, pounding the earth and throwing up mud all around in her panic to escape the storm.

Saskia held on with all her strength, the reins slicing into the leather of her gloves, and she managed to slow the horse's stride somewhat. When she thought it safe to do so, she let go one hand and reached down to stroke the mare's neck in an attempt to soothe her terror.

Just at that moment, however, they reached a swollen stream. Sunshine flew over it with never a check, and Saskia flew into the sir. Sunshine disappeared.

Everything seemed to slow down then. It seemed several minutes at least that she floated through the air, and the odd thought went through her mind that this

must be what it felt like to be a bird, soaring over the
fields. Then the ground seemed to rush up to meet her.
She landed with a splash of mud and a painful thud that
shuddered through her body. She was lying in a field,
the rain falling on her upturned face.

It is odd the thoughts that pass through one's mind in
such moments of crisis. It seemed to Saskia as though
her brain had split, one half of it in a panic, praying fervently, "Please God, don't let me have broken my neck,"
the other half noting prosaically, "I shall never get the
mud out of this habit."

She lay very still, afraid to try moving for fear she
would discover that she couldn't. She first became aware
of a vicious number of pains from all parts of her body.
Then, tentatively at first, she wiggled her fingers, then
her toes. Thank God they moved. She raised a hand to
wipe the rain from her eyes and slid her gaze to a large
oak not far from where she lay. If she could reach it, it
would offer some modicum of shelter until the storm
passed and she was feeling more the thing.

She didn't feel up to attempting walking just yet, so
she raised herself onto her elbows and began dragging
her battered body backward, slowly and painfully,
toward the tree.

It might have been five minutes before she reached it;
it might have been an hour. She couldn't say. But she
got there at last. Though far from dry beneath its
sparsely leaved boughs, the rain attacked her less
viciously, the lightning seemed less threatening, beneath
the canopy of the oak. She pulled herself upright and
sagged against the solid mass of the tree, sitting in the
mud.

"Thank you, tree," she muttered just before she passed
out.

Derek Rowbridge had had little more sleep than his
cousin on the previous night. When he did manage to
drift off it was to an agonized image of Saskia van

Houten and Captain Edward Durrant, arm in arm and with loving smiles on their faces, standing at the rail of a full-rigged schooner, waving good-bye as they sailed away in a glow of happiness.

Or there was the equally distressing vision of Saskia, in tatters and with all her brothers and sister in tow, appearing before a triumphant Derek, begging a shilling to keep the children from starving. All in all it was not a very restful night.

He awoke confused and irritable and very unlike himself. Pike was thoroughly grumbled at; the waiter who had the bad fortune to bring his breakfast was snapped at. His toast seemed to turn to cotton wool in his mouth.

Then over his second cup of coffee he decided on a course of action that brightened his outlook. This absurd rivalry must stop. He couldn't afford to lose the contest and he couldn't stand to win it. And he felt sure that Saskia hated the whole thing as much as he did.

He would speak to her this very morning. Together they could go to see Aunt Hester, explain their willingness to help her get Rowbridge Manor but say that they would no longer be pitted against each other in this absurd fashion.

Lady Eccles might be an eccentric, but she was not an unreasonable woman. And Derek had lately felt that she had grown genuinely fond of her young relations. Surely they could come to an arrangement that would suit everyone.

And perhaps, just perhaps, as the cousins worked together, Saskia would in time . . . He daren't complete the thought.

Pike was mightily surprised to see his master rise from the table with a smile in place of the black frown with which he had seated himself. The valet was treated to a cheerful good-bye, then watched out the window as his master stepped jauntily out into the light drizzle that had just begun.

Derek's cheerful air lasted only as long as it took him

to get to Laura Place, there to be informed by an apologetic butler and an abashed groom that his cousin had set out less than an hour before, quite alone, for Rowbridge Manor.

"And you let her go?" he berated the poor groom.

"Couldn't stop her, sir. Said as how I didn't work for the likes o' you, and I weren't to take no orders from you. Then she jest took off."

"I should have expected as much," muttered Derek, slapping his gloves against his thigh. "That girl would do anything she thought I wanted her not to do." The rain was falling steadily now, and black clouds hung low in the sky. "Damn!" he exclaimed. "Headstrong, mulish . . . I shall have to go after her."

"Beggin' yer pardon, sir," said the groom, "but I knows this sky. 'Bout to break wide open any minute now in a real nasty one."

"I know! I can't leave her out there all alone in it. Anything could happen to her." Buttoning his heavy cloak up to his chin and jamming his hat low on his head, he mounted the roan and headed into the rain.

Saskia opened her eyes with a convulsive shiver. She was drenched through, felt frozen to the marrow, and her chattering teeth seemed to have taken on a will all their own, quite oblivious to her attempts to still them. She had no idea how long she had lain here, but she knew she must get up. The rain had slowed somewhat to a steady drizzle, but it could go on all day. She was sure to freeze or drown or something equally uncomfortable.

She pulled herself painfully to her feet, calling on the support of the tree to help her. By leaning rather heavily on the oak, she managed to stand, waiting for the wave of dizziness that engulfed her to abate. When it had subsided a little, she took a tentative step, letting go the tree, and promptly sat in the mud again.

She didn't seem to be able to stand. What a scene this will make for one of Mama's stories, she told herself, in an attempt to joke away her rising panic. She wondered vaguely if one's teeth could be permanently damaged by so much chattering from the cold. With an effort that shot a pain through her whole body, she managed to regain the tenuous shelter of the oak which was beginning to feel like her only friend.

Another giant wave of dizziness poured over her, and she feared she would pass out again. She daren't do so. She must have something to focus her mind on, to force it into alertness, into full consciousness. She looked about her. There were a number of small pebbles around the tree. These she gathered into a little pile. Then she began painstakingly laying them in neat arrangements, concentrating all her remaining energy on getting them just so. Do not think of fainting, she told herself. Just concentrate on the arrangement.

First she lined the pebbles up into a long straight line. She added a graceful curve and saw that she had formed the letter "D". The next arrangement began to look very like an "E".

It was thus, propped casually against a tree, spelling out nonsense in the mud and looking as though she hadn't a care in the world, that Derek found her.

He had grown more and more worried with each mile, for it was shortly after he left the town that the lightning struck. But it wasn't till he spotted the frothing Sunshine, wild-eyed and riderless, racing back toward Bath, that real panic set in. He thought at first to chase the mare, but it was clear that he must find Saskia, and quickly.

Horrid visions of her broken body lying in a ditch filled his mind. His pace was slow for he had no wish to miss sight of her, but impatience at the snail's pace increased his anxiety.

He saw her before she was aware of his approach. The sound of Pasha's hooves was lost in the steady plop-plop of the rain, and she was so intently concentrated on her pebbles that by the time she saw him he had already dismounted and was striding toward her.

She quickly swept away the silly things she had been spelling out in the mud and looked up. A smile that mingled surprise, overwhelming relief, and something else she was not yet ready to name wreathed her face.

But her smile was not returned. In fact, Derek Rowbridge had never been so angry in his life. He had pictured her dead, or at the very least in deadly peril. At sight of her sitting there so calmly playing a child's game as though she were at a picnic, his overwhelming anxiety for her safety turned to overwhelming wrath at her thoughtlessness.

"Of all the pigheaded, stubborn, perverse females, you take the prize! You'll do anything, go to any lengths, to beat me in this stupid contest, won't you, Saskia?"

At his furious tone, she straightened up against the tree, all desire to faint now forgotten. "*I'll* do anything? But . . ."

"Yes, anything. You'll commit any folly! Riding out here in such weather, quite alone and on an inexperienced horse, for no better reason than to search for some phantom clue which may not even exist."

Her eyes sparkled, her anger rising at such Turkish treatment and acting like a tonic on her battered body and mind. "Oh, I see! And you, of course, just *happened* to be out riding for the sheer pleasure of getting wet. And of course it was the merest coincidence that you happened to turn toward Rowbridge Manor! How very convenient!"

"I came out here looking for you," he said in a voice of barely concealed rage.

"Doing it far too brown, Cousin. I really believe even you can come up with a better story than that. Why should you do any such thing? You don't give a fig what happens to me."

"I wish to God that were true!" he muttered as he removed his cloak. "Here, you're freezing." He wrapped it about her shoulders, giving her no chance to refuse. She was all but lost in its huge folds. "Come on," he said gruffly, reaching out a hand to pull her to her feet.

She didn't take the hand, however. "I'm quite comfortable where I am, thank you," she said stiffly and inexplicably, for it was obvious she was no such thing.

"Of all the obstinate . . . ! You'll do as you're told, my girl. Now get up and *get on that horse!*"

She stopped bristling—which was in any case rather difficult while she was shivering so much—and lowered her defiant gaze. "I can't," she said to the ground.

"Now what the devil . . . ?" Realization hit him, his scowl was instantly replaced by a look of grave guilt and deep concern. He kneeled in the mud beside her. "You're hurt!"

"Oh, no," she said. "It is only that I don't seem to be able to walk. I did try, but my legs wouldn't hold me up. I'm sure if I just sit here a bit longer . . ." Before she could finish she was scooped up in two strong but amazingly gentle arms. Her cheek was resting on a pleasantly scratchy coat, and she could feel his heart beating through it. Her own was pounding out a sort of tattoo against her ribs, and she wondered idly if she could have done it an injury in her fall to cause it to behave so strangely.

In a moment she was tenderly set on Pasha's broad back and Derek climbed up behind her, making a safe cradle for her with his arms. The anger that had kept her going seeped out of her, and she sagged against the warm safety of him with a sigh of relief.

He was uttering soothing sounds, and she thought she heard "poor darling", and "my poor little love" among them. She must be growing delirious.

They were no more than a pair of miles from Rowbridge Manor. Derek's frantic pounding at the back door was answered by a flustered Mrs. Gleason.

"Lawks, sir!" she cried at him and his wet burden, now dripping mud all over her spotless kitchen. "Why, it's Miss Crawley"s daughter! Oh, sir! She's . . . she's not dead, is she?"

Mrs. Gleason's alarm was understandable, for Saskia, ashen-faced, had finally given in and fainted once more.

Chapter Twenty

Saskia came around to discover herself under a quilted coverlet on a comfortable settee in the Gleasons' cozy sitting room. She was smiling as her eyes fluttered open to encounter the deep hazel gaze of her cousin. It was heavy with concern, and she realized that he was holding her hand, stroking it unconsciously. His touch was very gentle.

"Derek," she whispered. She tried to sit up but became conscious of a most violent headache.

"No, no," said Derek softly. "You mustn't even try. I'm going for the doctor now."

"Oh no," she exclaimed. "You needn't. I'm fine. Really I am. If I could just lie here a minute . . ."

"I am going for the doctor!" he said less softly and less gently. "And you, my girl, are in no condition to argue the matter, thank God."

He was right of course. She could barely speak much less read him the scold he deserved. She attempted a look of defiance, but the fire of their usual encounters was lacking.

He smiled back. "That's better. Now be a good girl for Mrs. Gleason. I shan't be gone long." He reached out a cool hand to smooth back her hair, and then he was gone.

"There's nought to worry 'bout now, miss," bubbled Mrs. Gleason. "Your young man'll be back with the doctor quick as ever you please."

"My young man," sighed Saskia as she fell asleep. She was smiling again.

When she awoke again a middle-aged gentleman in doctor's black was asking her where she hurt. He peered out from behind thick spectacles and his side whiskers bounced when he smiled.

Mrs. Gleason was readying a basin of herb-scented steaming water and a pile of clean towels and bandages. Across the room stood Beatrix, who Derek had thoughtfully brought back with him. There was a worried frown on her face and a tear in her eyes. Derek stood holding Trix's hand, patting it reassuringly.

"Everywhere," said Saskia softly. "I hurt everywhere." For in that moment, with all her natural defenses knocked awry, Saskia had had to recognize the thing that she had been pushing from her consciousness for days. She was hopelessly in love with Derek Rowbridge. She had been in love with him for a long time. She groaned and turned her head away.

"Yes, yes," chuckled the doctor. "I expect you do. That was a nasty fall. You've a bump there the size of an egg, and you're all over bruises, I'm sure. We shall do what we can to make you more comfortable, shall we?" He turned to Derek. "We must get her up to a proper bedroom. Will you assist us, sir?"

Derek was beside her in an instant. For the second time that day, Saskia was lifted in his strong arms. It was a lucky thing that his coat was still damp from the rain. He wouldn't notice the wetness of the tears she was unable to hold back.

"I went an' aired out Milady's room," said Mrs. Gleason, "an' there's fresh linens on the bed."

They entered the pretty bedchamber that had been

Saskia's grandmother's. Derek laid her gently on the bed.

"Thank you, sir," said the doctor. "You may go away now and trust the young lady to us. We will see to her."

Derek had no intention of leaving his poor broken Saskia. "Go away! But . . ."

"Sir!" admonished the doctor, peering sternly over his spectacles. "We must get her out of these clothes and into bed."

"Well, what's stopping you? I . . ." He was suddenly struck by the doctor's meaning and, to everyone's surprise and his own embarrassment, he blushed. "Yes, yes, to be sure," he muttered. "The lady's sister will help you." He turned to Beatrix. "I'll be just outside. You'll call me if . . . ?"

"Of course," she reassured him and Saskia saw her squeeze his hand. Oh, how her head ached!

The doctor set about bathing bruises and bandaging cuts and gingerly feeling the growing lump on the back of her head.

"Well, well," he said at last. "No broken bones, it seems. The cuts and bruises will heal themselves in a few days. It is to be hoped you won't come down with a fever from your wetting."

"Fair drenched through, she was, Doctor," said Mrs. Gleason, "and blue with the cold."

"So I heard," scolded the doctor. "Riding out in such weather! That was not prudent of you, my dear." He waggled a finger at her as though she were a child. "I'll send over a saline draught just in case, but I think you'll do. And now you are to rest, young lady. No doubt you'll be up and about in a few days, which is better than you deserve. In the meantime, I don't want you out of this bed. Understood?"

"Yes, Doctor," she mumbled. At the moment she had not the slightest desire to get up.

Mrs. Gleason's fears to the contrary, the promised fever did not develop. Saskia's body began to mend itself;

her heart did not. She was disastrously in love, and it was depressingly clear to her that Derek was just as deeply in love with her sister.

Oh, he had been amazingly attentive to Saskia, reading to her in his rich, deep voice or playing backgammon or just sitting and chatting. But she had no illusions as to why he was there. With Trix smiling so bewitchingly across the bed, he always had a reason to be there. It was surely not Saskia who drew him so often to the pretty yellow bedchamber.

She supposed she ought to be grateful. She had wanted a good, kind, wealthy husband for Trix. Now she had got him. Derek would be very wealthy, for he was certain to win the contest now. He might well have done so already, with so much time and freedom to wander about the house at will, searching out hidden diaries in libraries and other assorted clues of whatever variety. When he married Trix the family would be secure. He obviously liked them, except for Saskia, and would see them well provided for.

Saskia saw herself dwindling into an aunt, running the lives of her nieces and nephews as efficiently as she did those of her brothers and sisters. Derek was right. She was managing.

Even the masses of flowers from her many friends and admirers could not lift her spirits. They might as well have been funeral wreaths for all the joy they brought. She had often laughed when one of Mama's heroines suffered from a "hopeless passion" or went into a decline for lost love. She would not laugh in future. This was surely the most horridly uncomfortable feeling in the world, this business of being in love with someone who didn't love you.

She tried to go back to sleep to shut out the hurt. She accomplished the goal of slumber, but her dreams were all of Derek Rowbridge.

On the third day after her fall, Saskia was allowed to sit up and have a visit from her family. Jannie came in first wearing a look of stern disapproval. She had not at all liked being kept from her *lieveling*. She was finally convinced that she was needed in Laura Place, but she would never believe that Mrs. Gleason, a mere Englishwoman, could care for her darling. She marched about the room, adding a coverlet and a shawl to Saskia's already heavily draped form, and sniffing at every medicine bottle with a look of deep suspicion.

"Hah!" she exclaimed in triumph.

"What is it, Jannie?"

"*Hertshoorn! Ik heb hertshoorn nodig.*" And she hurried away to confront Mrs. Gleason about the missing hartshorn.

The twins entered on tiptoe, looking so grave and whispering so softly that Saskia had to laugh. She reassured them that she didn't intend to die anytime soon and asked them, without much real hope, if they were being good for Mama.

"They are perfect angels, my love," said Mama. "All my children are angels. But I am glad, darling, that you decided not to return to heaven just yet. We should miss you, you know."

"And I should miss you, Mama," answered her laughing daughter. "You and all your nonsense."

"Nonsense? But, darling! You know I have ever had the most serious nature. I quite rue it sometimes. And *why* did you never tell me about this wonderful house? Did you know that Queen Elizabeth actually slept here? Zounds! Methinks I feel a Tudor novel in me struggling to get out."

"Oh, dear," laughed Saskia. "We shall have you in a farthingale soon."

Her mother seemed to give the matter serious consideration. "I doubt I could find a proper one nowadays. But perhaps a red wig . . ." She hurried to the writing desk in the corner and began making rapid notes.

Saskia gave her sister a wry grin. "Mrs. Gleason must be in alt. She has finally met the famous Cornelia Crawley."

"She was speechless for nearly a full minute," said Trix, "which is quite an accomplishment for our Mrs. Gleason. But she finally came around."

"And what did she have to say?"

Mina, in a perfect imitation of the lovable little housekeeper, rolled her big blue eyes toward heaven, clapped her hands, and breathed. "Why lawks! Mercy me! My, my, my. Cornelia Crawley herself in our house. Well! I jest hardly know what to say."

"And won't that Mary Manners be green!" added Trix as they went off into a fit of giggles.

When she sobered sufficiently, Saskia turned to Neil. "And how does our budding mathematical genius go on?"

"Well," he demurred. "I thought perhaps I needed a break from my studies. Cousin Derek has offered to teach me to drive his curricle."

"Well, that's doing it in style, I must say."

"I should think so! A bang-up team, he's got. Sixteen-mile-an-hour goers. After I learn I might ask if I can drive round to call on Melly . . . uh, Miss Durrant."

Saskia twinkled in delight. Derek was turning Neil into a regular rounded gentleman. "Well, do give Melly . . . uh, *Miss Durrant* my best," she teased. Neil had the sensitivity to blush.

Looking around at them all, Saskia told herself again what a wonderful family they were. She would plunge herself into their cares and find her contentment in them. They were all she had now.

In a few more days Saskia was allowed downstairs to sit in the library or, if the weather were fine, to stroll gently in the garden or recline in the shade of a tree. One bright morning found her outdoors. Beatrix, in a villager hat and blue ribbons and looking pretty as Grandmama's portrait, was beside her.

"That hat becomes you, Trix," said Saskia.

"Do you think so? I thought it might be too large, but

Cousin Derek likes it. You know what good taste he has."

Yes," she sighed. "I know."

"I wonder if he will call today."

"It is very good of him to come so often,"

"Well, he *is* very good, of course," mused Trix, her eyes dancing. "But in this case goodness has little to do with it, I think. Something much stronger than mere goodness draws him to the Manor every day."

Saskia understood well enough Derek's reason for coming to see them so often, and if she hadn't she could easily read it in Trix's glowing face. She sighed.

The subject of this conversation interrupted it in person. Hearing the clip-clop of Pasha's hooves on the drive, two pairs of eyes, one pansy-brown, the other a remarkable blue, followed Derek's figure as he spurred the horse into a trot toward them. Beatrix cast a sidelong look at her sister to see abject despair. She was beginning to be just the tiniest bit worried about these two. Would they ever get around to admitting how much they loved each other?

"Good morning!" hailed Derek. Mr. Gleason ambled out of the stable to tug a forelock in greeting and take charge of Pasha. Derek dismounted lithely, said something to make the old man break into a toothy smile, then strode gracefully toward the sisters.

How handsome he is, thought Saskia. And how kind. How could I have ever thought him otherwise?

He looked at her with concern. "You look tired, Saskia. Perhaps you should have stayed upstairs."

"Not at all, Derek," she answered lightly. She tried to recall just when they had dropped the formal title of "Cousin". Their first naming each other seemed so natural. "I feel ever so much better. I am only a little homesick, I expect. I am not used to so much quiet."

"Well you shan't feel homesick today. They are all coming out to see you. And I do mean all!"

"*Opa* too?" asked Beatrix.

"*Opa* too," he affirmed.

"Oh, famous! The poor darling is probably wasting away without me to bully him into eating his dinner. I'll go see if Mrs. Gleason has any strawberries. He'll like that." Having thus dexterously managed to throw them together alone, she flitted off.

Derek watched her go with a smile. "What a constant delight she is, Saskia."

"Yes. My life will be far duller without her."

"Without her? But she isn't going away, surely?"

"Well, marriage does have a way of splitting up a family."

"Marriage? But . . ." His smile vanished. He knew that Beatrix had no thought of marrying anytime soon. She was enjoying her success as a Reigning Beauty too much to give up her crown yet awhile. So Saskia could only mean . . . "I saw Captain Durrant this morning," he said sadly. "He asked after you and sent good wishes for your recovery."

"How kind he is," she replied, thankful for this seeming change of subject. "He has sent ever so many flowers and books and such to keep me from dying of boredom."

"I know," he replied. How her face brightened at mention of Durrant, he was thinking. What I wouldn't give to see that sparkle in her eyes for me.

This unpromising conversation was brought to an end by the rumble of coaches. Aunt Hester's lozenge coach emerged from a cloud of dust followed by Mama's barouche. Seated proudly on the box, one each side of the coachman, were Willem and Mina.

The cavalcade pulled to a stop, and Willem jumped down with a whoop.

"Well, Mina," said Derek, assisting her from her perch. "You're looking smart as a parrot new-scraped." She giggled and curtsied. She had indeed taken pains with her appearance. Every tangle had been brushed out of her cornsilk hair, and her sprig muslin showed not a single grass stain.

Trix fluttered out of the house as the rest of the horde descended from the carriages. Mrs. Jansen, carrying an enormous hamper, accosted Mrs. Gleason over the question of luncheon. Aunt Hester surveyed the house dreamily, recalling her childhood here, and Mr. Weddington stood leaning on his cane until Beatrix took his arm and led him inside.

Apparently Mama had not given over The Tudor Idea inspired by the house. Her search for a farthingale had luckily been unsuccessful, but she had come up with a wide neckruff which kept her from lowering her chin and a bright red wig dressed in a tolerable imitation of the heart-shaped style of Queen Bess.

"Forsooth!" quoth Mama. "It doth appear unto mine eyes thou art not well, daughter." Saskia's eyes twinkled with suppressed merriment. "Have I got it right, do you think?"

"I am quite well, Mama, and you have it precisely right, I think," Saskia replied, brimming with amusement.

"Well, it is difficult, you know. Such a lot of 'doths' and 'quoths'. But now I am here, I daresay it will come easily enough. I shall go and dance a gavotte in the Great Hall." And Mama gavotted off. Derek and Saskia caught each other's eyes and broke into giggles.

"Yes, yes, children," said their Aunt Hester. "But I should like to go into the house now. Give me your arm, Rowbridge."

Soon they were all gathered in the library, the one room that had been made really comfortable, for a cup of tea.

It was Mr. Weddington's first view in over forty years of the Gainsborough portrait of his daughter. He gazed at it a long time, but oddly enough, he was moved a good deal less than he might have been. With Beatrix at hand, it was as though he had never lost Susannah. Trix sat him down in the comfortable wing chair and turned him to face the fire—his old bones felt the cold even on such a bright day—and plied him with strawberries and cakes.

Aunt Hester sat near them recounting one of her more

outrageous adventures. Something about a camel, a
fakir, and a traveling tent maker ...

The twins were behaving remarkably well, quietly
bent over a chess board, while Neil offered quiet advice
and instructions. Mama sat at the big desk, her spectacles at an angle over her nose, scribbling madly on any
slip of paper she could find.

And side by side on the sofa sat Derek and Saskia—
neither was quite sure how they came to be there together—chatting companionably. For a moment Saskia
almost forgot her unhappiness in the pleasure of his
company. They were now able to go anywhere in the
house without looking into every corner and cupboard
for some clue. Saskia assumed that Derek had already
found the answer. He, in his concern for her health, had
all but forgotten the matter. It would wait until she was
better.

All in all, it was a mellow scene, heartwarming in its
domesticity. Mrs. Gleason brought in a fresh pot of tea
and flitted about seeing that everyone was comfortable.
Everyone was.

Then quite suddenly the peaceful scene was rudely
shattered. The door was thrown open, and a bristling
Mr. Dawes surveyed the scene. "Mrs. Gleason!" thundered Mr. Banks's Bath agent.

The housekeeper yelped her surprise and dropped a
teacup with a crash. "Lawks a-mercy, Mr. Dawes! You
do give a body a start."

"Mrs. Gleason!" he repeated. "What is the meaning of
this invasion?" He was trying to look forbidding, but
when one is very thin, and very old, and only five feet
tall it is difficult. He went on. "I had heard *rumors* of
this, but I could not credit them. I had to see for myself.
Mrs. Gleason, *who* are all these people?"

"Well now, let's see," she answered, looking around.
"There's Miss Crawley, in course, and all her young
ones. Here's Mr. Rowbridge and ..."

"Rowbridge!" Mr. Dawes shot his pale grey eyes to
the sofa. He recognized its two occupants at once. "You

two! I might have known you were behind this. Well, we shall see what Mr. Banks has to say when he knows of this. Nice goings on, I *don't* think!"

"Shut up, Dawes," came a voice from the wing chair, the back of which was facing the door.

"What the . . . who . . . where . . . ," Mr. Dawes blustered.

Samuel Weddington peered slowly around the back of the chair, a look of unholy amusement in his eyes. "Mr. Banks knows well enough what is going on in his house, and he likes it very well indeed."

"Mr. Banks!" cried Dawes. "Sir! I didn't . . . I couldn't . . . why . . ." He trailed off in confusion.

A sea of heads turned toward Mr. Weddington, all save Mama who was scribbling away and had not, in fact, even noticed the agent's entrance.

Derek found his tongue first. "Banks? *You're Banks?*"

"Great-grandpapa!" said Saskia. "Is this true?" The old man only raised a bushy brow and gave her an elfin smile. The cousins turned to their great-aunt to be surprised by the expression on her face. She was looking . . . *guilty!* "Aunt Hester!" said Saskia as realization dawned. "You knew! You have known all along."

"Well, of all the shabby tricks . . . ," began Derek.

Aunt Hester thought some attempt at defense was in order. "You needn't get the wind up so. I didn't know it when I sent for you, I promise you."

"But you have known for some time, have you not?" Derek scowled.

"Yes," she replied calmly. "For some time."

"But Aunt Hester," said Saskia. "Why?"

"I think I know," put in Beatrix, looking from her aunt to her *Opa.* They were exchanging rather sheepish looks. "It was because you knew that Saskia and Derek were in love with each other, wasn't it?"

"Well, I didn't know that just at first, of course," said Aunt Hester. "I merely thought to divert myself with watching their antics, and I convinced Weddington to go along with me. But we have both long since seen which way the land lay. Why, it's been plain as a pikestaff for ages. It is amazing they haven't seen it themselves. Is that what they mean, do you suppose, when they say love is blind?"

"Never knew a Rowbridge so slow with his wooing," grumbled Mr. Weddington.

The two principal subjects of this discussion sat frozen. Saskia stared open-mouthed at her sister who was returning an encouraging smile. Derek's eye fixed on his great-aunt who shot back a look of challenge. "Don't you think," she said archly, "that it is high time you and Saskia went for a stroll in the garden, Rowbridge?"

The two of them slowly, almost reluctantly, turned to face each other, a look of speculation in their faces. "And," she added, "you needn't worry about that silly contest. You have both won."

A smile touched Derek's eyes, and Saskia felt something in her go limp. She felt him take her hand, felt him pull her gently to her feet, felt him lead her to the door, past the still speechless Mr. Dawes, and out into the garden.

"You know," said Mr. Weddington as the door closed behind them. "Never thought to say it of a Rowbridge, but I like that young man. If his grandfather'd been more like him, I'd have given him my Susannah without argument."

"Would you, *Opa?*" asked Trix. "Even with that marquis waiting in the wings?"

He thought a moment. "Well maybe I wouldn't," he admitted. "I've learned a thing or two since then, I hope."

"Of course you have. Isn't that the wonderful thing about growing old? I can hardly wait. Only think what a lot of things I shall know."

He beamed up at her, this child of brightness, then let his eyes wander to the painting she mirrored. He spoke softly now, to Susannah Rowbridge. "You know, he turned out to be a rum one, that marquis. Worse than Edward Rowbridge ever was."

Saskia and Derek made their way to a stone bench in the overgrown rose garden. They sat some little while in silence, birds twittering nearby. Finally Derek spoke.

"Saskia," he began tentatively. "Is . . . is there even the smallest shred of truth in what they've been saying in there?"

She stared at the ground and spoke so softly he could barely hear her. "I am so sorry to put you through such a scene, Derek. I know your feeling for Beatrix, and how much it must hurt. I honestly thought she returned your regard, I never suspected . . ."

"Beatrix? Why, what nonsense are you talking? My only feeling for Beatrix is that she is a pretty and charming creature who would make a delightful sister-in-law."

"Sister-in-law?" she said weakly.

"Yes, sister-in-law. I have had the effrontery to fall in love with you, you see, even knowing my cause to be hopeless."

She was still studying the ground, and he couldn't see the slow and totally transforming smile that crept up her face. "But it isn't hopeless," she whispered.

"Saskia." He took her hand once more and lifted her chin to study her face. "Can you mean . . . ?" He had no need to finish the question; the answer was writ large in her eyes.

Suddenly Saskia was taught that those strong arms, the ones that had gently carried her in from the storm, were not always so gentle. They were ruthlessly crushing her now as Derek's lips found hers. She felt not the slightest desire for the crushing to stop.

When the situation made breathing critical, they pulled apart, gazing into each other's eyes, quite lost in the wonder of it all. "Can it really be," said Derek at last, "that you are not in love with Ned Durrant?"

"Captain Durrant?" she exclaimed, snapping back to reality. "Good heavens, no! He is all that is kind, of course, but what could make you think I would fall in love with a sea captain who'd spend six months out of seven away from me?"

A warm smile touched his lips. "What a very *sensible* answer."

"Well, I *am* sensible, I'm afraid."

"I know, my darling. Sensible, practical, and often entirely wrong-headed."

"Well of all the . . ." She got no further as the sentence was bluntly cut off by another crushing kiss. When he finally released her, a pert smile appeared. "There is nothing at all sensible in a young lady who kisses a gentleman to whom she is not betrothed."

"Quite right!" he exclaimed. "We must remedy that." Before she could protest, he was down on one knee. "My very dear Miss van Houten," he began ponderously. "I have for long looked upon you as a paragon among women. My excessive admiration for your esteemed person has led me to hope that bountiful Venus, the goddess of love, will smile on our union with favor. Like Daphnis and Chloe, our love will be . . ."

"Derek Rowbridge! Get up this instant! I will not be proposed to in this odious 'Kneighleyish' fashion!" The wrinkles of amusement deepened about his eyes. "And how dare you laugh at me!"

"I'm not laughing, sweet termagant. I am only trying to determine if those remarkable eyes of yours are most beautiful when you are angry or when you are harboring a strong desire to laugh. The anger makes them quite magnificent, with little yellow sparks shooting out like fireworks. But on the whole I think I prefer the laughter." He leaned and lightly kissed each eye in turn.

"Then you will do well not to make me angry, won't you?" she teased.

"Ah, no such rash promises. I'm sure you'll be ripping up at me at regular intervals. And I am quite likely to do the same to you, for I shan't put you on a marble pedestal, you know."

"Oh, well," she answered. "It's just as well. I've been on one or two, you know, but the trouble with pedestals is that they are not very large, and one tends to get awfully cramped standing always in the same position. And then if one moves about at all and tries to get a bit more comfortable, one usually falls off."

Now he was laughing outright. "Dear delight! With you for a wife I shall never be bored."

"Am I to be your wife?" she asked saucily. "I have yet to hear you ask me."

"You will marry me, my girl, with no more argumentation!" He looked her in the eyes. "Won't you?" he asked softly.

"Yes," she smiled back. "I think I will."

"Sensible girl," he chided and proceeded to kiss her insensible.

It was quite some time later that the lovesick pair made their way back to the house. They returned to the library to discover that the family party had broken up. Only Mama remained, her pen scratching across the page. Her red wig had slipped to one side, and there were ink spots all over her neckruff.

"Mama?" said Saskia. "We have something to tell you."

Her mother looked up. "Hello, my love. Why, where has everyone gone? Are we to have lunch?"

"Mama, Derek and I are going to be married."

"Well, of course you are, dearest. I have known it forever. I can't think how it took you so long to learn it. You are usually so sensible about such things." The two lovers only grinned at each other. "Tell me, darling," Mama went on. "How do you spell malmsey?"

"Malmsey?"

"Yes. As in a butt of Malmsey?"

"Oh, dear, Mama. What shocking adventure have you got poor Magdalena into now?"

"Oh, it's not Magdalena. I've quite finished with her. About time, to. She was getting to be a dead bore. This is Lucinda." Cornelia Crawley, Authoress, pushed her wig back on top of her head and splashed her pen in the standish. Saskia and Derek, arm in arm, tiptoed out.

Lucinda's strength was ebbing fast. She couldn't hold on much longer to the rough stone edge of the battlements. Below her, the inky water of the moat loomed. In her heavy petticoats and farthingale she would sink like a cannonball.

A lantern swept the wall over her hands; she held her breath. It swung back, paused, stopped. The jingle of My Lord of Granthum's spurs sounded loud in her ears, and the yellowish light grew nearer.

"My Lady Lucinda," he intoned with malevolence as he caught at her bleeding hands and pulled her up. His sword and his leer glinted in the oily lamplight.

"'Od's death! What a beauty it is! Thou mayst love me, or thou mayst not, My Lady, but I'll have you yet!"

ABOUT THE AUTHOR

Megan Daniel, born and raised in Southern California, combines a background in theater and music with a passion for travel and a love of England and the English. After attending UCLA and California State University, Long Beach, where she earned a degree in theater, she lived for a time in London and elsewhere in Europe. She then settled in New York, working for six years as a theatrical costume designer for Broadway, off-Broadway, ballet, and regional theater.

Miss Daniel currently divides her time between her homes in New York and Amsterdam, together with her husband, Roy Sorrels, a successful free-lance writer. Her first two novels, *Amelia* and *The Reluctant Suitor*, are also available in Signet editions.

SIGNET Regency Romances You'll Enjoy

☐ **THE INNOCENT DECEIVER** by Vanessa Gray.
(#E9463—$1.75)*
☐ **THE LONELY EARL** by Vanessa Gray. (#E7922—$1.75)
☐ **THE MASKED HEIRESS** by Vanessa Gray. (#E9331—$1.75)
☐ **THE DUTIFUL DAUGHTER** by Vanessa Gray.
(#E9017—$1.75)*
☐ **THE WICKED GUARDIAN** by Vanessa Gray. (#E8390—$1.75)
☐ **THE WAYWARD GOVERNESS** by Vanessa Gray.
(#E8696—$1.75)*
☐ **THE GOLDEN SONG BIRD** by Sheila Walsh.
(#E8155—$1.75)†
☐ **LORD GILMORE'S BRIDE** by Sheila Walsh. (#E8600—$1.75)*
☐ **THE SERGEANT MAJOR'S DAUGHTER** by Sheila Walsh.
(#E8220—$1.75)
☐ **THE INCOMPARABLE MISS BRADY** by Sheila Walsh.
(#E9245—$1.75)*
☐ **MADALENA** by Sheila Walsh. (#E9332—$1.75)
☐ **THE REBEL BRIDE** by Catherine Coulter. (#J9630—$1.95)
☐ **THE AUTUMN COUNTESS** by Catherine Coulter.
(#E8463—$1.75)*
☐ **LORD DEVERILL'S HEIR** by Catherine Coulter.
(#E9200—$1.75)*
☐ **LORD RIVINGTON'S LADY** by Eileen Jackson.
(#E9408—$1.75)*
☐ **BORROWED PLUMES** by Roseleen Milne. (#E8113—$1.75)†

* Price slightly higher in Canada
† Not available in Canada

Buy them at your local bookstore or use this convenient coupon for ordering.

THE NEW AMERICAN LIBRARY, INC.,
P.O. Box 999, Bergenfield, New Jersey 07621

Please send me the SIGNET BOOKS I have checked above. I am enclosing
$_____(please add $1.00 to this order to cover postage and handling)
Send check or money order—no cash or C.O.D.'s. Prices and numbers are
subject to change without notice.

Name _____

Address _____

City _____ State _____ Zip Code _____
Allow 4-6 weeks for delivery.
This offer is subject to withdrawal without notice